# Hybrid

# Hybrid

BY

## Diane Cilento

**HODDER AND STOUGHTON**
LONDON · SYDNEY · AUCKLAND · TORONTO

Printed in Great Britain for Hodder and Stoughton Limited,
St. Paul's House, Warwick Lane, London, EC4,
by C. Tinling & Co. Ltd, London and Prescot.

For my mother and father

# Part One

# 1

## Matthew Jackson

MATTHEW JACKSON HAD peculiar eyes. The centre of each was a bright, top-of-sky blue which graduated into brown around each rim. They were the legacy of an African grandmother and a Scottish grandfather. These two had produced a number of children of varying colour, depending on which race had proven genetically dominant, and so on and so on, until Matthew arrived to show the world that sometimes there can be a true hybrid.

Matthew Jackson looked out of his blue and brown eyes, he saw things, and he was a lover.

There are men in whom the ability to love has withered away like a hot-house plant put out in frosty ground. They look about them, they register the sky and trees and sea and flowers, but they are not lovers. They do not experience small secret bursts of joy when confronted with sparkling morning light filtering through fragrant new leaves as Matthew Jackson did, nor do they sit suspended in time, watching the intricate lacy patterns forming and reforming around foaming coral reefs; they do not gaze (for minutes at a time) into the perfect purple depths of a double hibiscus; they do not lie on their backs on grass and let the whole busy, blue, insect-ridden sky swarm above them, balanced beautifully on the tips of their noses. All these things Matthew Jackson did frequently, though, at the same time, it is important to note that in his early manhood he was not so entranced by people. They had taught him to be wary of them, to approach with caution, to proceed with extreme care, and to withdraw at the first sign of hostility. Those same eyes that regarded the growing things with wonder, began to watch people with less and less of their customary blue and brown candour.

*     *     *

Matthew Jackson was born on Hambro Island in the West Indies. His skin was a splendid café-au-lait, his teeth were large and tombstoney and, because he had never been made to wear shoes, he had prehensile toes that could pick up pebbles and play the piano. In fact, he was the only boy at the Hambro Island Mission School who could play 'Good King Wenceslas' with his toes. At school he was known as 'Jumpin' Jackson', he was 'Matthew' at home, but when he came to England people called him 'Jackson', 'Hambro Jackson', the creator of the Cult, the leader of the New-Chosen; 'Hybrid', 'the Speaker' and 'Two-Tone'. He came to London to learn about earth.

There is very little earth on Hambro Island: it is made up of lime-stone and coral, pockets of dirt in crack and creek bed and an inch or two of top-soil that winds and birds have left behind them over the centuries. Consequently, trees do not grow very high on Hambro Island, the sugar-cane is spindly and bananas are apt to get bunchy-top.

Jackson decided at an early age to change all that. He leafed through his grandfather's books and found pictures of forests and lawns and great walled gardens, high hedges cut into precise shapes, long paths through avenues of flowering shrubs. It was not the order and precision of everything that obsessed him. It was the profusion. He dreamt of his land, acres of tall coconut-palms, cane, akkee trees, breadfruit and a canopy of fat, green banana leaves stretching out. When he woke up and looked around him at the stunted vegetation, he asked why.

His father, Sidney, said the soil was 'mean'; his uncle, Hector, said it had 'gone sour', but his grandfather took him out with a small pick-axe and dug a hole to show him where the top-soil stopped and the chalky lime-stone base began. His grandfather told him that this island, like all the islands in the West Indies, had once been a mountain peak in a huge lost continent which some people called Atlantis, and that this great continent had sunk and shifted and that was why the sea around them was never any deeper than twenty feet, and then, where the continent's coastline ended, suddenly dropped to a depth of thousands of fathoms. His father, Sidney, said that Hambro was just a little coral atoll in the middle of the sea. His uncle, Hector, said that nothing except coconut-palms, whose roots push through coral and filter up the sea water, would ever grow on an atoll and that fishing was the only answer.

He believed only his grandfather.

He walked along the beaches, savouring the soft pink coral-sand between his prehensile toes. He played in the shallows and squirted water at his cousins through cupped hands and he tried to imagine himself on top of a mountain. It was very hard because he had never even seen a mountain in his life.

He asked his grandfather what it was like to stand on a mountain and for answer his grandfather took him to Jamaica in his boat. They sailed into Kingston harbour and his grandfather held his hand and walked him through dusty streets, the midday sun bleaching all colours and people textureless.

They got onto a bus with a group of American lady tourists, dazzling in blazing silk prints, straw hats and costume jewellery.

"Oh, just look at that cute little coloured boy. He's got two-tone eyes!" cried one marsh-mallow-armed matron.

"Am I coloured?" whispered Jackson to his grandfather. "What colours am I?" he asked, peering down at his arms and legs.

"Everybody's coloured, except dimduss albinos, and that's only because they got no pigments. It's all a question of pigments, boy." His grandfather was looking out of the window at the clapboard houses on the outskirts of town, paint peeled and blistering in the heat.

"What's pigments?"

His grandfather turned away from the window and pulled at his moustache a minute before answering. "Well, pigments . . . pigments . . . yes . . . well, for instance, I'm a good shade of pink, I'd say, with brown spots . . . rum and sun, y'see, light complexioned like my father; he had red hair . . . that's bad for your hot climates—burns and freckles; and that's your pigments too, not coagulating."

"What's kwagling . . . kwaglating, granpaw?"

"Coagulating? . . . That's . . . er . . . uh . . . well, that's getting together, son. Then there's yellow people, ivory-coloured, black and sometimes purpley-black . . . Take old Carley Fish-Hook at the docks—a beautiful deep plum is old Carley."

"Then there's red people, red around the gills, comes from too much gin, though they say there's a race of red indians in America—never saw one myself but heard they were a real rusty colour; and there's chocolate, caramel and coffee . . . and maybe there's a few, a few lucky ones like you—coffee and caramel mixed." He smacked his lips together. "Very good flavour!"

"Is *she* an albino?"

His grandfather peered balefully at the lady in question.

"Could be, sonny. She looks kinda washed out to me," he concluded and turned back to the window. For Jackson for many years afterwards, an albino was a middle-aged Caucasian lady with glasses attached around her neck by a little chain and the suggestion of a moustache showing on a glistening upperlip. He watched the woman for any other phenomenon, as the bus climbed laboriously up the steep winding road. At each bend the driver blasted the air with a piercing two-note klaxon and stepped firmly on the accelerator.

"Where're we going, granpaw?"

"Newcastle, sonny, four thousand feet above sea level so's you can look down on everything. Highest point around. Cooler too. You goin' tuh de top uf de mountain, man." Jackson's grandfather patted the top of the boy's head and used the special caressing island voice that was reserved for renewing affection after hidings and telling bedtime stories.

Jackson grinned, screwing up his nose to show the serrated edges of his two large second teeth through his upper gum.

"But yu said we *lived* on top a mountain granpaw, and we don't have to take no silly old bus to get *there*!"

*　*　*

The view from Newcastle was heat-hazy, the coastline lay fuzzily below them, the long strip of Palisadoes and Hunts Bay. Jackson looked down disappointed.

"But ah can't do nothing with that, granpaw, I'd prefer be down yonder than up here on top."

His grandfather seemed not to have heard. He breathed in deeply, his eyes staring sightless out over the big ocean. He stayed motionless for several minutes with his head thrown back, a sort of defiance that accepted infinity and death in his stance. Jackson watched him and wondered what it meant. He tried standing with his head thrown back, one foot thrust forward and gazing downwards like his grandfather.

It was still a remote and misty scene that lay beneath him, and no joy.

He tapped his grandfather lightly on the leg, fearful of inter-
rupting, but feeling suddenly lonely and confused.

"What you thinkin' about, granpaw?" he asked. "Ah don't
like it up here."

"You've got to stand back and look at it all sometime, boy.
That's why I come here every so often. I expect it's in my
blood." He took hold of the boy's shoulder and pulled him
against his body. "You see, boy, my father come out here from
a country where there are big mountains twice as high as this
here hill. He come here from those big, cold mountains and he
brought me when I was about the same size as you. We look
around these islands and my father settle on Hambro; he was
a poet, my father was, always singin' songs and makin' up bits
of verse about Black Beard and Captain Morgan and old tales.
A dreamer, too, to pick an island like Hambro, a speck in the
sea and nothin' else to recommend it."

He laughed and took hold of the nape of the boy's neck with
strong, stubby fingers.

He sang gruffly, a strange song about the Lord Donegal and
a queen called Isabel (pronounced Eye-sabell) who died and
grew into a briar rose, all the while kneading the boy's neck
and looking out over the sea.

When he had finished Jackson turned his cheek into the
palm of his grandfather's hand and tried to imagine his father's
father's father, the poet, who had sung these strange, sad songs.
He had once seen a faded sepia dengue-type of his great-
grandfather—all he remembered was a large handle-bar moustache and limpid eyes that stuck out like two slit door-knobs.
It was impossible to believe that that dreaming young man
could have been the daddy of this crusty old one with his
shining bald pate, brown cancer spots and shaving brush
moustache all yellowed with rum and tobacco.

He saw that his grandfather's eyes had reddened and that
the flesh around them had somehow folded in and left him with
the look of an old sandstone statue, beginning to subside with
the seasons.

He felt embarrassed by his grandfather for the first time in
his life, uneasy in the presence of his groping sentimentality.
He hated to see the great male symbol of his childhood crying
and whimpering like everybody else did; and at the same time
Jackson was crying too, tears of sympathy and dismay welled

into the corners of his eyes and dribbled down his cheeks. He snuffled and shifted under the old man's heavy hand, wanting to disengage himself from age and grief and misery that he could not understand. He looked up through his useless tears and knew that he loved his grandfather better than anyone else in the world.

"There're all dead now, boy; those lads, all dead or away yonder over the water."

"Which lads, granpaw?"

"The lads I went to war with, boy. We sat in trenches together for a year or more . . . stinking holes in the ground; sat, while our feet and our teeth rotted in those rotten cold French trenches. I dreamt about coming up here to this place all the time I sat there, somewhere high up, y'see, and the other poor lads, they dreamt about their places. We used to swap places and wonder if we'd ever visit each other's place. Everybody's got to have a place to dream about."

Jackson's grandfather held up his left hand to show the missing index finger, the stump that Jackson had seen him touch with his thumb a hundred times when agitated, or beat time with when they sang hymns on Sundays.

"And that's all I left there in France, boy!" he cried, stamping his foot down on the ground. "The rest of me is going to be left *here*, in these Islands, and you're the boy to see they do it right."

Jackson looked away and blinked his eyes.

He knew that his grandfather was talking about death again, his own death . . . an event which occupied him more and more lately, and one which Jackson had come to dread with breath-stopping anguish.

\*   \*   \*

Jackson's grandfather was his only one. That is to say—Jackson's grandfather had sired both his parents. To explain this it is necessary to understand both the geography of Hambro Island and the rather precarious sexual relationships which exist in this part of the world.

Jackson's father, Sidney, was the legitimate son of old man Jackson, and May, a black-skinned, broad-hipped woman of pure African blood. She was a deliciously wide woman, wide-set teeth, generous, wide-set eyes, wonder, and wide hips capable of bearing many children and many loads. Jackson's grandfather had married her for these attributes and kept her near him like a life-belt, handy in all crises.

Jackson's mother was the result of a brief but delightful sojourn in Kingston in the summer of 1927. A year or two later he had moved both mother and daughter out to Hambro and set them up in a small house on Snipe's Bay by the sea, with a few coconut-palms, chickens and mangrove crabs to keep them company. This little house was twenty-three miles, the whole length of the island in fact, from his and May's house.

For two years he kept up the liaison; travelled up and down the island in his buggy drawn by the good quarter-horse (there were only three on the island at that time); he pretended not to notice the shadowy male figures that melted into the mangroves at his approach or were to be seen emerging at his departure.

Then in the beginning of 1932, after arguments over money, frequency, or rather infrequency of visits, status, rights, etc., Jackson's grandfather gave up his mistress, who disappeared back to Jamaica on the next boat and was never seen again. She left her daughter in the care of neighbours who brought up the child with good-natured affection and had soon forgotten all but the most essential facts of her origin.

Jackson himself was already conceived and well on his way into the world before either of his grandfather's children knew of their connection. And so, he became his grandfather's child, the fruit of an incestuous union, however innocent, and the apple of the old man's eye. Nobody whispered about him in corners or even considered him unique, except for his eyes.

\* \* \*

At school he learned his sums and spelling and geography, and at home his grandfather read poetry aloud in the evenings and showed him through mounds of National Geographies and books filled with pictures and descriptions of every fish and shell in the sea.

He had a museum of his own filled with bailer shells and cowries, brain coral, lace coral, mushroom and branch coral, smooth sea-urchin shells and turtle backs, carefully blown eggs and a precious piece of petrified wood, identified by his grandfather and, according to him, further proof of the existence of

15

Atlantis. His museum was actually the second and third shelves of his grandfather's glass-fronted bookcase in the library, the one room in the sprawling wooden verandah-surrounded house that nobody entered without first asking the old man's permission.

A roll-top desk, kept locked by his grandfather, an ancient stuffed kiwi in a domed glass case (sent all the way from New Zealand by a wartime comrade), Jackson's museum and a ten year supply of National Geographies, a leather-bound set of Encyclopaedias and some beautifully illustrated pornographic books in French—these were the sacred possessions that his grandfather guarded so jealously. Also a banjo gathering dust on top of the bookcase and sometimes played at Christmas, a small supply of the best liquor rum to be had, (small—but always a replenished supply), two riding crops, a pineapple grenade and a heavy useless German pistol—relics of the Great War. Jackson had discreetly examined every item in the room at one time or another and knew them all intimately. He had fingered the prints of coy ladies being covered by moustachioed gentlemen, who in turn were covered by rice-paper fly leaves, yellowing with age. He had gingerly strummed the banjo when his grandfather was well out of ear-shot, climbed through the window and sampled the rum with distaste. The room drew him like a magnet, as it did all his grandfather's children and grandchildren. To be *invited* into 'The Study' was a great honour which the old man bestowed only occasionally, and on few. Jackson fossicked for hours on end to find something worthy of his museum. In this way he was able to enter the study more often than his cousins and in this way he became his grandfather's favourite.

\* \* \*

The rest of the house was Grandma May's. She had decorated it with the flamboyance of a bazaar. Chairs were covered with heliotrope-and-blue patterned chintz, faded red and yellow curtains, ink-stained jade and lilac bedspreads—the profusion of colour splashed haphazardly about the house was evidence of visits to the sales in Kingston, where she picked up bargains in large rolls of material, and used them with marvellous abandon.

Sunday was the important day of the week for Grandma May. She baked at least a dozen banana and nut loaves, chicken

16

and hot peppers, ribs, grouper with ginger. Calulu soup, huge plates of okra, red peas and sweet potatoes to fill her teeming brood on the Lord's Day. The house was jammed with bellowing children, dogs, pregnant women in cotton smocks, laughing, sparring men and boys, music, palaver, hullaballoo . . . NOISE . . . and in the middle of it all sat May, serene after her orgiastic culinary efforts, supreme with goodwill, crushing various small children to her huge bosom, that shelf of maternity. She dispensed valuable advice to daughters and daughters-in-law on cooking, weaning babies, starching shirts, lumbago pains, teething troubles, potency and contraception. She vetted all her daughters' lovers, supervised their pregnancies, acted as midwife at most of the deliveries, and could be counted on to take over when any delinquent mother left her children to disappear to Jamaica with some new lover, sometimes forever.

Arguments would break out and one segment of the family would be missing from the table for several Sundays, only to reappear again later on in the year in need of succour and attention, and be encompassed once more by those big black arms that welcomed with no heed for apologies. She also kept a herd of goats and called them each by name. Her cheeses were a delight. She hung them in dripping muslin bags from the clothes-line to mature.

May was well known throughout the island (indeed, her reputation had spread as far as the mainland of Jamaica) as a great procurer of potions for unrequited lovers, charmer of warts and cysts off the lumpy, and it was whispered that she would use 'the evil eye' and put a double whamee on those who crossed her. At the same time, she was to be heard leading the choir of voices in the small, mud-floored shed that served as church on Sundays and as the Hambro Island Mission School on weekdays. Wearing a voluminous white dress (she actually possessed *two satin* ones) and a straw hat covered in flowers, she was a truly formidable woman, and the whole island recognised her as such.

The grandfather, Jackson, who owned most of the island, with the exception of a couple of miles of coastline on the southern shore, and Snipe's Bay, also sang in church. His voice was harsh and nearly always out of tune, but he sang the words as though he meant them and sometimes delivered short sermons on 'Saving for a rainy day' and 'The fruitfulness of nature'. 'Saving for a rainy day' was incomprehensible to most of the parishioners as the rainy season was a time of rejoicing and delight. Children took off what few clothes they wore and slid about on banana leaves in the mud, women saved buckets full of the lovely, fresh rain-water to rinse their hair, and the fishermen thankfully sat indoors with their rums, swapped stories and listened to the pleasant drumming on the roofs.

'The fruitfulness of nature' was better understood judging by the number of babies born every year.

Jackson's father, Sidney, was a sometime fisherman who enjoyed life immensely. He hung around the house on the days when smells from the kitchen promised succulent meals, he drank rough rum in large quantities, remembered dirty stories and brought home a new woman every couple of years. Jackson had at least six half-brothers and sisters, all of whom Grandma May coped with, Sidney being a man blissfully untroubled by guilt or responsibilities.

When times were bad, and there *were* times when the sugar cane was hardly worth cutting, corn shrivelled and red beans became the only staple diet, he would disappear to Kingston. Once he was gone for a whole year and came back laden with trinkets and shrunken skulls, telling tales of months on a merchant vessel that had taken him through the Panama Canal and as far as Montevideo.

A few tourists in their fancy yachts came to the island but they stayed only long enough to note that there were no night-clubs, no proper restaurants and only two houses which provided accommodation. No picturesque seventeenth-century settlement houses beckoned them and swarms of naked children followed them wherever they went demanding cigarettes. They usually upped anchor and were away within a couple of hours.

\* \* \*

There was a doctor on the island called Bates who had left his wife in Nottingham in 1934. He had lived with Grandma May's eldest daughter, Libby, for twenty years and was accepted by the islanders as one of their own. His surgery was at his house and was run with great efficiency by Libby and her sister Kay, who was one of 'Nature's Virgins' (Grandma May's description) and had spent three years training to be a nurse

18

at the Kingston General Hospital. Dr. Bates was old man Jackson's drinking partner and friend and unless some emergency called the doctor away, they spent each evening with long glasses of rum in their hands, sitting on the verandah of Jackson's house, watching the children play and discussing astrology, crops, deep-sea fishing, politics, war, medical discoveries, the possibility of an airstrip being built, anything that they deemed worthy of the consideration of two sage and venerable gentlemen sitting on a verandah drinking rum.

Doc Bates was a massive man. He had a huge cranium and hardly any neck, his hair was cropped to about half an inch all over his head and stood out at right-angles to his skull no matter what contours were involved. Rum had loosened his vocal chords to such an extent that his voice came out like an incredible talking ratchet, and his hands were thick lumps on the end of his arms, hairy and covered with freckles on the backs. His fingers were also thick but far from unwieldy. In fact, many islanders bore the fine, fine scars of Doc Bates's nimble fingers on their bellies, where he had performed appendectomies or caesarians or other intricate surgical work.

Jackson had always been fascinated by Doc Bates. He would lie along the front steps and watch his grandfather and the doctor sip their rum and ruminate. He never tired of the rumbling voice, though he could not follow half they said; he would puzzle for hours over the deep guffaws and fruity chuckles that followed some spicey story, or listen with bulging eyes to the doctor's horribly graphic description of the removal of a brain tumour or the lancing of a monstrous carbuncle.

Once the doctor took him to witness the birth of a child. It was down at the other end of the island in the small settlement which had sprung up there in 1946 after the war. A clutch of about ten fishermens' huts edged the sea and behind them some half-acre of fenced-off chicken farm, where an enterprising man called Noakes raised Rhode Island Reds, and supplied eggs for most of the island.

It was a Tuesday evening and Jackson had come home from the beach to find the two men drinking and chatting just like any other evening. He sprawled out on the verandah watching the sunlight change position and creep up the wall as the sun went down. He listened dreamily to the sound of the soft, deep voices and drifted off into his own world in the silences—

winning fights at school, finding new treasures for his museum, owning a bicycle, discovering Morgan's treasure.

Suddenly up the stairs ran a buck-toothed, crimpy-haired boy of about the same age as Jackson, who gasped out "Doc Bates! Doc Bates! You have fe come now, Doc, right now!"

Jackson did not recognise this boy, though he thought he knew every face on the island. He sat up and eyed the boy uncertainly. It was not that it was such an unusual occurrence; people were always rushing in calling for the doc, knowing that he spent most of his evenings on old man Jackson's verandah, but this boy was sweating and white spit had gathered at the corners of his mouth as though he had been exerting himself furiously for a long time. He put on a little red cap that had been cut in scoops around the edge and which he had been holding in his hand. It was studded with Coke bottle tops. He was breathing heavily and chewing a wadge of gum in between breaths.

The doc looked rather startled but sat still and finished his rum. He belched and rose to his feet. "All right, Quincey, I'm coming, boy."

One half of Jackson's fascination for Doc Bates was his car. He owned a 1948 Riley convertible which Jackson thought perfection and delighted to climb into. There were only five or six other cars on Hambro in 1956 and Doc's was by far the finest.

This night Jackson scrambled to his feet and ran down the stairs behind Doc, partly out of curiosity to see how the boy, Quincey, had arrived and where he had come from, but also because Doc had brought his car with him—a thing he rarely did as he lived only a hundred yards down the street.

Jackson saw that Quincey had ridden on an old, blue-painted bicycle which he had left on its side by the front gate.

On an impulse he said, "Can I come along with you for the drive, Doc?"

The big man looked down at him. He screwed up his eyes, pressed his lips forward and then opened the door of the two-seater. "Hop in," he said briefly.

Before he got into the car himself, Doc called up to old man Jackson: "Look after that boy, will you, Matt? His name's Quincey! Ridden all the way up here from Snipe's Bay. Give him a bed for the night and some dinner. He can go back tomorrow. I'm taking yours with me. Do him good."

He climbed in, folding his great bulk into the seat and Jackson felt the car sink down on the other side.

Doc hardly ever spoke while he drove. The road was only a dirt track but it went the length of the island, and crossed two rivers, the Clyde and the Hambro. Jackson loved the sensation of speed and ownership as he swept along in the car. They raised a column of dust behind them that blotted out everything in their wake. It was that last moment of daylight which outlines everything with devastating clarity before darkness rushes in to blot and smudge the shape of trees and hills and rivers. "One day all this land will be covered with growing things," thought Jackson. "One day there will be copra and bread-fruit trees and jacaranda, poiciana all along this road and people will come from all over the world to see the green garden island."

Doc was humming, at least Jackson thought it must be humming. It sounded a bit like someone sharpening a knife on a grindstone, a sort of deep chest grumbling that wavered on tunelessly while the car sped along and darkness fell and crickets scraped their legs together.

They had gone about eight miles before Doc broke his silence.

"How old are you, boy?"

"Twelve and three-quarters."

Doc mused on this for another mile.

"Twelve! Good," he said finally. "Yes, that's good."

They saw the lights from Snipe's Bay long before they got there. Someone had lit a bonfire just outside Noakes's chicken-yard and all the children from the settlement were squealing like piglets and throwing themselves about in the firelight.

They rushed forward as the car came towards the light and swarmed over the mudguards, tapping on the bonnet and the windows, grinning brown faces lit to auburn by the fire, little-boy legs and arms never still, and gleaming new sets of incisors that always look too big for the mouth of a child.

Doc Bates heaved himself out of the car, patted a few finely-moulded heads and marched purposefully towards the huts scattered about in the direction of the sea. Hurricane lamps lit the huts as there was no electricity at this end of the island. The light they threw was softer and more beguiling than electric or sodium or magnesium glare, and Jackson followed the huge pale bulk of the doctor in a sort of dream, in love with the sight of the frail lights reflecting delicately on the water beyond them,

21

the inflated rising moon giving back a reddish path across the ocean that led straight to himself. "It's the heat waves off the earth make it look bigger," his grandfather had told him.

The smell of frangipani, of night-blooming jasmine, cinnamon and port-wine magnolia, the sound of laughing, whispering boys, the distant yapping of a dog—it all combined to make one of those hallucinatory seconds in time that came back to Jackson at moments throughout the rest of his life. For no apparent reason he would have a half-second of total recall until he was quite familiar with the remembrance of Snipe's Bay on a Tuesday night, the retreating back of big Doc Bates, and the engorged red moon whose path led to himself.

The doc had to bend down to get in through the doorway of the hut. It had been put together from bits and pieces of every imaginable thing that came to hand; kerosene tins, half a galvanised iron tank, driftwood, packing cases, old doors and bed-frames and there was a sign written outside on a child's slate, 'Bewar Dog'.

No dog presented itself as Jackson went in after the doc but there was such a clutter of goods strewn about the place that it could easily have been asleep behind one of the piles of fishing nets or old magazines, empty cornflakes packets and hessian sacks that littered the corners.

A kitchen table occupied the centre of the room and on it lay a girl.

The girl was very black, very frightened and very pregnant.

She held herself up on her elbows and looked down with pain and disbelief at the huge contracted mound that was her own stomach.

Over the table hung a bright, chromium-plated lamp which gave a light of extraordinary brilliance for a few feet but whose rays did not reach the corners of the room. To Jackson, the light seemed to have concentrated its beams on the belly of the black girl in the white shift.

He stared at her contorted face and rolling eyes and watched as the doctor's huge hand covered the hill of white shift and somehow diminished it, muttering, "Good girl, Lily, look what a beautiful contraction that is, you're goin' to have a lovely baby, Lily, that's a very clever girl."

The girl's face relaxed and she lay her head back as Doc's other hand caressed her cheeks and wiped the sweat back into her hair. He glanced at his watch and Jackson could also see that it was registering eight o'clock and some minutes between ten and fifteen.

"Now let's see when your next one is, Lily girl; I'll be here now all the time, be with you, you don't need to worry any more. You're going to do everything I say and it will be perfect. See?"

Jackson wondered at the gentle rumbling voice that the doc used as he pinched the girl's cheek. She giggled and rolled her head into his hand but kept her eyes great trusting black eyes turned up on the doc's face.

"Who that funny boy gawpin at me, Doc?"

"That's Matthew Jackson. One of old man Jackson's boys. Come and say hello to Lily, boy."

Jackson came into the light and held out his hand; Lily held up her right hand and her fingers fluttered over his palm like moths. She was beautiful in the light when he looked down on her. Her face was broad and the eyes long and Egyptian now, nostrils flaring proudly; her mouth was a smiling mouth whose lips had opened slightly in the horizontal position in which she lay and Jackson could just see the gleam of teeth through their purple inside pleats.

"You goin' see Doc pull out the baby, boy? You goin' see him pull baby outa me?"

Jackson nodded and looked to Doc for verification but Doc was busy opening his black bag and bringing out his stethoscope.

He pulled up Lily's shift and placed the hearing end on the swollen lump of flesh, listening intently to the whisper of another heart that beat inside her. With a satisfied grunt he straightened up and hit the top of his head on the lamp which wobbled on its wire and set all the shadows in the room jiggling and dancing. They both laughed as Doc rubbed his skull ruefully.

"Hmmmmn," he breathed (like a bubbling whale). "Nice and steady, a pleasure to confine such a . . ."

Lily's neck muscles suddenly tautened into two thick converging cords. She threw back her head and stiffened her legs and Jackson could see the mound under the shift bunch into a rigid ball. Her lips unfurled to reveal two rows of even teeth and her eyes slitted up in agony. A snarling, guttural sound like Jackson had heard dogs make when they walk around pre-

23

paring to fly at each others' throats, came from Lily and she clutched the sides of the table as though she would wind them around herself like a shroud.

Doc looked at his watch again. "Seven minutes," he said to himself and put one of his great, stumpy fingers to Lily's mouth.

"Bite on that, Lily," he said. "Breathe even and slow if you can. Don't push too hard, lovely, it's not time just yet . . . Ow! . . . That's better, isn't it? Turn on your side, little girl, and I'll rub your back for you . . . There, little Lily, there . . . Slow down . . . slow . . . that's it, girl . . . easy and slow."

Lily's contraction had quickened her breathing to a wheezing pant that ended in a whimper each time, but the doc's big hand rubbing on her back seemed to regulate the rhythm of the breaths and after a few more moments she sighed and relaxed once more.

"Dat's a real bad one, Doc. Dat baby tryin' to get out real hard now."

Doc nodded and turned to Jackson. "Here you, boy, come and rub this girl's back while I go out to the car and get some things. Come on, she won't have pain for a few more minutes but it feels good to have someone near, eh, Lily? By the way, where's your daddy?"

Lily squirmed around before answering. "When he know me time come, him put me on the table and light up, send Quincey up to yu, and him gawne down to Mrs. Winnie Hart house see if she come as well. I think him just havin' a bitta rum with 'er, pass the time." Lily showed no signs of her recent pain and talked in a sing-song little girl voice, unrecognisable as the same which had produced such vicious snarls only moments before.

Jackson rubbed Lily's back with the same rhythm that Doc had done and the girl purred and moaned with pleasure beneath his hand.

"Matchew Jackson," she crooned, "you a sweet kind guava-face boy, and I goin' eat your guava-face one day, Matchew Jackson."

"It don't hurt now, Lily."

"No, it nu hurt. I just have a little sleep before next time round, eeooow . . . that real good, Matchew . . . that so nice . . ."

Her voice trailed off and it seemed to Jackson that she was dozing, though small sounds escaped her every few seconds, sounds of a child dreaming and chittering in his sleep. Jackson decreased his efforts and gently stroked the smooth black back under the shift.

Doc returned bearing blankets and a rubber sheet. Jackson felt the muscles of Lily's back arch like a bow and she rolled onto her back again swearing and fighting out with her fists.

"Calm down, calm down, Lily. Don't fight, lass, it only makes the pain worse. Shhhh . . . Shhhhh . . . don't bear down too hard, you'll bash the poor thing's head to a pulp on your pelvic bone. Too strong, Lily, you're too strong. It's all that swimming and jumping about . . . Shhhh . . . Good girl . . . "

Doc parted her legs and placed the blankets and the rubber sheet under her hips as he talked. He crooked her knees up, pushed back the shift and felt her belly with a gentle, exploratory hand.

"Yes, girl, that's very good, head well down, three fingers dilation; five shilling pieces. Not long before the waters break now, girl. How you feel now, Lily love? Breathe slow now. Try to count with me . . . "

Lily muttered a few obscenities and said she'd rather bite his finger, but she was exhausted by this contraction and did not offer any resistance when Doc hoisted her further up the table so that her head was in the shadow and her legs and abdomen fully exposed to the light.

Jackson was astounded and fascinated to see between her legs, between those other purpley-brown lips and dark thighs a tiny patch of head, baby's head, that showed lighter than the rest. He gasped as the tiny patch grew larger and larger and Lily gasped and cried out too, and Doc was suddenly busy, his big hands moving deftly and cleverly, assisting that little head to emerge from the body that enclosed it. Lily moaned and tried to thrash her legs, anxious to be rid of the growing thing that had lived inside her and drained her energy for all these months.

"Here, boy, hold her leg; hush, Lily, you're doing beautifully, don't push so hard, girl, hold back a little. Pant! Lily! Pant like a dog! Hah-ah-hah-aha-hah-aha-hah! Yes! Hold it back a little or you'll hurt yourself . . . Good . . . good girl . . ."

Jackson watched the little head come forth with so much wonder that he almost forgot to hold the flailing leg. He was not frightened by the gush of fine fluid that flowed out over his

25

hand. He was not shocked by the pounding urgency of birth that pushed the whole of Lily's body into action; her womb, her bowels, the muscles of her abdomen all worked to push the tiny creature out of her body with the utmost speed.

Jackson saw Doc's hand clasp the small, tight head covered with fine black down, wet and crisp, and gently urge the shoulders out, his deep voice hypnotising, always confident and confiding, always demanding obedience from Lily's striving limbs.

"Come on, now Lily, here's your baby, Lily, and it a fine, healthy one, gel, a little beauty, Lily. Don't push so hard! Pant! One more push, Lily, and we'll see if you've got yourself a boy or a girl. That's it, my beauty. Something you be proud of all your life. You're a brave, good girl Lily. Here he comes . . . No, no, not yet . . . pant again, Lily, I don't want to do any stitching tonight . . . Hush now and gather your strength, my girl, my pretty Lily . . . Give yourself time . . . Now? Now!"

And out he came, a compact, high-chested morsel with flattened ears and squirming reddish limbs, flesh folded and covered with a whitish substance, face like a bemused old pixie, and with him came the knotted umbilical cord looking vigorous and heavy in the white beams of the lantern.

The doctor cut and tied him off from his mother with unhurried dextrous hands, and suddenly there was another human being in the room who had not been there a few seconds before, a squalling, hot-headed human being with open mouth and kicking frog's legs, who demanded attention and who fought to catch his first breaths with an amazing life force.

Jackson was unaware of the figures that moved into the room around him.

Blood and cries and pain and birth were too strong to enable him to note anything but them. Doc thrust the baby into his arms with a towel and said to rub the white stuff into the skin as best he could; he found himself chaffing the small, hot body, cradling its heavy head and tiny body in his arms. He sat down on the floor for fear of dropping it and felt an enormous lift of responsibility in his chest as he held the new soul close and heard the roars of expectancy of life in his ears. A lift and a weight.

It was unbelievable that everybody started like this; that his grandfather had once been a puling, purple, mosquito-armed midget, that Doc Bates had been a helpless thing with an open squalling mouth and unused lungs, that even old Joanna 'Windy-Belly', (one of the Misses Clark who ran the Post Office Trading Store and was the children's natural butt) had had tiny unformed features and a soft, vulnerable pulse beating on the top of her head instead of a cavalry moustache, wheezing walk and huge bunions sticking out of her slippers. How was it possible that these wispy little beings could grow into such monsters? Jackson looked down at the thing in his arms and his own wonder encompassed him.

Someone grabbed the baby out of his arms and up it went, shrieking and squirming, as a man's voice shouted above Jackson, "Let's 'ave a look at yu, yu raw-bummed little bastard, let's see if yu take after your grandpapa. Can't you wash this white scum off him, Doc, he look *horrible!*"

"That's vernex, Samuel. Insulated lanolin, super hormone variety . . . " said Doc Bates over his shoulder. "He's a great boy, isn't he . . . good pair of lungs, last a lifetime. Ha! Ha! Ha! Lots of fight."

Lily shouted out that she wanted to look at him, but Doc said, "Just you finish what you've got to finish and then you can have him."

Jackson felt both relief and loss that the baby had left him. He sat still on the floor and stared up at the thick black limbs of the Doc and the man Doc called Samuel silhouetted in the glare of the light, the legs of the table, the murk beyond. A wet nose was suddenly pressed behind his ear and dog's breath fanned his face as a large grey one inspected him. It did not seem very ferocious so he patted it and watched as it moved near to the table to make further examination of who was invading its house and what all the fuss was about.

"Get that beast out of here, Samuel!" Doc commanded, and Jackson saw a foot kick out and catch the dog's rump. It scurried for cover in a corner.

"Come on, Lily, one more push and it'll be done . . . uh . . . mmm . . . yes . . . here we are . . . perfect, girl . . . you're a marvel, no trouble, ahhh . . . " Doc let out a great gravelly sigh as the after-birth came away and the room was filled with the mysterious smell of newly-turned earth, of blood and birth.

A woman stepped into the light and moved to the end of the

27

table where Lily's head was. Jackson could not see Lily, could only hear her smothered breathing and sobbing, but he saw the woman—a large-jawed, grey-skinned lady with hair as red as cooked lobster-shells, lean down and whisper. She whispered for a full minute, her big jaw moving in the light, but Jackson could not make out what she said. Lily giggled weakly and then began to laugh a gusty, hysterical laugh.

"Let me look at him now, Doc, let me see me little pink and white baby," she gurgled. "Him pretty, Doc?"

The baby had quietened down but was still being held in the arms of the grandfather, Samuel, who was rocking and crooning to him above Jackson's head.

Doc was busy clearing things up and had moved out of the room for a moment so there was no answer.

"Do—oc!" yelled Lily, suddenly fearful, "where you gawne? Doc? You there, Doc? Ah want fe see the baby."

Doc came lumbering back into the room and took the towel-covered creature from Samuel and brought it to its mother.

"Here, Lily, here he is. What are you going to call him?"

"Oooeow! Him so little! Him so pretty! Look pon him fingers, look pon him nose . . . ha, ha, ha, ha, you the best little youngest child in the world! Look pon him, Doc, him got *blue* eyes!"

"Oh, they'll probably change, Lily. Go brown. See, he can't focus them yet. Oh, yes, they'll end up brown."

"Ah goin' to call him Baby-Doc, Baby-Doc Bates, after you," Lily announced breathlessly. "You like dat?"

Doc rumbled deep in his chest, "Baby Doc Bates," he said, "Poor little bugger."

\* \* \*

When Jackson followed Doc out of the hut he had lost all sense of direction. There was no moon now and the night was black and near and breathless . . . quiet, too . . . There was no glow of fire and the children had all gone home; only the night song of cicadas and soft shushing of the sea were to be heard. Then, surprisingly, they were on a beach. Jackson kept close behind, stepping warily on bare feet through coarse runner grass and then onto the delicious cool fineness of silky sand. Doc scuffed along ahead of him, the sand shrieking small protests under his old army boots while Jackson wondered where they would end up this time. He did not dare ask, and Doc seemed preoccupied and unaware of his presence.

A slight breeze was coming off the sea and the water lapped limply on the shore. Phosphorus made fleeting pretty appearances on the top of the few waves that broke on the shallow reef a little way out to sea as Jackson's eyes accustomed themselves to the darkness that had seemed to envelop them only a few moments before.

On the rise of sand at the end of the beach Doc sat down heavily and brought out an old pack of cigarettes, a box of safety matches and a hip flask. Jackson stopped and stood in front of him and watched as a flame flared in the blackness and lit the rugged face for a minute. He waited anxiously for any indication of what was to be the next move but Doc only grunted, rubbed his knees and offered the boy a cigarette as an afterthought. Jackson took it and waited again as the match rasped out its warning and another tiny flame gave no clue as to why they were here, though he searched Doc's face for information in the ten-second glow it made.

He sat down and sucked on his cigarette in the silence.

"Well . . ." Doc said finally, thick crumbling voice in the night, "now you know how we all get here."

The boy hesitated before he spoke, blowing smoke and hovering in the bewildered limbo of not knowing what was expected of him.

"Oh, ah seen kittens and bitches and goats havin' them, but it's different for people . . ." He trailed off into the silence. "Isn't it?"

"Mmmmm," Doc grunted again and drew a long, deep drag on his cigarette and Jackson could see the red glow that lit his nose to a transparent ruby in the darkness and, for an instant, two rheumy pea-soup eyes that stared balefully out into the Atlantic. Doc unscrewed the top of the flask and took a mighty swig, a swallow that sounded like a small explosion in the quiet night.

"You're twelve, mmm?" Not waiting for the reply. "Twelve . . . yes . . . I expect you'll be more interested in how they get in there than how they get out, eh, lad?" His belly shook slightly at his own joke, but no sound came out of his mouth.

He drank again.

"Some of them jump like frogs, some of them lie there like

little blubbery jelly-fish and some are tough red gnats with no flesh on their bones."

"Who?"

"The babies, boy, the babies. I can watch them grow up and they're always the same as that first moment they come out, the same personality as the gnat or the frog or the jelly-fish, that they were when they came out . . . its uncanny . . . the gnats have drive, but the jelly-fish probably live longer."

Another musing silence followed, broken only by Doc's harsh breathing and a swift expectoration of phlegm that landed on the sand with a squat, splatting sound.

"What was that one who just got born?"

"That one's a tiger, I hope. He ought to be . . . with a mother like that Lily and a rum-soaked old alligator like me for a father . . . he ought to be something . . . Baby Doc Bates . . ." The air seemed to tremble and swell with his great guffaws, "BABY DOC BATES, HIMSELF!"

It took Jackson a full minute to assimilate this fantastic disclosure. He did not know whether to laugh with the doctor or to shout out the amazement that he felt and he was glad of the concealing darkness.

"Twenty-five years I've been waiting for Baby Doc Bates to turn up and now he's here I don't know what to do with him!" Doc flicked his cigarette out towards the sea and it lay, a pin-prick of light in the black.

"Wasn't sure he was mine until I saw him, you know, but he's too light to be anyone else's around here. Good girl, Lily!" He up-ended the flask and drained it, smacking his lips and wiping his moustache with the back of his hand. "Happy Days," he said.

Jackson was still trying to imagine the mating of the monumental doctor and little Lily, as the voice in the darkness continued . . . "I had a daughter in England once, but she'd be over twenty by now . . . took after her mother though, always whining and grizzling around your legs, the mother yapping at eye level and the daughter girning at thigh level; gutless wonders, both of them, so I left them to get on with it. Hmmmmm, Baby Doc Bates . . . not much of a start in life . . . little cross-breed bastard, father over fifty, mother sixteen, pushing forty in guile, and black to boot . . . he'll have to do some travelling to make his mark in the world . . . I suppose it's no skin off his nose on Hambro but put him out into the big world and his chances are close to zero unless he's a genius . . . No, worse if he's a bloody genius, they're always being shit on from a great height . . . It's unlikely he's a genius, after all . . ." Doc's reverie was so entirely self-directed that the boy listened with mounting anxiety and a vague sadness that he could not understand. "Give him five years down this end of the island, let his animal instincts get full sway, and then up our end for as much education as I can cram into his head . . . Libby won't mind. That's one of the things I love about this island . . . it's the only place I've met true liberalism in my lifetime. Not like those turds on sticks in England who cleverly harness their hate and shriek invective against 'Injustice', 'Insanity', 'War', 'Poverty' and 'Disease', all big words and easy to say—they disapprove of them—they've made their statement and that's it—that's the only sort of liberalism I've ever met there and about as useful as rusty razor blades—but here they adapt to the situation and then gradually absorb and change it until it is not a 'situation' anymore . . . I admire that, lad, I admire that very much . . . Libby the Liberal, huh . . . I wonder what Libby is short for? Libby . . . let me see . . . Liberty, perhaps, or Libertine. No, not libertine . . . she'll look after him anyway when my flighty Lily finds fresh fields . . . poor little Baby Doc Bates . . . couldn't send him to University I suppose . . . pity . . . if he's the right stuff, maybe . . . mmmmn . . . poor little bugger . . ."

Jackson could not understand why Baby Doc Bates should be so poor; Doc was a better father to have than Sidney and Lily was not going to run away and leave him like his own mother had done. Libby, Doc's faithful Libby, would be a good mother even if she did. How could he be so poor?

"I think he's a lucky little bugger," he said.

Doc expelled breath and ran fingers through scanty hair, feet thrust out in the sand and big khaki shorts hung in dark loops that scalloped below the backs of his knees.

"Well, young Jackson, I suppose his is not such a different case from yours; both born in Snipe's Bay, both half-castes, both born at this end of Hambro Island; you'll both try to conquer the world—God help you, if I know your grandfather's blood, and there's a lot of it in you; . . . we'll have to see how the rest of it turns out."

31

"What's a half-caste?"

"A half-caste—hmmmmmn—a half-caste is a person who's half one thing and half another, like half black and half white would be; half English and half Chinese, no—that's a Eurasian . . . No, but that's a half-caste as well."

Jackson was puzzled. "Does it feel any different to be a half-caste, do you think?" he asked tentatively. "I don't think I feel different."

"Well, some people say it's different, son, though I've never seen anything in my time that would corroborate it . . . there was a theory about a hundred years ago that the sutures in the negroid skull (that's those small joins in the scalp that you saw tonight in Baby Doc Bates's head) came together earlier in the negro skull thus making the brain smaller, but it's been disproven years ago . . . No, a half-caste is not a man who is envied in the big world because he belongs to no one . . . he's not white, and he's not black, so he's in the middle and he's got to pretend he's one thing or the other, or else become militant. Here on Hambro nobody bothers because everybody is mixed and the society caters to anybody, but in the United States or, in fact, in any white community in the world, they'd question your colour."

Jackson took more time to digest this. He felt himself suddenly the victim of a new and virulent disease for which there was no cure.

"Hasn't your grandfather ever talked to you about this?"

"No," said Jackson. "I've never heard him even say the word 'half-caste' . . . Oh, I always knew my grandmother was black; no, not black, I used to try and bite into her when I was little, she looks like she made of chocolate . . . and once when my granpaw took me into Kingston when I was eight, a lady said: 'Look at that coloured boy', but he told me that everybody coloured except albinos and that it horrible to be albino like her because they can't look at the sun, or open their eyes in bright light. They got no pigments. Anyway, I've never felt any different from my grandfather or my grandmother," he finished lamely.

Doc did not say anything for some time after this outburst. He sat still, holding his two knees wide apart with his hands and whistling through his bottom teeth.

"Looks like you and Baby Doc Bates are going to have the

same problems, lad, if you ever try to leave this island. I would like you to look out for him when I can't do it anymore. Is that a bargain?"

The boy nodded.

"You can be the youngest godfather on the island, how's that?"

"O.K. Doc, but *what* problems?"

"Ah . . . you'll have to talk to your grandfather about them. I don't suppose you've decided what you want to do, but you won't stay on this island for the rest of your life and when you visit the big cities like London and New York you're going to have problems, son, take my word for it . . . and so is *he*."

"Because we're half-castes?"

"Yes," with finality.

Jackson sat on his haunches and dribbled sand through his fingers. He wanted to pursue the subject further but Doc was already gathering himself together to stand up, stowing his flask in the back pocket of his voluminous khaki shorts; cigarettes, matches went inside his shirt.

They marched solemnly back along the beach and Jackson wondered why it had seemed so dark before. Now he saw everything; black sea-weed lining the shore, the curve of white sand, rocks jagged and teeming with scuttling crabs, even a ragged spider's web stretched precariously between two bushes he saw, but only with his outward eye; inwardly he was surveying the many impressions and happenings which this night had brought with it . . . Doc's retreating back in the firelight; Lily's sweating face and her snarling in pain, sweet sing-song voice: "I goin' to eat your guava-face one day, Matchew"; the funny little head coming out light from between her dark and lovely thighs; holding the baby on the floor, the fear for its frantic vulnerability; Doc's hands busy in the glare of white light, blood; the dog's breath fanning his ear and the shifting jaw of the strange lady with hair the colour of cooked lobster shells . . . It was like remembering the whole of one of those truncated dreams where everything seems normal while the dream lasts, but totally bizarre, worrying and fragmented when it is over—there are large gaps of non-recall which the dreamer has thrust from his conscious mind in fear or in repulsion. The rest of the evening had not been like a dream though, trudging along the beach, smoking, and hearing Doc's voice pour out 'problems' in the darkness. He thought about Lily and the doctor doing what he had seen many couples do, perhaps on the very beach they had just left . . . his mind seemed magnetised by sex these days, pictures of naked females lurked in his semi-conscious like greedy cats who rush forward at the sound of a spoon on a plate and he masturbated frequently. He had never felt any guilt about this as he knew that all his half-brothers and younger uncles did the same and they all compared notes jauntily on how it was, and how it felt, and boasted of the size and endurance of their personal apparatus. The picture of Doc and Lily was not an easy one to conjure up, but once conjured, it was also impossible to dispel it from his mind and he laughed aloud, seated beside Doc in the lopsided car, at the sudden thought of the baggy shorts and bristling ugly head both giving way to passions that Jackson had previously thought belonged only to the young and beautiful.

Doc looked at him sharply but said nothing.

"I was just thinking of Lily's daddy's big, grey dog sticking his nose in my ear," Jackson explained hastily.

The 'half-caste' business he pushed aside until he could talk to his grandparents.

Strangely enough, it was to neither of them that he spoke; it was to Elliot Brodie.

# 2

## Elliot Brodie

ELLIOT BRODIE WAS a Canadian who arrived on Hambro Island several weeks after the birth of Baby Doc Bates. He came on the weekly boat from Kingston, bearing a sleeping-roll, battered, bestickered Samsonite bag and a guitar. He wore a large straw hat, frayed and yellowed, low on his head.

He was crane-like, rangy and stooped with straight tow hair and a long nose, twenty-eight, still a perpetual student though he held a degree in construction engineering; he was looking for Old Man Jackson.

He came to the house armed with a letter from his father who had kept up desultory postal chess games with the old man over the years, and was greeted by him as a long-lost son. He had spent several months on Bimini, "just bumming around," he explained; a week in Nassau, which he hated for its blatant tourist atmosphere; nearly a year in Jamaica, where he worked on the construction of a new hotel in Ocho Rios. He was immediately much enraptured by the old man and adored Grandma May whom he followed around for the first week or two, fascinated by her variety of interests—her skill and practicality in all the pursuits of goat-keeping, honey-gathering, wart-charming, cooking and other forms of housewifery. He was also delighted with Hambro itself and decided in the third week of his visit to walk right around the island, taking notes and making a rough geographical survey as he went. Jackson was allowed to accompany him as he knew more about the topography of the island than any of his contemporaries in the family. His frequent forays in search of items for his museum had given him a good working knowledge of the whole island.

Grandma May gave them honey and goats' cheese, bananas, home-made liquorice to chew when thirsty and brown nut-loaves. Old Man Jackson presented Brodie with a gallon of his best rum and they set off carrying haversacks and water-bottles, underwater equipment, compass, Brodie's guitar (because he never travelled without it), a Leica camera, twenty precious rolls of films, and a sextant, which old man Jackson had unearthed from the depths of a mouldering trunk that lay in the tool shed.

The island was shaped roughly like a horse-shoe with the opening on the south-east corner and Snipe's Bay like a hand grabbing out into the Atlantic on the eastern end of one tail. Old Man Jackson had built his house right at the other tail of the horse-shoe, the western end. It was from here that the boy led Brodie down to the sea (the western extreme of the island) to commence their exploration.

Brodie carried with him a thick notebook in which he wrote continually and a large sketch pad. It was slow going. He had one of those perpetually enquiring minds which did not allow him a moment's relaxation, and he was as thorough in his examination of a butterfly or a spider, as he was in measuring the density of coconut-palms, or gauging the depth of a particularly prolific coral reef. On the second day out they discovered a marvellous reef and dived all day, collecting specimens of 'gor-gonians', those strange skeletons of a flexible, horny substance which form themselves into branching bushes, lacy fans and tapering whips and give the appearance of wonderful swaying gardens in transparent waters.

Jackson was very excited at finding a huge chunk of organ-pipe coral and immediately claimed it for his museum. It was one of the few species that was badly represented in his own collection. Brodie acquiesced, reluctantly, and they carefully stowed their finds in a well-marked deposit to collect at some future date when less encumbered.

On they went, Brodie taking readings each night with compass and sextant which he taught Jackson to use. They supplemented Grandma May's provisions with fresh fish caught on the reefs and shellfish which they threw in the fire and which roasted in their own juices.

At first they did not talk much. Jackson was shy of this peculiarly donnish man. His long, pink nose which peeled regularly once a day, his prying mind, his huge knowledge and his dedication to detail, were all very foreign to someone brought up in the easy-going atmosphere of Hambro Island.

36

The boy was wary, but as polite as he could be for the first two days, listening to all that Brodie had to say, but offering very little information himself, though he knew much more about the coastline and layout of the land than he admitted. At night they sat on either side of the fire and Brodie plucked at his guitar and sang songs in a thin tenor, while the boy whittled away on sticks and watched Brodie's long fingers changing position on the strings of the six-stringer.

On their fourth night out he picked up the guitar, held it as he had seen Brodie do and tried to reproduce some of the chords. Brodie, who had been writing furiously in his notebook came over and showed him how to place his fingers to get a harmonious chord and Jackson spent the rest of the evening practising. He sang a few songs of his own, but his voice was just breaking and sometimes the notes came out on three levels like 'a raging cockatoo being attacked by a crow'—that's what Brodie said it sounded like.

They established a much more equable relationship after this. At night Brodie talked about his home in Canada and showed Jackson more chords to practise. During the day he was not so preoccupied with beetles' legs and gnats' wings that he would not stop and have a smoke or swim with the boy. In short, Brodie began to consider him as a person, a noteworthy creature, and not just as 'one of Old Man Jackson's dingy progeny' as he had at first described Matthew Jackson in his diary. He called him 'Matt'.

They were now halfway down the island though still travelling very slowly and, by this time, had finished most of Grandma May's supplies. They lived on fish, sea oysters, coconuts and rum for which, through necessity, Jackson had developed a taste.

\*     \*     \*

The day they crossed the 'Clyde', squelching through mud two feet deep, bitten by swarms of sandflies who took full advantage of their exposed bodies, cursing the pointed mangrove shoots that pierced the soles of their feet and the great gnarled roots that stood out of the mud and made progress into an obstacle course, Jackson felt so tired that he would cheerfully have sunk into the swamp and been incarcerated there for ever. They camped on the other side in a small gully where the wind

37

blew the tiny vicious sandflies back to their own stagnant breeding ground and the air was not sour with the fetid smell of disintegrating mud. The boy threw himself down on the ground and allowed Brodie to prepare food, forage for wood, make the fire, put up the tent and light the hurricane lamp. At last, hunger stirred him and he ambled over to the fire where Brodie sat neatly penning his diary.

"*Thursday 17th of September, 1956.* Feathery Cirrus clouds high in the western sky. I went down to the beach early to fish for rock cod. Used crab bait which Matt procured for me. He impales the unfortunate crab on a long wire spike as it lurks in a crevice of a rock and brings it out triumphantly, all eight legs and both claws waving about in a frenzy of impotence. Today Matt was irritatingly slow, being slightly hung-over . . ." he read over Brodie's shoulder and then glanced at the heading of the page.

"Is that the date today?"

"Yes," snapped Brodie, flicking over the pages. He did not like Jackson even reading through his notes, but his diary was sacrosanct.

"It's my birthday tomorrow! I forgot all about it. How could I forget my own birthday?" The boy swerved about the fire kicking sand and punching brown fists into his own belly in frustration.

"Grandma May was goin' to bake me passion fruit cake and make Calulu soup . . ." He slumped into a heap of leaden arms and legs on the ground. "Christ, I'm hungry!"

Brodie took off his glasses and rubbed the bridge of his nose delicately. He was not accustomed to this sort of problem and had to give himself time to adjust to the violence of adolescent emotion which he himself had put so far behind.

"And how old will you be tomorrow?"

"Thirteen."

Brodie pondered on this for some minutes still gently moving the upper bridge of his nose between forefinger and thumb. Then he rose with his customary stooped dignity and made his way to his haversack which lay on its side next to the tent. He rummaged through the outer pocket for some time and then emerged smiling with a thick bar of dark bitter chocolate sunk with silver paper, melted and hardened in turn by ardours and temperatures.

"Here," he extended it towards the boy. "Here, I was saving it up for something, I don't know what, but it will serve for your birthday. Take it. It's yours. Eat it now, if you like. It'll do you good."

Jackson took the proffered gift with a gasp of joy and began to pick lint, fluff and silver paper from its edges. He smelt it and licked a corner lovingly. Then he took a huge bite that filled his whole mouth with the brittle limpid ambrosia and lay back sucking and sighing, while saliva and juices of chocolate ran over his taste buds and did him good.

Brodie put back his spectacles and watched the boy with a solicitude that was quite foreign to his nature. He remembered his own thirteenth birthday especially . . . that was the day when both his mother and his father, who were divorced, had given him a bicycle. Two brand-new mint-fresh bicycles, a pair of binoculars and *The Omnibus of Scientific Facts* had been presented to him that morning with his cornflakes. After much deliberation he took the second bicycle to a dealer in town and received sixty dollars in return. His father was a millionaire, a self-made man who had made his pile in lumberyards, timber and papermills, but who preferred a solitary life in the backwoods to the bustle of Montreal. Elliot lived in that city with his mother, who had married again. A substantial trust fund had been set up for his education.

His had been a lonely childhood spent mostly in a modern apartment block in the centre of the city. Every summer he was sent to camp while his mother and step-father travelled. He received cards from Mexico, Ecuador, the Virgin Islands, Portugal, and always carefully removed the stamps for his album. They bore messages like "Went round Cintra Castle today. Very baroque", or "Have just visited Chichinitza, home of the ancient Mayan civilisation", or "It teemed with rain here in Kobe. The smell of drying fish was unbearable."

He searched them for some hidden meaning and, finding none, finally resigned himself to non-communication with both his parents. He spent two weeks of each year with his real father fishing for salmon, and playing chess with him in the evenings. When they spoke at all it was about fishing tackle or bait, sport, (his father was a great ice hockey fan) or chess finessing.

He thought about Matt's grandfather, the old patriarch Jackson, surrounded by his prolific children, his sprawling wooden house, his industrious black wife, his island, his drinking partner, Doc Bates, and he envied him. He envied the boy, too, for his ability to lie savouring chocolate in the glow of the fire, wallowing thoughtless in the comfort of drowsy well-being; he envied him for the nearness of brothers, sisters, uncles, cousins, aunts, dogs and goats . . . an animal proximity that made him part of a whole, unquestioning of his own existence, alive.

"Do you go to school?" he enquired, knowing that he was about to embark on one of the sort of cross-examinations that he himself had loathed being subjected to as an adolescent.

Jackson mumbled assent, but was not distracted enough from his stomach to notice Brodie's attention.

"And do you learn much there?" persisted Brodie.

"Oh, just sums and readin', writin', that's about all." The boy rolled over on his belly and examined the chocolate for more embedded silver paper.

"What would you like to do with yourself when you grow up?"

"I'm goin' to grow things," answered Jackson unhesitatingly.

"Where?"

"Here. All over the island. It goin' to be a garden island."

"But there's not enough earth here. Your grandfather has the only workable land on the island . . . and that's about twenty-seven acres . . . the rest is scrub with no top-soil. You can't grow things where there's no earth."

Jackson, unconvinced, chewed his chocolate in silence. The fire crackled. Brodie went back to his diary. He felt a twinge of guilt at dampening the boy's hopes so brusquely. He could not concentrate on the events of the day.

"Wouldn't you like to go to a proper school?" he said finally.

"Our school's proper."

"No, I mean a school on the mainland, say in New York or Montreal."

Jackson stared into the fire bemused.

"Or even London. There's a place in London where you can find every known plant, tree and flower that's ever been categorised. Kew, it's called."

"I couldn't go any of those places yet."

"Why not, Matt? I could pay your way. I'd like to do something for you. Let me speak to your grandfather about it when we get back."

"No. I don't want to go to any those places yet," said Jackson, "it would be bad trouble."

"But why?" Brodie now felt impelled to force the boy to agree to a formal education. Part of his insistence was a genuine desire to see an intelligent human being given every assistance to achieve his potential, part was a vague yearning that he should understand *him*, Brodie, resemble him, feel the insularity of lonely years of study in a cold, distant climate.

"They probably wouldn't accept me anyway. I'm a half-caste."

Brodie was stunned into silence.

"Doc Bates told me that it was trouble to be a half-caste in those big cities."

"And what else did he tell you about being a half-caste?"

"Nothin'. He said to ask my Granpaw."

"And did you?"

"No. I forgot."

"Do you know what a half-caste is?"

"Of course, man, it's being half one thing and half another—grandmother black and grandfather white—they don't like half-castes in big cities, Doc says."

Brodie went back to his diary with this information resounding in his ears; but Jackson's hereditary problems, his education, his future, his implicit acceptance of the situation, stood bulky and immovable between him and the jottings of the day.

His mind sifted through methods of approach, discarding the ones which smacked of patronage or pity. After a careful consideration he cleared his throat pedantically, collecting all the gravel in his larynx and thrusting it into a corner so that it might not interfere with his intention.

"If you want to grow things you have to know everything about the half-castes of the vegetable world too, because they are nearly always superior to the parent plant. They are called 'hybrids' and every farmer knows that hybrid corn, strawberries or tomatoes are the best . . . Oh, practically every variety of fruit and vegetable has been improved by hybridisation . . . animals too . . . they've crossed buffalo with domestic cows and got terrific results, 'Cattalos', I think they're called; donkeys and mares make mules; chickens; pigs; they're experimenting with all sorts now . . ." He began to doodle in his diary as he talked.

"I've always disliked the use of the word 'half-caste' . . . it has so many unfortunate associations . . . 'half-baked' or 'half-cut', 'half-cock', 'half-hearted', 'half-mast', 'half-truth', 'half-pay' . . . They're all words that imply something unpleasant and because of them, I think 'half-caste' has come to mean an untrustworthy person, a sinister, skulking *side-kick* who lurks about in lurid tales of the South Seas, never the hero certainly, not even worthy enough to be the villain . . . no, I disapprove of the word."

He was expanding nicely into his subject now, not noticing that Jackson's eyes had glazed over and that he had finished the whole bar of chocolate . . . "They should ban the word from our language and apply the use of 'hybrid' to *people* as well as plants and animals . . . It is a dignified word hybrid, yes, hybrid. It conjures up pictures of cobs of corn and honeysuckle to me, but that's probably because I took part in an experiment in pollination one year at camp . . . of course, it's well known that hybridisation in plants is more successful than in animals, but why shouldn't there be a strain of man, hardy and resistant to disease, who's known as a 'hybrid'?"

Jackson was sound asleep.

"He could have eyes featuring both his genetic antecedents like yours do; mmmm, yes, come to think of it, we are all hybrids of one sort or another and becoming increasingly more so as travel facilities shrink the world. I suppose students of ethnology would say that each variety of the human race commenced with some repeated physical characteristic— Mongoloid—slit eyes, folds in the inner corners, skin from saffron-yellow to light shades of brown; Caucasoids—no corner or lid fold, skin from pinkish-white to olive and brown; Negroids—nose, broad and flat with flaring wings, skin from light to dark brown and black. Surely there could be a fusion of Caucasoid and Negroid to produce a 'Hybroid'."

He realised instinctively that he was talking to himself and stood up wearily to prod the dying fire and pull off his sneakers.

"Hmmmmm, wery in-triguing, Brodie, a fascinating prog-nostication!" (He imitated the thick accent of Mendel, Professor of Anthropology at Montreal University). "You should write a thesis and expound your subject, Brodie; Ex-cept-ion-al vork, my poy!"

"What I advocate, sir, is that they declare a week of National

Orgy in the United States of America. During this week every fertile white man must copulate with one or more fecund black women, while every fertile black man must cover at least six fecund white women—thus taking care of the population ratio. The resultant children will form the basis of a new race of 'Hybroids' and discrimination, of course, will be a thing of the past, sir."

"Good vork, my poy, excellent!"

He giggled at his own humour and picked up his diary again. He had drawn a scribble of adjoining squares, some jagged with triangles, some divided into two parts, one of which he had filled; a cockatoo's head with raised crest which had started as a chicken and got out of hand. He had written 'HIGH' and drawn a large phallic tree stump. He took a sip of rum, tore out the page and threw it in the fire.

Years later, going through old diaries, he could not remember why the 17th of September, 1956 had so mysteriously disappeared from his life. When he read the 16th and the 18th of that month, he suddenly had a vivid picture of Jackson, flat on his back beside the fire, still clutching a handful of crumpled silver paper, his face blissfully unconscious, sleeping the deep adolescent sleep that lengthens limbs overnight. He had covered the boy up and determined to do something about his education that night, he remembered, but there was still a worrying gap as to why that page of his diary was missing.

\*   \*   \*

The next day, Jackson's birthday, they journeyed on, arriving at the Hambro River in mid-afternoon. This was a twin of the Clyde, another turgid mangrove swamp widening into mud-flats before it emptied its chrome waters into the sea, staining the ocean for about fifty yards and then dispersing into wisps that clouded the iridescent blue for half a mile.

Jackson threw off his clothes and hurled himself into the cool, green sea. They had made the tedious crossing. His body sang and his pulses beat loud through him as he washed off the offending sludge that clung between his toes and in the backs of his knees. He swam away from the scum that had come off him and lay motionless on his back, letting himself be held up by the buoyancy of salt and the small flirting of his hands in the water.

43

He lay, dreaming, seeing how little movement he could make and still stay afloat, suspended in his element. Golden light filtered through closed eye-lids and flooded his brain. He wished they would reach Snipe's Bay soon and see Lily and Baby Doc and old Samuel. He wondered what they would look like in the daylight, whether they would remember him after the drama of that evening, only three months ago.

He was continually hungry now and that was an added incentive to reach Snipe's Bay. Huge helpings of treacle pudding and loaves of crusty bread, savoury rice, chicken with fried bread-fruit, hovered in his head sending groans of anticipation up from his stomach and groans of frustration down from his throat.

*    *    *

Entry in the diary of Elliot Brodie:

*21st of September, 1956*
SNIPE'S BAY

A hot dry wind blew us into Snipe's Bay yesterday evening. It blew sand from behind us that stung the backs of our legs and hurried us along like two tattered terriers, tired and tremulous. (Alliteration, full marks Brodie!)

The light was failing as we entered the village and I could not make out much of our surroundings. A few asymmetric huts dotted about, a long low shed that housed chickens from the sounds issuing forth, skinny dogs that nipped our heels, sussing bums immediately. ('Sussing' is an island word for recognising or understanding. I think it is a bastard form of 'Assessing', but am not sure. Matt uses it all the time). He (Matt) led me to a sagging shack where an old man with fewer than five teeth in his head, welcomed us with a steadying dram of rum. There was a laughing girl there as well, holding a tiny naked baby out to make water on the dirt floor. She gave Matt a kiss which embarrassed him into a corner and she told me her name was Lily. We were so tired that after she had given us another tot of rum and a plate of beans flavoured with pork (delicious), we both fell into respective corners and slept until morning (our first night under cover for two weeks).

I was startled into wakefulness this morning by the baby mewling and for a few moments could not remember where I was. After a wondrous breakfast of papaya and goats' cheese,

44

coffee and bread, Lily took us down to the beach where I got my first view of Snipe's Bay proper. It is a long, wide crescent with rocks at one end rising to a hill at the other (snap-shots included), coconut fringed; the hill is densely vegetated. The inevitable mangrove roots surround the creek which trickles clear fresh water out into the sea from the centre of the bay, but I counted at least seven different types of tree including cinnamon, so perhaps there may have been ancient deposits of guana to enrich the soil and bring about all this verdancy? (N.B. have taken specimens from different parts of the bay marked 'Snipe's Bay' 1, 2, 3, 4 and 5 for analysis).

Lily came with me on my exploration while Matt took the underwater equipment and made a survey of the reef which lies about sixty yards from the shore. He brought back an assortment of reef fish including two 'Grunts' and a large grouper, a red one, which we ate for lunch. I found out that the old man is her father. Lily's, I mean. The baby is called 'Baby Doc Bates' after the doctor who delivered him. Quaint. Still cannot figure out who can be the father. No likely candidates in evidence. She is a very attractive girl!

*22nd of September, 1956*

More exploration of Snipe's Bay. Lily showed me the remains of a house set among the mangroves on the far side of the creek. She said the house had been built by Old Man Jackson for the boy's grandmother and was originally occupied by her.

"Oh," I said, "before they moved down to the other end of the island?"

"No," she said, "his other grandmother . . ."

"And what happened to her?" I asked.

"She go back to Kingston . . . she fancy lady. Old Man keep she here three, four year, sar." (More complications of hereditary for poor Matt to cope with?)

It is a mysterious and rather disturbing place. Not revealing its secrets and yielding nothing at all to strangers. Yesterday when I undressed to swim from the beach at the far end of the bay, I had an odd sensation that the trees were watching me. Not people behind trees, the trees themselves. But it is lovely and wild, untouched. Above all, untouched. I have discovered frangipani, the wild pink one and the fleshy white and port-wine magnolia; the smell was overpowering last night (like the essence of all that is best about bananas), a cocktail of smells, which include dog, chicken, pig and baby.

A vague plan to build a house myself on the crest of the hill and overlooking the bay has formed in my head. Maybe *then* it would yield me up its secret . . .

The natives of Snipe's Bay are a mixed bag. I have met a man called Noakes who owns a much-mended Ford pick-up, about two hundred chickens and the only house worthy of the name in the settlement. He is acknowledged squire by the other inhabitants and has a vast number of children by several women, judging from the pregnant ladies and ladies lugging infants who passed to and fro taking a look at me as I sat sipping rum on his verandah. He also has a brilliant long-tailed macaw called Seraphina which shrieked incessantly throughout our interview.

There is also one expatriate white woman in the colony, a certain Mrs. Winnie Hart, who is quite hideous, pretty ancient, and who obviously dyes her hair with red ink. She lives in a tumbled-down shack at the rocky end of the bay and there is some liaison with Lily's father as he spends a good deal of his time down there. She is garrulous, but gives away nothing about her past, which I suspect has been notorious. Says she has lived here since the end of the war. I would say she was American from her accent, but who knows about anyone in these remote little back-washes? She could be a German spy stranded here during the war, a missionary fallen from grace, a has-been 'Madam', anything . . .

Lily is beautiful. I decided that fact today. She has the agility of a cheetah, and the face of a naughty kitten with brown eyes. Quite a devastating combination! She has a moth-eaten brother called Quincey who works for Noakes and appears every lunchtime for a grumble.

She and Matt are very thick, giggling and whispering secret jokes. I am jealous, but I suppose it is ridiculous, as the boy is only thirteen.

I have come to realise that he (Matt) is extremely intelligent. He has that strange island aptitude for looking stupid when it suits him and then suddenly one is aware that not only has he understood, but is generally several steps ahead and *predetermining all one's moves*. It is most off-putting, but I will allow my misjudgement and treat him differently in future. Incidentally, I think he has a great one, given the right education and environment. I will foster it if possible!

*　*　*

Brodie never finished his circumnutation of Hambro Island, at least not on that trip. Early next morning Doc Bates arrived, bearing news that spoiled all his plans of further exploration. The Misses Clark from the Post Office Trading Store had received a message through their pedal radio (the only one on the island) that his father was dying, and that he must return to Canada immediately.

They drove back to Old Man Jackson's house in style, Brodie craning out of the car beside Doc and pondering on the possibilities of an air-strip in the flat lands in the centre of the island; Jackson spreading himself out like a pasha on the back-seat with most of their gear and a cheeky three-day-old kid which Lily had given him: it butted its head into his belly and tried to suckle his fingers all the way back.

*　*　*

Brodie did not return to Hambro Island for over a year and a half. He spent his time pulling in all the far-reaching assets of his millionaire father's empire, consolidating his new position, selling stocks, disposing of a vast proportion of the responsibilities of timber-yards and saw-mills, planning his own migration to the island when he had accrued a large enough working capital. He arrived back on Hambro, pale and purposeful, ready to start on the construction of an air-strip halfway between Old Man Jackson's house and Snipe's Bay. He had made elaborate plans.

He found the Jackson family just as he had left them, except that there were two new members and Jackson had grown four inches; his voice had matured to a steady baritone not given to sudden soprano squeaks. No one was surprised, except Brodie himself, when he stepped off the clumsy, but sea-worthy tub that brought him in from Kingston. He felt greatly honoured and relieved to be welcomed with such affectionate acceptance.

Both Old Man Jackson and Doc Bates were thrilled by the

47

idea of an air-strip. It was agreed that the land would be leased to Brodie for a period of seven years in which time he would complete the work, set up two hangars, and begin trading with Kingston and Miami on a commercial basis.

Brodie imported a bull-dozer, a caterpillar, three jeeps, a station-wagon and a cement mixer from Kingston, and work on the Hambro Island Airport commenced. Every available man was employed and Brodie proved an efficient painstaking boss, who was constantly on the site and who displayed an infinite patience with the foibles of his workmen, even when they disappeared on fishing trips or lazed about in the shade on sweltering days.

Sidney was a willing, if somewhat irresponsible overseer, but valuable because of his knowledge and understanding of the men he was dealing with. Jackson learned to drive a jeep. He was used as an errand boy to liaise between jetty and air-strip. When the first shack was erected on the work site, Jackson lived in it with Brodie, and thus began the true education of Matthew Jackson.

Brodie filled the shack with books. There were books on soil conservation, land erosion, books on crop-rotation, insect pests, butterflies, birds, Ancient Egypt, the Fall of the Roman Empire, pole-vaulting, One Hundred Famous Lives, Shakespeare, Tolstoy, De Maupassant and Flaubert. There were books on art, finger-painting, exploration, botany, flowerarrangement, chess and anthropology. Each weekly visit of the boat from Kingston brought more books, until they had to erect a lean-to to house them all.

Brodie scheduled Jackson's day so that it included at least two hours of reading time, which, at first, was an interminable fatigue for the boy. But after three weeks he accustomed himself to it and slowly began to enjoy his continuous expansion of knowledge.

Brodie took great pleasure in explaining the functioning of some hard-to-grasp theory, though he would become irritable when Jackson put on his non-comprehending face. He could not abide feigned stupidity, which was the commonest excuse for shoddy work that he found on the island. He talked it over with Old Man Jackson and Doc Bates one night after a particularly gruelling week's work on the air-strip—men had fouled cables, put a bull-dozer and a caterpillar out of action and deposited twenty tons of wet cement a mile away from where it was to be used.

Doc Bates propounded a concept that it was the congenital hang-over of the slave, his only means of retaliation. Play dumb and thwart the white man. Old Man Jackson poo-pooed this idea, saying that the only reason for the men's lack of enthusiasm was the fact that they had never worked on any project which called for combined effort—that they had never taken orders from one man before—never exerted themselves beyond a few hours fishing and a desultory dig in their small plots of earth; why should they suddenly adapt to a strenuous nine-hour day? It was ridiculous to think that they could.

Slowly, ponderously, and with a multitude of set-backs, work on the air-strip continued.

Jackson earned enough money to buy himself a bicycle. It was a bit of a come-down after the jeep, but it got him about, and he spent every Sunday at Snipe's Bay. Lily was the attraction, though some Sundays the lure of Grandma May's feasts were too much for him, and he cycled down after gorging himself at midday.

Lily had seduced him several weeks before Brodie came back to Hambro Island.

One calm Saturday evening after she had brought in the goats, fed the baby and left him with Mrs. Winnie Hart, she took Jackson by the hand and led him down to the old ruined house by the creek.

He had been at Snipe's Bay all that day. Had a lift down in Mr. Noake's pick-up truck. All day he had watched Lily. He watched her milk six goats (the same straddling stance that his grandmother used), squirting jets of frothy white into a giant pail; he watched her, while Baby Doc Bates took uncertain steps and sat down heavily, waving a stick around his head and crowing with delight when the small black kids leapt in the air and stamped their neat hoofs down together; he walked down to the water's edge and held the squirming brown body of the baby while she washed him with incredible thoroughness. He lay back on his elbows on the sand and watched her as she tucked her skirt up around her hips and heaved her baby through the small waves breaking in the lee of the reef. He watched her scale and gut a fish, while the flaking white sequin scales flew back and caught in her hair. He watched her eating the same fish which she had wrapped in banana leaves and steamed with herbs over hot coals. He watched her black eyes beckon him in the shadow and change to amber in the sunlight. He watched the drops of salt water slide off her seal-smooth shoulders after she had raced him to the reef and back and they lay panting on the beach; the shadows of the palm trees lengthened above them, and then she took him by the hand and led him to the ruined house by the creek. And all the time she had been watching him watching her.

So she took his hand and put it on her breast under the old faded blue T-shirt that she was wearing and he remembered Doc Bates talking to his grandfather on the verandah one afternoon . . . "Breasts like bullets", he had said, "put your eyes out, they could . . . like bloody bullets, they were."

"This your grandaddy's house, Matchew. This *your* house, *my* house. You like it here, Matchew? I goin' eat your guava-face today, Matchew. You see."

And Jackson felt a groan growing inside him. A groan that would not escape from his body until he had invaded *her* body, a groan that filled him as he wanted to fill her. She would not let him grab or be incompetent. She led his hand to touch and explore until the groan was a roar of blood in his head and every piece of clothing that touched him was a clinging, poisonous vine that held and choked and fettered. He tore off his shirt and shorts while Lily carefully put aside her clothes and they faced each other naked in his grandfather's termite-ridden house with the crooked floor.

"You got the same colour like my Baby Doc Bates," said Lily. "You a real man now, Matchew. One day my Baby Doc Bates goin' look jus' like you. Real pretty boy."

Jackson did not make sense of anything she said. He took one step towards her and held the burning heat of himself against her cool, sleek length.

\* \* \*

And afterwards he ran, ran and ran all the way down the beach and all the way back again. He was surprised that his legs transported him with such ease. He felt as though the bones inside them had turned to honey. Then he threw himself into the water and let it engulf him. He sank beneath its surface

50

like a piece of water-logged driftwood and very slowly expelled every ounce of breath from his lungs. It was what dying must be like, he thought, sinking into a marvellous labyrinth of thoughtless, timeless, weightlessness . . . a different sort of dying than he had done with Lily—that had been a climax and a death of the senses which left him fearful and elated by his own virility—he needed respite to gestate his new status and responsibility. Under the sea he ceased to exist and even the bubbles that escaped his mouth stopped breaking the surface of the water to disclose his whereabouts. He felt that he had died and was reborn in the two minutes he spent slowly sinking in Snipe's Bay.

When he came up, he swam out to the reef—a lingering crawl keeping time, in long over-arm strokes to the song in his head . . .

> O Li-ly, O Li-lio,
> Lily, Lil-lil-lilio,
> O Li-ly, my lo-ove.

By the time Brodie came back, Jackson had established a routine of going down to Snipe's Bay on Sunday morning or Saturday night depending on when Mr. Noakes made his rounds. He and Lily made love on the floor of his grandfather's toppling house, they made love in the disused goat shed, they made love on the beach, in the shallow water, under the trees and on the hill.

They planted a garden near the old house and Lily put in some beans and sweet corn. Sometimes they would stay there all day, just he and Lily and Baby Doc Bates, drifting up and down the beach, cooking fish over the open fire, prodding at the earth, drinking clear water from the spring, sleeping . . . And Lily would sometimes cuff him and treat him just like the baby, and they would wrestle on the sand until Jackson proved himself the stronger and Lily would writhe and twist in his arms and then collapse, pleased and giggling, defeated, to bite his lips with bird bites, stroke his neck and call him her sweet guava-face boy.

His world was in Snipe's Bay and in Lily's body in Snipe's Bay and there wasn't time to think that it wouldn't always be there.

# Part Two

Part Two

# 3

## *Colonel Francis Omerod M.M.*

*September 1966*

Quite a number of odd chaps have passed through my office here at Kew Gardens. Whenever any of the other administrators get some cranky fellow to handle, they pass him on to me.

"Send him up to old F.O.," they tell their secretaries, "he'll know how to deal with this."

I've always been known as 'old F.O.' When I was at school in the early part of this century, it would have been inconceivable that it meant anything but *Foreign Office*. Times change, of course. Sometimes they call me *U.F.O.* which I take to be more affectionate.

I interviewed one chap who was convinced that he could irrigate the desert by imbedding miles of string in the sand and then impregnating the string with moisture; another one had invented a rice-planting machine which he intended to use on a stretch of Norfolk Broad in the summer. Wanted us to subsidise the scheme.

A Greek once tried to inveigle me into allowing him to install hi-fi equipment throughout the hot-houses at Kew. He assured me that plants thrived on the sound of Bach or Mozart.

This particular fellow came into my office on a Thursday. I remember distinctly that it was a Thursday, because that's my Golf Day and I'm always itching to get off; never feel right until I've actually thumped that first ball off the tee. Doesn't matter where it goes—the ball, I mean—shanked, hooked, sliced, or topped—just so long as I get it off. And it *is* a fact that I always have trouble settling in on those first few holes—I expect it's the impatience to get cracking that tenses one up and destroys the rhythm. Silly thing, really.

To get back to this young fellow. Yes, he came into my office on a Thursday and told me that he owned an island in the West

Indies. Curious-looking chap, early twenties, I'd say, something odd about this eyes, and obviously a generous helping of the tar-brush there somewhere.

My first impression was that he was a bit of a crank, you know, not the sort of fellow you'd go into the woods with, sort of thing. I wasn't feeling particularly inclined to listen to a lot of guff about soil distribution on coral atolls in my golfing time, but he had the gift of the gab all right, spoke up well and know-ledgeably about the ambitions he had for his island, and finally I became as engrossed as he was.

Seems his grandfather had bought most of the island for a song in 1920 or thereabouts, and had evidently decided to make it (or try to make it) self-supporting. He had experimented with cotton, tobacco, corn, bananas and sugar-cane. The first few crops would be satisfactory enough, but then the quality would suddenly dwindle, and the old man would have to cultivate another piece of land and sow a new crop.

The boy claimed that there just wasn't enough earth on the island, which, of course, is a common failing of all these piddling little atolls stuck out in the middle of some vast bloody ocean as they are. That and no water.

I started to question the boy closely about the actual assets of the place, wondering in fact if there *were* any. Stupid to waste one's time worrying about some bird-dropping in the middle of the sea that has about as much chance of supporting inhabitants as the top of Mount Everest.

He sat across the desk, twiddling his fingers and every now and then turning his hands over to examine the pale palms, the lines of which were deeply ingrained and seemed marked out with a pencil. His answers grew softer and softer. He *knew* that I was about to tell him that I thought it would be totally impractical to cultivate anything seriously, and to advise him to stick to tourism and the stamp trade for an income. I had to ask him to speak up several times, and I was beginning to find him annoying, when suddenly he stood up, walked back to the door and took up a long cardboard tube that he had left in the umbrella rack. Out of it he brought one of the most beautifully executed pieces of cartography I have ever seen, especially as you could see that it was the work of an amateur. Every creek, river, knoll, lagoon and ditch was lovingly marked, the depths at which limestone started and soil ceased, the vegetation and the lack of it, he had even brought little plastic bags with deposits of earth from various parts of his island to have tested. Round the edge of the map were pen-drawings of various shells, coral, fish and birds found there.

I pored over his map for a long time. It was like a personal document recording his life, and I could feel the boy's reluctance to have me touch it. He wanted me to look, admire, but not to handle. He stood stiffly behind my chair, clearing his throat and bristling his chin with forefinger and thumb. I remember being surprised that he hadn't shaved.

"And what are you planning to do with your property, Mr. Jackson?" I asked, pushing up the special glasses I use for close work and leaning back in my swivel chair to show him that I had finished perusing his work and was not about to harm it. He moved slowly round my desk touching the elephant's foot that I use as an ash-tray, the silver topped ink-stand given to me by my wife on our fifteenth anniversary; his fingers came to rest on my letter opener, a relic of my days in India.

Holding this delicately between his index fingers he stared down into my eyes and said, "I'm going to make it grow things. I'm going to cover it with earth."

It was at this time that I noticed the colour of his eyes—the pupil was an opaque blue, like the inside of a glacier, and around the edge was an etched brown line. The eyes of a visionary or a fanatic, I thought; the only other time I'd seen eyes like that was in Northern India, the eyes of some of the ancient tribesmen who live their lives out in the mountains. I remember thinking at the time that *their* eyes must have been bleached to that colour through continually scanning the horizon in glaring sunlight, or perhaps, like eagles, looking straight at the sun.

I leaned over and glanced at his map again, "You mean you're going to cover all . . . ah . . . 54.3 square miles . . . of it?" I allowed my voice to be sceptical. "You realise it would take at least eight inches of top-soil to do the trick and *that* would obviously mean millions of tons of earth—no, but literally! Have you any idea of the cost?"

He smiled for the first time since entering my office, "Well I wouldn't do it all at once; just a few productive acres at a time. In a year's time, some more, until we have worked up maybe one thousand acres of real land. That would feed a lot of people,

Mr. Omerod, if it's worked properly, rotated and kept productive. What I want to do here at Kew is to learn about the earth itself—what it needs done to it to get the best out of it forever, what to grow in it, how to rotate crops, how to transplant trees, what chemicals to use to bolster it up, anything and everything you can teach me here, I want to know. That's what I want from you, Mr Omerod, that's why I'm here." He was a persuasive fellow, I suppose.

I pulled my spectacles back over my eyes and dragged his precious map towards me again. I wanted to give myself time to decide whether this fellow was genuine, or just another audacious bag-of-wind who'd wandered into my office with nothing more to recommend him than a map, some earth samples, and a pair of peculiar eyes.

"And what made you come to us rather than the Jamaican Government, Mr. Jackson? Surely they'd be more interested in your venture?"

It's always good to sound them out about their motives. I've learnt that if their reasons for undertaking these schemes are too glib there is generally more volubility than sincerity behind the words. But this chap replied with a certain amount of reluctance, choosing his words hesitantly.

"We—ell, there's a guy who came to live on Hambro about ten years ago . . . name of Brodie . . . he came from Canada . . . he built the air-strip you can see marked on that map. Ever since I can remember he's been going on about Kew Gardens . . . how I should come over to London, learn all I can before I start somethin' I don't know enough about. He says this the only place . . . the best place where I be sure to learn it all."

"But didn't he tell you that you need three years' experience before we consider you for a place as a student here?"

"No," he said, "he didn't tell me that."

"That's a pity." I was about to roll up his wretched map and terminate the interview, but he stood so still, so immobile and undefeated before me that I was unable to move myself.

I studied him again. His eyes had an open but watchful expectancy that reminded me suddenly of Rufus . . . poor dead Rufus . . . who had waited for me to make decisions with the same stoical acceptance.

I cleared my throat and looked away.

"Then what would *you* say were your qualifications, Mr. Jackson? What have you done since you left your island?"

"Been a merchant seaman. Seen a bit of the world. Earned enough money to come to London, try and get accepted into Kew."

I picked up a magnifying glass and put it over the map, covering a section at the mouth of a river called 'The Clyde' on the Western coastline; alongside it there was a homestead marked 'Jackson', with a cemetery at the rear of the property boundary.

"Is this where your grandfather lived?" I asked.

"Yes," he said, "he's buried there."

"Was he Scottish?"

"I dunno."

"Anyone who calls a river 'The Clyde' can't be a Sassenach and the Scots seem never to be able to get away from their origins no matter how far they wander."

"If you look a little further to your right you'll see a village called 'New Aberdeen' and there's a beach called 'Portobello'; Scottish by courtesy of the Romans, my grandfather said."

I thought of my own grandfather, that dour old crofter who had survived on a bottle of whisky and a thick Highland stew a day, (never eaten above body temperature), until the excessive age of one hundred and one; I pictured him the last time I had seen him, a wispy white-headed figure with watering eyes still gleaming from under sparse brows, "Aw, Cm'mon Francis, gie the wee laddie a chance."

"All right, my lad," I heard myself say, "I'll take you on, but it has to be on a temporary basis. Every three months I shall have a recap on your work here and see whether it's worthwhile keeping you. I will see that you get a grant of five pounds a week starting at the beginning of next month. After that, it's up to you."

I looked at him again only when I had made the decision and said the words. He was still standing holding my paper-knife between his fingers and I had the impression that he hadn't moved or breathed until my words were out. Immediately, he relaxed and placed the knife carefully back on the desk, rolled up his map and took up his earth samples.

"Thank you, Mr. Omerod," he said, making for the door, "I'll be here on the first of next month."

"We'll write and confirm things. Give my secretary your address on the way out," I said.

As soon as he was out of the door I had second thoughts. The boy was a half-breed or some such mixed blood and I have very strong views in that direction. It's as useless as farting against thunder to think that you can mix the bloods without evil results. Why, I had a perfect example of this with my own dog, Lucy. Beautiful Boxer bitch was Lucy, full brindle, good pedigree, intelligent. Well, we had her covered by another good dog, Jack Poynter-Orme's dog, in fact, a handsome black beast.

Puppies were duly born and we suspected nothing; kept one and sold the rest—always thought there was something a little leggy about the animal, but when it started stealing eggs from out of the chicken-house and sucking them, I *knew* . . . I was *sure* that Lucy must have got out, or some cur had got in to her. I *knew* that that pup was not a full-breed. Nothing surer . . . had to have it put down finally. You see, you can never trust a mongrel; they inherit the worst traits from both parents . . . and it's the same with the human animal.

"Damnation," I thought, "It's all my grandfather's fault, *and* I've missed my golf game."

# 4

## Maggie Truro

*December 1966*

I am sitting in the Glass House in Kew Gardens. You know
the one. It's shaped like a big Swiss Roll with a blob on top, and
all the Queen's beasts are standing round the front. I think old
Victoria had it put there for Albert. Anyway, I am sitting in it
because it's warm—always heated to at least seventy-five
degrees even in winter—and it's one of the few public places in
London where you can go most afternoons and stay warm,
without being bothered by shrieking kids or dreary fellows
hanging about . . . and it smells nice; all those palm-trees and
flowers growing away there in the warm, spicey air, and outside
the grey frost and desolation.

I discovered it in my first year in London and I've been
coming back for three winters now.

Well, I'm sitting there smelling and thinking and I see this
boy, kneeling down under a group of trees and he's digging—
digging away happily and singing . . . No, not exactly singing,
it's a sort of humming.

And then quite suddenly and for no reason, I have this
terrific sense of well-being. There's nobody there, only him and
me, and everything sort of damp and new, and the only other
sound apart from the humming is the clicking of the big, fat
pipes that run round the edges of the glass walls to heat the
place.

I try to see his face, but he has his head down.

I can see that his hair is very dark and I wonder if he is a
spade with such a good voice to hum so loud in Kew Gardens.

After five minutes I can see that he is not going to look up,
so I walk over to the path near the lacey spiral staircase that
goes up to the walk around the tree-tops, and start to climb up.
Then I pretend to change my mind and come down the other

side so that I end up next to where he is kneeling; I stop and say, "That is a very beautiful song you are humming. I never heard it before."

He looks up, not hurrying, and stops humming—and I see that he is sort of dark—like maybe he could be an Indian from India or even a Red Indian, but his eyes are blue in the middle and brown round the edges and the combination is knockout—weird and wonderful. Really.

I know I'm staring at him but he doesn't seem to mind—just goes back to his digging and says, "It's a little Sunday song my Grandma May taught me."

I just stand there waiting for him to say something else, but he doesn't, so I say, "Do you work here?" I know it's pretty obvious but that's all I can think of.

"Yes," he says, "I am learning here."

"Oh," I say, "are you going to be a gardener?"

"A sort of a gardener," he says, and he's got this crazy, clipped sort of jazzy accent that I can't place, so I say: "Where are you from?"

"Hambro Island, West Indies," he replies.

"Sounds nice and hot and hammy." I giggle a bit and then I lean over and say, "I come here nearly every day to keep warm. I hate the winter, confidentially."

He laughs and I see that he has big teeth all the way back and no fillings.

"Maybe I'll see you again sometime," I say, and then I walk away quickly and I'm pleased because I know I will, and that he will remember me.

That's the first time I ever met Jackson.

\* \* \*

The next morning I have a red rinse put through my hair so that it's this really eye-catching chocolate-chestnut colour and I go down to Kew in the afternoon.

It's even colder and my breath unfurls in front of me as I walk down the wide avenue, a few months ago crowded with rhododendrons and people, and now dead and brown for the winter.

I pass the lake with the poor statue stranded remote and chilly in the middle, pass the Griffin and the Unicorn, and on to my favourite glass dome. It is really fabulous some days when there's a little touch of winter sunshine. The inside gets all steamed up and you can see splodges of green tree through the glass and the whole thing shines and shimmers like a huge green and white jelly on a plate.

Anyway, *this* day there is no sun, but I don't feel bad. The sky has this low-ceiling head-crunching aspect to it that usually throws me into a terrible fit of depression, but not today. Today I am dedicated to pleasure.

Who cares that I haven't worked for three weeks?

Who cares that I have exactly ten shillings and threepence in my purse, four guineas in my Post Office Savings Account and only a faint hope of getting the twenty-five pounds they owe me for a gig I did in Luton a month back and they never came through with the bread . . . the loot . . . the loot from Luton.

Who gives a hoot for the loot from Luton.

SAPPY WHAPPY FLAPPY DAPPY

ZOINCK ZOINCK BOUM!

GERASH! GERONCK! GULINCK! GULANCK!

THWAP THWOP BOUM! As Superman said to the Actress.

You see, that's how I'm feeling today . . . sort of cocky and confident with my new red rinse.

I hurry through the first door, anticipating the sudden relief of warmth that will envelop my legs (I am not wearing stockings either, as my last pair gave up yesterday) but the inner door is locked for some reason. I rattle it: no reply. I go back through the outside door into the bleak old day again and round to the door on the other side. There is a dismal card in the window that only says 'Closed'. No explanations, just 'Closed'. A small piece of my delight breaks off and my knees begin to feel icy where the boots stop.

I look back across the lake to where one small, blue-hooded child of indeterminate sex is being shown to the ducks and water-hens, and then I remember my second favourite place to go in the winter at Kew Gardens.

This is a tropical greenhouse, but much smaller and less interestingly shaped. Inside, there is a pool surrounded by banana trees and filled with goldfish and big waxy water-lilies. You have to go through the Orchid House to get to it. I suppose they use the same boiler to heat them both up; next door is where they keep the Venus fly-traps. Once I spent all afternoon trying to feed flies and moths and insects that I had saved into the Venus fly-traps, but I think they have covered them up now to stop people from playing their games and getting their jollies from the Venus fly-traps.

"Presenting Maggie Truro—Miss Venus Fly-Trap—The World's Subtlest Stripper". Almost worth a try, I am thinking as I walk back around the lake.

There is a dribble of doubt seeping through in the back of my mind, that things will not turn out well today, and that I may miss my lovely singing spade, and *that* is bad for me. Once that dreary old Doubt starts I am dead. The Doubt begins to block out everything else in my head until I am just a big Doubt-on-legs, and I have to hide out for a day or two until it goes away like the 'flu or rabies or something. Anyway, the big Doubt only happens about once every couple of months now, so I am careful not to let this niggling little Doubt out of its box as I approach the entrance of the Orchid House.

I do not like orchids very much. They don't smell and there is something a bit phoney about them. Once a boy sent me an orchid, and the stem was in a little bottle like a tiny test-tube. That's *just* what it looked like—a sort of monstrous growth they had produced out of a tiny test-tube. Anyway I could never wear one. I always hurry through the Orchid House.

When I get to the pool there is a bunch of art students standing around sketching the banana trees. It is funny to watch people drawing. Some of them are so concentrated and anguished-looking; others get the dreamy far-away look of a baby dirtying its nappy, and others screw up their faces as though they're going to spit on you any minute.

So I stand around watching their faces for a while and just enjoying the streaming sensation of warm wet air, and then I go over and sit by the pool and let my hand touch the water—just touch it—so that the hundreds of baby fish think they're about to be fed and come whooshing up to examine my fingers and nibble at the quicks of my nails.

"Hello," he says, as though he has made the appointment and is sorry he is late. It is him. He is wearing navy-blue overalls and gum-boots and has a big wire broom in his hand.

"Hello," I say, "fancy meeting you here." And I laugh to show him that I am not really surprised.

He laughs too, and then begins to show me around. He knows all the long names for trees and plants and I can see by the way he touches the leaves and bark and buds that he loves them like most people love money.

He tells me that his name is 'Jackson' and I tell him my name is Maggie Truro and that I'm a singer. What I like about him is that he is so interested in everything and at the same time he doesn't try to push me into behaving like 'boy meets girl', or chatting me up in that goading way, like most of the boys I meet.

Outside it is beginning to get dark and they will be urging everyone out any minute now.

"It's going to snow," I say, looking out at the murky sky.

"You mean it?" he says, and starts to jump up and down and get all excited.

"Do you really think it *will*? You mean real white Christmas-card snow!!!"

"Well, it's not the kind you sniff," I say.

"Real snow! Real snow!" he cries, making all the students turn round. "I never have seen real snow!"

We walk around a bit more until he looks out and sees that the sky is murkier than ever and that things are moving up there.

So he grabs my hand and drops his broom and away we go through the old Orchid House and out through the double doors to the path overlooking the Rockery; and luckily for me, lovely little flakes are just beginning to steal down out of the slate-grey and darkening sky. He puts his head back and opens his mouth wide, wide, to catch them or feel them on his face, or maybe just because it's suddenly so cold out there after the hot-house, and we do a polka down the path and he keeps saying: "It's fantastic!" and "Wow", "It's like salt and spice", "I like it, I like it," he croons, "Snow, snow, cold floating snow", and "Feathers from heaven." Things like that.

And somehow I feel like it's the first time *I* ever saw snow too, and as he runs and leaps now, I can see the steam rise out of him, and as it gets darker so *he* gets darker, and by the time we get near the gates he looks really black, a big steaming black animal, laughing and leaping about in his overalls; and I think he's the most alive thing I've seen in my whole life.

And now the snow is really coming down strong and they've

already turned on the lights in the square, and he runs and stands under one of the lamp-posts and stares up to watch the snow flurrying down through the light as though it can't wait to get there. I have no feeling in the tips of my fingers or my cheeks, and the tops of my ears have started to freeze too, so I run . . . and run . . . and when I get to where he is, I can see that the snow has begun to settle on his hair and eye-brows; even his eye-lashes.

He is all white and black and lovely.

*　　*　　*

He gets hold of my hands, pulls them down to my sides to keep me still, and takes a long, hard look right into my eyes. I think, "Oh stink. Interrogation Look. Always means they're going to ask you some dreadful question that you can't answer . . . or say something stupid that spoils everything." But he doesn't say anything, just drops my hands and laughs.

Laughs and laughs like there was some big joke.

"Yahoooooo!" he yells like a cowboy. "Yeweeooow!" he yells and picks me up in a bundle and runs with me bumping up and down right into the middle of the commonland in front of Kew Gardens where they play cricket in the summer. The snow's like fine white powder covering the grass and all sounds are muffled except for him yahooing and me laughing, and we tumble to the ground and start scratching and scraping up the thin snow and throwing it at each other, and it's like when I was ten again and nothing mattered except the fun you were having at that very and precise moment.

And he rolls over and over in the snow like a dog in manure after you've given it a bath—just for sheer ecstasy; and so do I. It becomes a game.

Everything he does, I do.

He gets up and starts to do a little soft-shoe shuffle, shaking himself about to get the snow off . . . so do I.

He scoops up some snow, pats it into shape and throws it high into the air, heading it towards me as though it was a football . . . so do I. Splosh, it hits his head. It misses mine and lands on my boot.

He runs in a circle and throws himself forward on his knees, leaving two trails of dark grass behind him. I try it, but snow

66

gets down my boots, and my knees burn with the friction of hitting the ground with too much force . . . I'm laughing and sucking in air in great gasps, and puffing like a porpoise.

Then we wander off towards Kew Bridge and the lights of the main road, where the rush-hour traffic is already starting to pile up. We stop and look at the churchyard where the grave stones are turning white, and he clears the snow off one and we sit there to take a breather.

"Maggie the Ice-Maiden," he says, taking my hand and rubbing it between his two. "My little snow-flake girl."

My hands and feet have lost their feeling, so I give him my other hand and the wonder is that his hands are so dry and warm.

By this time, the trees are beginning to be outlined by snow and it's still coming down thick and heavy. We just sit there watching it all happen and getting more and more covered in snow like two orphans of the storm in one of those old Victorian novels.

"Time for us to go, girl," he says, ruffling the snow out of my hair. I'm worried in case the rinse might be dripping out of it as well, so I race him to the pub on the corner and in we rush and go and stand near the fire to thaw out.

He orders two rums and we gulp them down. I can feel mine hit the bottom of my stomach like hot treacle, and then my cheeks are on fire and he laughs as he touches them and pretends he's been burnt.

"Wow!" he says, and jumps back blowing on his fingers.

We have another, and this time it hits the back of my skull and I hear myself say, gazing into his strange eyes, "I never met anyone who looked like you before. Are you a throw-back or something?"

"A throw-back?" he says, screwing up his nose, "That sounds like a very small fish, or a reject singlet . . . No . . . No, if I'm a throw-anything, it's got to be *forward*." He takes a quick nip of his rum.

"Yes." he says. "That's definitely what I am, I'm a throw-forward."

"No, but seriously, what are you *really*? Scandinavian and Singhalese?"

"Nope."

"German and Arabic?"

67

"Nope."

"English and Pakistani?"

"Nope."

"I know. Your father was Enoch Powell and your mother was Queen Salote . . . Ethel Waters? . . . King Farouk?"

"Nope."

"Well, what? I give up. You must be a mixture of something, with those eyes?"

"Mmmmmmmmm, yes, well, I suppose I am what one would call a *hybrid*. At least that's what Elliot Brodie called it and he is about the best educated person I ever met. I looked it up in the dictionary once and it said, 'Produced by the union of two distinct species, a thing composed of incongruous elements'. You are probably one too, only it's less obvious. One day it will be one of my sort who will be saying 'Are you a throw-back or something?' to a girl who looks like you."

I laugh. "But I don't suppose she will be able to answer that she's a throw-forward."

"No, that's true," he says, "but your girl would always answer something bright, I bet you. She'd say she was a 'throw-up' or a 'Throw-out'. Oh, she'd very likely have something to say for herself.

"But to return to the question of the mixture that I am. Well, I am half African, probably West African, and half Scottish. A half-caste, cross-breed, mongrel, mulatto, half-breed, hybrid, mustefino, what you want to call it . . . Neither black nor white, and therefore considered an outcast by both sides. Oh, if I earn more than a hundred pounds a week, I can decide which side I wish to be on, though of course a hundred pounds, economically, says I'm as white as you. To be a hybrid, a half-caste, is like taking part in a very nasty compulsory game where all the rules favour your antagonists."

I sit there feeling ashamed without knowing why.

It's not my fault if I'm all white and he's not.

Perhaps if he sounded more bitter and angry I would feel less uneasy, for though he is talking and the words are unpleasant, he makes it sound as if he's telling about last year's summer holidays.

"The rules of the game state first and foremost that you have to decide which team you are going to play on, don't they? Well, first off that creates a big problem for me, because truly,

68

*I will not make the choice*. I will not say I am on the black side or the white side because I'm not going to be pushed into behaving how they want me to. I will have to create my own side—the non-players—'Hybrids of the World, Unite! You've got nothing to lose but your chips!' "

He is still speaking in a bantering way but I can tell he's got down to bed-rock, something that has kept him awake at night, his credo. Then he stares at me for fully thirty seconds before speaking again, sorting me out with a look that is at once clinical and quizzical.

"Do you realise," he says at last, taking a big breath, "that of the twenty or thirty millions of black people, so-called, in the United States, only ten per cent are full-blooded Negroes. The rest are partly something else. You can be one-eighth black man in some countries and still be considered coloured . . . like Cape Coloureds in South Africa . . . Cape Gooseberries, they sound like, but they are discriminated against just the same. In the West Indies, where nearly everybody has a touch of ju-ju, it's a question of *economics*. I know a boy who would be called 'little black Sambo' here, who is lily-white out there, because his family is one of the richest in Jamaica. He been pushed in society like a white boy, son of two rich parents, off-white but rich enough for it not to matter. It can't be helped that he just happens to be darker than both his parents, he's white, man, he's white. Of course, if he goes to America or South Africa or Rhodesia, that's different. Nobody cares what his social or economic position is in Jamaica or anywhere else, he's lumped in with every man and woman whose skin happens to be darker than the Miami sun can burn it, and he's black, he's segregated, forced to live by a set of standards that he probably knows nothing about. He's *black*. He's got to make that adjustment immediately and without turning one hair . . . there's no way that he can do it, of course, but there's no way that he *can not* do it either, if he moves into non-integrated society."

He stops abruptly and holds up his glass to the fire watching the deep ruby of the rum through the light. "That's a lovely drop of bottled sunshine to see me through me first day of snow in poor, swung, old London."

The change in him is so sudden that I am thrown for an instant, unable to find any words to say where we can meet again. All my Doubts, big ones and little, seem paltry things of my own making compared with the things he is talking about, so I peer into my glass and say nothing. He lifts his hand as though he knows that he has stepped outside the limits of my understanding.

"You don't have to look so innocent and forlorn, I'm not attacking you; not *you*," he repeats.

The rum is knocking at my temples as I reply: "I honestly don't care if you came out of Cambodia, you're just a boy I heard humming in Kew Gardens, and it doesn't mean a thing to me even if you are a . . . a . . . a whatever it is you call it."

"Hybrid," he says calmly and takes my hand and my glass.

"I never meant to frighten you, Maggie, little girl," he says; but I take my hand back fast.

I sit there for a while not saying anything, pulling my fingers through my hair to dry it off, and he watches me, smiling a little, but with a wary look in his eyes, and waiting for me to make a move.

I try to think what it would be like if I was partly coloured, what it would be like if my mother was black. How she would hate it! No, it wouldn't *do* for my mother, but it makes me giggle all the same. Then I have a sudden explosive picture of my father in one of those pink turbans and a beard held in with a hair-net taking fares on top of a bus, and that makes me laugh even more.

He doesn't ask me why I'm carrying on, so I say, "Don't you want to know what's broken me up?"

He nods and looks down at his gum boots; at the dirty snow melting off them onto the floor.

"I expect you're trying to imagine yourself as a half-caste," he says. "It generally gives people a good laugh."

"Of course I'm not," I lie breathlessly, "I'm laughing at you sitting there in your overalls and runny boots, trying to be a whole minority group in one man."

He squints at his rum, runs a finger around the rim of his glass and his face is wearing a rare ambivalent smile-frown that shows I have hit a chink in his armour. I have thrown my dart into one of his vital organs, and he is trying not to show it.

"Is that so funny?" he says. "I *would* like to make people aware of what it feels like to be unacceptable to any race . . . yes, I would . . . " he says quietly to his rum. "You see, I would be a good person to do it, because I have been lucky, I have not suffered much for what I am and I'm not bitter, at least not very. I have had a whole childhood untouched by all this nonsense . . . came to discrimination very late, you might say. But the thought of thousands and millions of poor little bastards born into a society that condemns them because they don't look right—the thought that those same kids have to make an agonising choice, whether consciously or unconsciously—Are they going to be black white-men or white black-men?—the thought that being forced to sit on either side of the colour fence automatically denies them part of their blood heritage or even one of their parents . . . that turns my guts—"

He drains his glass and sets it down on the mantelpiece above the fire.

"Yes," he says, "I am a minority group—a whole one—in one man. I am Jackson, the original Hybrid, and I want the world to be different!"

I think he is very impressive standing there in front of the fire with his arms outstretched. He is laughing at himself, but not laughing . . . Oh, I can't explain it exactly, but I think he is fantastic and marvellous secretly.

"Have you got a girl-friend here in England?" I ask, and it's out of my mouth before I even knew it was in my head.

This is the first thing I've said to him yet that seems to take him by surprise. "We—ell," he swivels around on his heels to face me. "We—ell, little Maggie, I've got a few friends, and some of them are girls, but I don't like girl-friend girl friends. They take up too much time, and I've got too much to do."

"Oh," I say, "but I expect you've got dozens of them out on that island, waiting for you to come back."

"Dozens and dozens," he says grinning. "All pining away on the jetties and lining the beaches."

"Maybe you'd like to come and hear me sing one of these days, if you're not too busy?"

"Sure," he says easily. "I'd love that. Where are you working just now?"

"Oh, I'm not working this week," I say hurriedly, "*next* week, but I'm not sure *where* yet. My agent never tells me until a couple of days before. Anyway, I will drop in at the Gardens in the next day or two, you can show me some more plants and I'll tell you where it will be. Is that O.K.?"

"I'll be there," he says.

I stand up, determined to move fast and remove every obstacle that stops me from getting myself fixed up with a good gig for the next week. I will show him that I *too* am a busy formidable career-lady with no interest in having boy-friend boy friends.

"I must fly," I say.

"All right, little Maggie, you fly; I have to go back and change my clothes. See you soon. I won't forget."

And out into the snowy night I go, feeling purposeful and flushed from the rum and the running. We part outside the door with a squeeze of hands and I hear the muffled sound of his boots clumping off into the snow as I turn up towards the lights.

I wonder how I'm going to get a definite offer to sing in some decent place before the weekend.

All the way back on the bus I apply myself to the question, going over possible contacts and places where I have played that might re-engage me at short notice. The list is not very long and less than exciting. I look out at brown slush churning around the car-wheels, at neon lights glaring harshly on the whiteness of the snow—the benediction of snow lying graceful on bridges and neatly on roofs . . . It is the 12th of December, and all the Christmas bookings have already been made. Oh, what a drag it is to have to cope with cumbersome detail; to *always* have to prove that you have talent, to be *always* in competition, to *have* to audition, to *have* to try to impress! Why can't I just walk in somewhere and say, "I want to sing here tonight because I feel like singing, and this is where I fancy doing it" or "I'll sing here for nothing as long as you'll give my friend a drink and let him listen to me." But the rules don't ever make things easier or more pleasurable, and like it or not, we are all barricaded by the rules, hemmed in, and bleating like mutton.

Still, I have met a human being today who believes in something, who is alive and cares about something important that is not just *himself*; who has pride and vigour and is not trying to *make* me, or impress me, or do anything except be with me. And that's not nothing . . . that's not nothing today.

# 5

## Francis Omerod

EXCEPT FOR THE usual brief meetings in corridors, my next encounter with the half-caste fellow Jackson was a few months later in my office. I had to call him in and give him a good tongue-lashing about leaving his locker door open.

I usually make an inspectional tour of the premises every week, including in my rounds the locker room where the students keep their belongings and change in and out of their working clothes. Noticing that one of the doors was open, I walked down the corridor to investigate. That sort of thing is an invitation to a plague of petty pilfering and I have had to cope with several outbreaks of it in my time, needless to say.

The inside of the offending door was plastered with photographs . . . not the usual assortment of pneumatic breasts and inflated haunches which generally spread themselves around young men's work-benches and lockers these days.

There was a recent photo of Jackson with the sea behind him, laughing and naked, holding two air rifles crossed in front to cover his vital parts, and a more professional colour picture of a skinny blond fellow standing on a beach clasping a black girl in a bikini in his arms. The Negress was ogling the camera and thrusting her pelvis against the man, while his hands caressed her black flesh and he stared out of the photo with a silly infatuated expression on his face. Disgusting really.

Alongside these two there was another of the enlarged colour snaps. It was a close-up of two heads. Jackson and a red-headed girl. He was grinning out and wore a green muffler around his neck. She regarded him with a look of such melting adoration that it quite turned my stomach.

At the bottom, set apart from the others, there was a blown-up snapshot of an enormous black woman seated in a peacock-backed cane chair and fanning herself with a round palm fan.

Her knees were wide apart and there were four or five lighter-shaded children squatting around her feet. One of her hands rested heavily on the head of a kneeling boy. What a monster she looked, like a big black Amazon gone to seed. The kneeling boy was recognisable as Jackson. There was also a faded portrait of a young corporal in the familiar uniform of the Great War, puttees neat, boots shining and turned out at the regulation thirty degree angle so favoured at the time. I supposed he was the Jackson fellow's grandfather, the one who owned the island. He was white, though, and had his hair parted in the centre. Poor chap, to saddle himself with such a great black brute and so many rabid little half-breeds. Still, it was his own fault. Looking at the photographs, I thought once again of my own grandfather, a fire and brimstone lay preacher from the high-lands of Scotland. I cannot imagine him having so little pride as to mate himself with a woman of any other blood but his own; even the English were a suspect race to him and anybody from across the water was beyond the pale. He preached monogamy and gave terrifying descriptions of what would happen to those excessive souls who dared to leave the path of righteousness. He himself produced only one son, my father.

I was born on the 4th of January, 1900. Evidently I should have arrived three weeks before but must have stubbornly refused to appear until the twentieth century.

My father was a cavalry officer in the Indian Army stationed in Poona and that is where I first saw the light of day. My mother had been a Miss Paynford—a niece of the colonel of the regiment—visiting her uncle with the intention of procuring a husband, which went under the name of 'broadening the mind' in those days. She must have captured my father's heart with-out much effort, because they were married only two months after her arrival. I was not her first child. She gave birth to five children before my advent, only one of which, my brother Radnor, survived. I remember her only vaguely as a lavender lady with a frilly parasol and sad dark eyes looking lovingly (but fearful for me) into mine. She died when I was six, finally giving in to the rigours of childbirth in a climate that resembled not at all the cooler climes of Kent.

My brother and I had a forebidding governess, Miss Chivers, who kept us rigidly correct and God help the boy caught with his hands in his pockets on a Sunday, we were looked after by an *amah*, Maia, who loved us and pressed sweet things into our mouths when Miss Chivers' back was turned.

When I was ten my father remarried and I was sent back to England to school. I remember crying my eyes out every night as the ship forged its way farther and farther away from everything that I knew and loved. I had to hide my tears from Radnor, who was three years my senior and not given to emotional displays, even at that tender age. He was the perfect example of every father's dream at that time—fearless and upright, phlegmatic but alert, and good at cricket. I never liked him, as he beat me unmercifully for small misdemeanors, always finishing his performance with a stern lecture on how good it had been for the strengthening of my weak character. He is now a High Court Judge and is meting out his punishments with just as firm a hand to this very day, I expect.

I was fourteen when the Great War began, a gangling, pimply fourteen, full of raging ideals and patriotism. I believed in comradeship between men, the British Empire, God, and the sanctity of women. I was tremendously anxious to prove myself a man and a soldier, someone to contend with, a cavalry officer's son, True Blue. I was terrified that the war would end before I was old enough to participate. At that time news from the front was fed to us at school as glorious adventure stories from *The Bumper Book for Boys*. When my brother Radnor joined up at eighteen I was beside myself with envy. I ceased any serious thought of study and spent my time planning elaborate methods of escape from school to join up. I was sixteen before I achieved my desire and found myself a private soldier in the Infantry. Ah, the disillusion! The incredulity, the pain of discovery that army life—or at least that of a private soldier—was drudgery, injustice, indignity and stupid bull-like devotion to an absurd ritual which I instinctively despised. It took me six months to find my feet and not burst into tears in the latrines, not stagger under the weight of a full pack; to refrain from covering up my ears at the ferocious obscenities of the men, to swallow the vomit that sprang up my throat when fed pig swill, bully beef, weevilly biscuits and slops. The toughening-up process happened so violently and so quickly that I had no time to think, least of all to resist. I survived; and six months later was a smoking, swearing, spitting, stinking soldier in a trench like the rest of them. I believed that there were two sorts of men . . . those who stand up, and those who sit down to pee; the ones who have their balls in the right place and those who don't. Keep your mouth shut, your bowels open and don't volunteer. Of women I knew nothing; I was a virgin.

At school I had once entered a cubicle to discover two boys twined together in an embrace which did not suggest that they were wrestling, but I had put the incident out of my mind and avoided the two ever afterwards as filthy cads, and once I had been thrashed by a house-master for self-abuse.

Now, suddenly, all around me, I saw men in close proximity; I saw them love each other and die for each other, hate, mistrust and admire; all the human emotions and some very inhuman ones squeezed into damp traps six feet beneath the earth. I saw men dismembered and disembowelled, headless and bleeding, memories too painful to linger in the conscious mind, but returning in those moments before wakefulness and sleep to rip and gouge my brains apart.

\* \* \*

Because I had never really lived, I had a double fear of death. The child in me was petrified of the hurt of death and the new man of dying without ever having had a woman or got really drunk or been to the races or read books, all the things I heard the other men discussing. Somewhere deep inside me, I had an aching hope that God might protect me if I threw myself in the path of danger, that He would see me through because I had never done any of the things that seemed the cement that held other men's lives together. I talked to a Chaplain but he spoke only of 'God's will', and 'King', and 'Loyalty', and though I struggled to comply with all these agonising ideals, they finally left me more wretched than before, and sank into the mud of my fear like ships that leave no trace behind them. I looked around me for some raft to cling to and found it in the form of Captain Milton. Here was an officer who had come up through the ranks, fearless and practical, who treated his men as individuals capable of thought and feeling, not just as lumps of turd to be left in the ground as fertiliser. He stayed with us and learned our names, he knew our faults, our hopelessness, our helplessness and despair, and unlike the other officers who wore handmade gloves and disappeared from the Front on sprees behind the lines, who were as far above our heads as the Kaiser's Zeppelins, he stayed and talked and joked to fill the endless hours and give us a little of the courage that had disappeared so disastrously after the first stench of corpses hit our nostrils.

He took me under his wing and there I flourished. I told him all about my fear. I told him about how I was frightened to make friends with anyone my own age or near it because each time I did, they were killed the next week or even the next day. I was a Jonah. I told him about Dickie Jobson walking into the trench on his own two feet holding his elbows close into his sides. "I'm all right, Roddie," Dickie had said. "I think I'll be all right," he said, sat down, took his elbows away from his sides and died. Just let go of his guts, out they came, and he was dead. The Captain had seen it all for himself a thousand times I expect, but he still listened and understood and I was comforted.

I became one of his junior subalterns and we made a pact. We'd see it through together, the two of us, we'd live to tell the tale.

I hurried into action after that, I used my head and I became a good soldier. I loved Captain Milton, Rufus Milton, with a love that was near to worship, as near to complete love as I have ever been, I think. I followed him and stayed as close as I could get, and there I felt secure; not safe, because no one could feel safe in that inferno of slush and rats and daily pounding with the big guns and shrapnel flying, but secure that here was one man who was indomitable, that he was my friend, my mentor and my friend. If he had been killed I think I should have gone mad. But he lived and so did I.

*　　*　　*

Towards the end of the war I was commissioned and I walked about carrying my new-found status with me like King Arthur's sword. I tried to grow a moustache like Major Milton's (he had been decorated and given his Majority a month before my commission) but I fear that all my strength had gone into growing five inches in height since I had joined the army, and the result was an unqualified failure.

So there I was, a beardless wonder, at eighteen, a veteran, unmarked on my skin, professing to be twenty-two, a tough disciplinarian, wise in the ways of war and as accustomed to death as most boys are to eating. I have a photograph of myself taken on my first leave in Brussels and I still cannot look at it without a momentary clutching at the throat. It is the picture of a serious-eyed, tight-lipped boy disguised as a man, standing stiffly to attention with his baton under his arm, but leaning forward slightly as though he is about to step off but doesn't know which foot to put forward first.

*　　*　　*

Rufus took me to my first brothel in Brussels. It was a very grand affair, rather like what I imagine Sarah Bernhardt's mansion must have been. A vast entrance hall with blue and white tiles and wide centre staircase leading up to a long balcony with alcoves and parlours in which sat the beauties, combing their hair; sewing, sipping, giggling, entrancing beauties. The walls were covered with tapestries, the floors with animal skins. Tigers opened their jaws and bears stared back with glassy eyes.

There were aspidistras crowding into every corner and a huge chandelier to top it all off. Beads and muffs, white rice powder, red rose-bud lips and black-rimmed eyes, the tops of chubby-women arms, and hair, a profusion of curling, luxuriant hair; and breasts seen fleetingly through sheer blouses of rainbow silk, breasts and eyes, little teeth, laughter and the click of beads. I had walked into my own dream, to life, to lovely, throbbing, wanton, whispering, spangled, gaudy, precious life.

The Madame who presided over this realm of delight was a thin imperious woman with very black hair, cut short and curled around each ear. Her ears were pierced and from them hung threads of jet. The place was jammed with officers and the language was a jumble of English and French, but Madame threaded her way dexterously through the crush of uniforms, her jet earrings swaying, her voice rising above the rest, cajoling or coquetting or commanding champagne from liveried waiters, who flitted in and out of the khaki and blue uniforms like tropical fish through sea-weed.

She came to a halt in front of Rufus and me. I had been

78

transfixed by the scene before my eyes, drinking in its disorder and colour, gaping and dazzled by all this splendour.

"*Ah!*" she cried, clapping her hands together in the air, "*Un enfant! Qu'est-ce que tu fais ici, mon brave petit soldat?*"

I flinched involuntarily and looked straight into her piercing black eyes. She must have seen the fright and pain in my own because she was immediately contrite; she took hold of my arm firmly above the elbow and led me through the throng to the foot of the stairs.

She told me that her name was Hermine, Madame Hermine, and that we would become great friends.

Not having known a woman's touch, or smell, or caressing hand, for as long as I could remember back to my childhood, since Maia, my *amah* had fondled me, I was thrown into a state of trembling excitement that was near to panic. My limbs refused to obey me and I stumbled up the stairs with as much fear as I had experienced in climbing out of the trench on my first sortie into enemy territory. With Rufus behind me and Madame Hermine at my side, tenderly grasping my quaking form, I ascended the battlement and found myself in that open fortress of delectable ladies who had observed my progress with amusement and concern. Madame led me past her ranks on an inspection tour. I scarcely dared to look into the eyes of these unbelievably glamorous creatures arrayed before me. I was terrified for Rufus's sake lest I make an absolute fool of myself and I watched him covertly in order to ascertain what was the correct behaviour. He strolled nonchalantly along, stopping in front of each alcove and perusing the languishing beauties that it held. His eyes were gleaming and his small, red moustache seemed to bristle more than I had ever seen it do, but these were the only outward signs by which Rufus showed that he was inspecting anything more than a batch of raw recruits sent up to the front.

No human beings in the world could have looked less like those haggard, whey-faced youths, weedy clerks, red-fisted plumbers, apprentice printers and farmer-boys, who had answered their country's call, however laggardly. Here we had sleek, powdered blondes with surprised blue eyes, generous olive-skinned roses with clouds of black hair floating, plump girls, girls as thin as nails, girls with slanting eyes and girls with fat, pale thighs and naughty garters showing. Some stared back at me and nodded their encouragement, some whispered and snickered as they saw me on Madame's arm, others again looked hypnotised with all the whites of their dazed orbs showing, and all the time Madame pointed out her best wares, "*Irma, et ça, c'est Claudine, Meg, et ça, Ernestine, Mouchette—Mignonne et la petite chinoise là, c'est la belle Chi Yung—Maria et Carmen-Louise.*"

"*Vous avez de vrai delices, Madame,*" murmured Rufus politely, but I could tell that he had already settled on the dark, scowling Maria. His eyes kept coming back to her as though they would devour her, but still she would not glance up at him and stared fixedly at a little sampler that she stitched to fill the time. She was older and more Latin-looking than the rest of the girls and she seemed to me the least attractive of all the women present; I would even go so far as to say that she was a sullen creature. I looked at my friend in surprise but he had no eyes for me at that moment.

Madame Hermine beamed her approval at his wise choice and then turned to me expectantly. I hurriedly pointed to the little Mignonne, a flaxen-haired minx with darting eyes, who had winked and stuck out her pointed pink tongue at me during our first 'tour'. The two girls rose as one and Madame parlez-voused them for a minute or two (the commanding officer briefing his men before the action). Just before we left, she patted my cheek again and hissed "*Merde!*" into my ear and off we went.

I remember every detail of that evening as though it had been tattooed on my brain, perhaps because it set a precedent in my life which I have been trying to recreate ever since, perhaps because it was my first woman, perhaps because Rufus insisted on paying for the whole evening and it was his way of showing that our friendship was cemented forever. Who knows?

We drank Krug Champagne, '09 Vintage and ate a lot of oysters. Mignonne buttered my bread, squeezed my lemon, and managed to feed me several dozen oysters off a little silver fork. The whole operation was an amazing feat as she sat on my knee to perform it. She squirmed and wriggled and giggled, and bit into the brown bread with her savage, little white teeth, until I thought my head would burst. She commanded me to eat and so I did, and even tasted the sea-fresh limpid morsels as I have never done before or since. She commanded me to drink and down my throat obediently flowed the delightful, straw-coloured liquid.

I tried to observe if Rufus was as filled with joy as myself; I could see that one of his hands had disappeared under Maria's plum velvet skirt, but that her face was still frowning, her upper lip still curling up, and she sipped her champagne in angry dips like a bird. I wondered at his seeming immersion in this contrary creature.

When we parted, he patted my back and shook my hand and said, "See you later on downstairs, old man." He winked. "This is something we promised ourselves, isn't it, old son? Not such a bad ending to the story, is it?"

Six months later he was dead. Dead of influenza in the big epidemic that carried millions away with it. I would not believe in his death, could not and would not, took to my bed for a week to cry and bite the covers, sleep, and wake sweating, in a nightmare of swollen corpses and gaping soundless mouths. But I am jumping ahead of my story and must get back to my rosy night at Madame Hermine's.

*   *   *

My first attempt to justify my manhood was a fiasco. I was too impatient; my little Mignonne had excited me beyond the powers of human endurance, the bursting wave had broken on the shore and receded back to sea before she had time to divest me of my newly-acquired uniform. A shame spread through my limbs and paralysed me and I lay on Mignonne's bed and wept. When I was empty of tears, I slept, probably for about ten minutes, the sort of cat-nap that we had learnt to snatch in the trenches when things were going badly.

I awoke startled to find myself naked on a soft satin counterpane with Mignonne leaning over me, her tongue gently parting my lips, and her hand already exciting me again. This time I acquitted myself well and Mignonne had some words of praise for me. I lay with her afterwards, toying with her hair, her nose, her pert little breasts and her tiny feet and then I squeezed her to me, until she cried out '*Assez, assez!*' and I was suddenly stopped short, remembering that I had heard some French deserters shouting the same thing as they threw down their guns and ran. Their own Captain shot two of them, after calling out 'Halte!' three times and the others were brought back to face charges.

I lay and stared up at the ceiling after that and tried to clear my mind of everything except the painting of nymphs and centaurs chasing each other all over it. Mignonne lay beside me stroking my hair and sometimes blowing in my ear, but I would have none of her. After a while, she became bored and went to sleep herself.

I listened to her breathing deepen to a steady sigh with a little whistle at the end of each breath; I knew she was really asleep; I got up, crept into my clothes, pressed two pounds into her pretty sleeping hand, and left the room. Even if Rufus *was* paying for the evening, I had to give her something for herself.

Downstairs, even though it was already the early hours of the morning, traffic had not ceased. It had diminished but not ceased, and waiters still scuttled about bearing champagne and snacks to jaded campaigners. I even smelt hot chocolate wafting past. I caught one waiter by the arm and ordered beer, feeling buoyant, light and restless. I saw Madame welcome an ancient French General and launch him up the stairs. He was wearing all his medals and clanked his sword on the bannisters going up. The Colonel of our own regiment sauntered by, very much at home. Of course, in the last year he had visited the Front less and less frequently, and I had actually held open the door of his taxi when he arrived back, looking rather the worse for wear, after perhaps just such an evening as this.

Rufus appeared and ordered bacon and eggs and beer. I followed suit, and we both tucked into a full English breakfast with yards of tangy Belgian beer to wash it down. He was talkative and lively but did not belabour my inauguration into manhood.

We discussed what we would do after the war. It was then September 1918, and peace was imminent.

"It's going to be dashed difficult for you to settle down, Roddie. What do you want to do with your life?" He asked briskly wiping his egg up with bread, French style.

"Oh, the Army, I expect. But I'd like to transfer to the Cavalry like my father. I'd like to be posted to India. I suppose a career in the Army is about all I'm fit for now."

Rufus laughed his clear, bright, three-note laugh. "You've

got the world before you if you want it and you talk like one of my old campaign sergeants whose wife had run off with the milkman. He was invalided out finally; been gassed, poor fellow. 'Me bellows is busted, Captain,' he'd say. 'Me wife's done a flit, me bellows is busted—so the Army can '*ave* me now, that all I'm fit for.' "

Rufus paused to drain his flagon and when he had finished, his moustache was covered with beer froth. "Not so odd, really, old man, after all, that's exactly what you are—one of my old campaign sergeants!"

I felt a swell of pride and took a huge gulp of beer to cover my beaming face.

"Why don't you come out to India too, Rufus. It's fantastic! I mean I can only remember our own garden and rivers all yellow, filled with boats and people, thousands of people with great black eyes and dressed in saffron robes; green, blue, saffron, purple, robes. You can keep polo ponies too. You'd love it, I know."

"I'm sure I would, old man, but not going as a sort of glorified policeman, keeping the miserable coolies down, so that we in the Old Country can still live in the manner to which we have become accustomed. I don't believe in it."

"I don't understand. Do you think that being an Army officer in the East means being a glorified policeman?"

"Nothing surer. Look, to a certain extent we all live by our economical dependence on the vast trading companies in the East, i.e. by systematically robbing coolies, keeping them at such a low standard of living that the price of labour is negligible. Now, those of us who feel we are 'enlightened', maintain that these coolies should be set *free*; but our standard of living, and hence our 'enlightenment' demands that the robbery should continue. That's why we keep such a large military force in India—to ensure that our 'interests' are secure; we police our colonies for the protection of our economic interests and for no other reason. Most armies are economic machines and most wars, in fact, I venture to say *all* wars, are the culmination of arms manufacturers machinations. Take this one we have just fought in. Nobody knows exactly what it is all about idealogically, but in practical hard-cash terms it has kept arms manufacturers frantically busy, churning out guns and grenades and more guns for the last five years. Thousands of people have been employed making them, millions of people have been killed by them, and a good time has been had by all. End of lesson one, my son, in how to understand the wicked ways of the world."

I had never heard Rufus talk in such a fashion. Some of what he said was so cynical pure horrifying that I could not eat. It seemed to me that he was negating all the deaths of our men, the brave men, whom we had seen die beside us. I did not speak, but sat staring down at my plate, trying to work out some of the things that he had said.

"Ah, but the worm will turn, my lad, you'll see, in fact the worm has begun to revolve alarmingly already. Look at what's happening in Russia. The coolie class has risen up and smitten its rulers with the force of avenging angels. God knows what will happen to *them*, whether they burn themselves out in private struggles for power, or whether they form their own 'ruling class', who knows? Russia, yes, that's where I'd like to go, Russia, Tolstoi, *War and Peace*, Chekov, where East meets West, Rasputin and Felix Youssoupoff—you know I knew him at Oxford, strangely enough . . . Youssoupoff, I mean . . . He's escaped now and lives in Paris. Russia, yes, but not just yet. I've had enough of chaos for the moment, I think I shall wait until they get things a bit better sorted out—then go! I'll be fascinated to see if the Bolshevik ideology can actually function."

It was then that I realised that Rufus was very drunk and was not speaking to me at all. He was sitting there talking to himself. I had tried to follow what he was saying but it didn't make much sense. I wondered if the sullen Maria had been unsatisfactory and searched his face to discover any tell-tale signs of disappointment or frustration, but there were none. His eyes were cool and bland and blue, his fair hair was neatly parted in the middle and his mouth relaxed and smiling. He must have noticed my intent regard, because he suddenly leaned over and clapped me on the shoulder, "All right, Roddie, lad, there's no need to look so glum, I haven't gone mad or anything, I'm just trying to collect my scattered thoughts now that peace is upon us." He poured himself the last of the beer. "And where better to do it than here, sated with women and beer and eggs and bacon."

"And are *you* sated?" he squinted up his eyes, tilted his head back and glared at me like a myopic mother.

I laughed. "After all," he added, twisting the short ends of his moustache and slicking down his hair on either side like a true villain of the melodramas, "we are fully paid up all-night members of this elegant establishment, heh, heh, heh. Shall we re-join the ladies?"

We linked arms going up the stairs. With Rufus in this jaunty, exuberant mood, my own spirits rose, and I laughed inside myself with the knowledge that God had fulfilled his part of the bargain—I was alive, I had had a woman, I could get drunk if I wished, go to the races, read books, eat bacon and eggs, link arms with my drunken friend going upstairs, pat dogs, ride horses, kill pheasants, swim in the sea, pick my nose, anything I desired was mine. I wanted to shout out that I was alive and that I loved the world!

On the first landing Rufus stopped me and said, "I say, Roddie, what say we swap women? I mean, you'll be getting the thick end of the wedge, and I don't know whether I can cope with another bout myself. Now *you*, on the other hand, are at the height of your sexual drive according to Plato, so a tumble with Maria would be the perfect ending to a delightful evening and truly complete your education."

I thought of surly Maria versus pretty Mignonne and I must admit I became very tentative.

"But Rufus, what if I can't cope with her either?"

"That, my son, is indeed a question which puts your virility to the test . . ."

So saying, for the second time that memorable evening I was dragged up those daunting stairs, hurried along the passages, and deposited outside the door of Maria's room, breathless and disconcerted. I stood there for a full minute while Rufus weaved off down the passage, and would probably never have entered had not someone opened a door behind me. The fear of being caught standing outside like a nervous school-boy sent me sliding through faster than I can say. I closed the door soundlessly and turned round to be confronted by a scene which has never left me. There was Maria, sprawled on the bed, her legs and arms thrown out every which way, her black hair tumbling about her shoulders, her eyes half shut, her big, wide breasts pointing east and west—Maria, smoking, in the rosy light of the bedside lamp and watching herself in the huge black mirror that hung above the bed, contemplating the voluptuous movement of her own olive limbs, the black mound of Venus surmounting all.

I smelt the acrid undergrowth smell of kief for the first time in my life, only registered it as part of the scene, the smell of sex and woman—undiluted woman—and like a frog transfixed in the thrall of a snake, I croaked and shuffled forward to show myself in the light.

\* \* \*

I only met Rufus once more before his death. It was in London after his demobilisation. He was wearing a pair of green tweedy trousers and a grey flannel shirt. I thought he looked much better in uniform and I dared to say so.

"Ah, Roddie, we all must wear costumes, and if mine doesn't fit the role *you* want me to play, it's too bad." That was all he said.

\* \* \*

I left England several weeks after Rufus's death—as soon as I had recovered from the shock in fact, and rejoined my father and his new family. Nine long years had passed since I had seen him and now I had several half-brothers and sisters to contend with me for his affection. I think he was proud of my achievements in his own way, but jealous of my youth, the active service I had seen, my freedom to come and go as I pleased.

I took up polo and bought myself a pony and then two more. Mothers of marriageable girls invited me to cocktail parties, supper, and on picnics. I became the sort of equivalent of 'The Deb's Delight' in India, could always be counted on as 'extra man' by distraught hostesses giving dinner parties, was a six handicap polo player, and enjoyed pig-sticking.

I had transferred to my father's old regiment, the 71st Light Horse, and though my duties were very minor—I reviewed troops in the morning, was officer of the watch two nights a week—I often thought of Rufus's words that night at Madame Hermine's. I must say I did not consider myself a 'glorified policeman', but then, nor did I consider myself much of a soldier.

A curious thing had happened to me after that fateful night. I found the idea of approaching a lady, any lady, with the intention of making love to her and then not paying her, quite impossible. I had visited the best brothels in Paris, London and even went back to Brussels; I was always easily excited, indeed, I might even say that I was athletically inclined sexually, but, let even the little finger of a young lady whom I had met in Society or who was the sister of one of my contemporaries, touch my hand, or let her put her little mouth up to be kissed, and I flew like a dog from thunder, my tail between my legs my ears flattened.

I shall not belabour you with accounts of my social activities in India between 1920 and 1937, vouchsafe to say that they were lively in every direction except towards the altar. Many ladies of varying attraction tried to coax, lead, push and even drag me in that direction, but I resisted valiantly and won the enviable title of 'confirmed bachelor' from the community. I paid regular visits to all neighbouring brothels, first making absolutely sure that they were clean and hospitable and, I am proud to say, that in all those seventeen years I was caught only twice with venereal diseases; once by a dark snake-like Tamil they had brought up from Ceylon and not yet vetted; and once I was drunk in Bombay and allowed myself to be inveigled into accepting the attentions of a kohl-eyed beauty of the streets.

\* \* \*

Early in 1938 I returned to England—Captain F. Omerod, M.M., and was stationed in Sussex, quite near to Brighton. I had brought my three best polo ponies over with me and I settled into a delightful cottage near the barracks and bought myself a boxer pup which I called Rufus.

There were several reasons for having left India. The first was an incident which happened in a village near the border of what is now Pakistan. We had been sent down there to give support to the troops who were keeping looters and rioters in check after a series of clashes between Hindus and Muslims.

We rode into the market place flanked by troops, to be confronted by a mob of stolid silent people, standing, sitting, holding children in their arms, edging forwards and staring at us. We were quite used to this sort of greeting in a trouble spot and were unperturbed. In all, we must have been thirty men and fifteen mounted escort. The men marched into the centre of the square dividing the crowd as they went and we followed behind them and stood our horses, waiting for a proclamation to be read by the Chief of Police, warning all people to return to their homes and create no more disturbances, otherwise action would be taken against them.

The first sign that everything was not under control, was a scuffling sound behind me, and I saw that the attention of the crowd had been diverted by two youths locked in a vicious embrace and rolling about in the dirt. I turned my horse around and noticed that all the open area in the square was now completely filled with people and more were infiltrating from every side. The troop was now surrounded on all sides by a crowd of more than five or six thousand people, at a rough estimate.

A murmuring replaced the silence and scuffling and, as the bespectacled Chief of Police appeared on the verandah of one of the buildings at the far end of the square, the murmur grew to a shout and the shout to a tumultuous caterwauling that continued for several minutes. Just as I thought my ear-drums were about to burst, my horse reared up in the air almost unseating me. Someone had thrust a dart or some sharp instrument into its flank and the poor animal was mad with pain, bucking and neighing and kicking with all its might.

I shouted to my sergeant but saw that he was in the same predicament as myself, shots were fired into the air, then pandemonium. The troops had fixed bayonets and were endeavouring to throw back the surging mob that flailed at them from all sides. My horse had already bloodied my nose with its tossing head and, as we converged—the teeming mass of humanity and my horse and I—I saw its front hooves descending onto the head of a woman carrying a small child. She was knocked out of the way but dropped the baby and I caught a glimpse of it as it curled up into an embryonic ball once again, blood spurting out of its mouth, its chest crushed under one hoof. Profoundly shocked, I jumped off my horse, to try to curb its madness and recover the child, but a new wave of people hurtled forward and I was trampled into the dust with the rest. Fists pummelled me, feet kicked out at me and I felt a chilling fear of the mob. The sound of gun-fire was now constant and I drew my own pistol and rose to my feet knowing that in the panic, there was no way other than force to stop its spreading and getting completely out of hand. I fired some shots into the air to try to make a space around myself and find my way back to the rest of the troop, but these people seemed impervious to noise, so I fired at the legs of the pressing, hissing crowd. As soon as any of their number fell, there was a sort of communal gasp of breath and half of them began to retreat; another few shots and they turned tail and ran.

In ten minutes the square was empty, save for the miserable little bundles of dead or wounded that they had left behind, and quiet, save for the whinneying of the horses, and the wailing of the mother of the dead child. Our troop was busy dusting itself down, recovering the horses and seeing to our two wounded men; one had sustained a nasty gash in his thigh and the other had concussion. There were seven of *them* dead in all and ten wounded, one severely. I had a broken nose and already one of my eyes was closing with a shiner the size of a toffee apple and about the same colour. A curfew was placed on the town, the dead were buried, and we were sent back to barracks.

But the whole incident left me with a taste of alum in my mouth. Here was I, trampling down children—even if they were half-starved bundles of misery—shooting unarmed people in the street—even if they were WOGS. Rufus's words came back to me and with a vehemence that resounded through my head . . . not *even* a 'glorified policeman', just an ordinary brutal one on a horse, and carrying a gun . . .

The second reason for leaving India is much more difficult to explain. The fact is, I had begun to talk to myself . . . At thirty-seven I was fit, tanned, balding it must be admitted, but starting to talk to myself like some old codger of seventy. I became very sensitive about it, especially as some of the junior officers in the Mess cracked jokes about me and would often pretend to be talking to *themselves* in my presence.

Having no intimate friends that I *could* talk to, and no women except whores to whom I could unburden my heart, I thought that a complete change of scenery and society might jerk me out of this unfortunate habit. I bought a dog and took him with me wherever I went so that if caught in the act of uttering lonely sentences, people would automatically take it that I was addressing the hound and not think me a crank. I had never been an excessive sort of fellow as regards money, only splurged once or twice on buying polo ponies. I had no wife and children to support, so I had saved a goodly amount. This I invested and was making a fair income from the revenue. Thus, I packed my worldly goods and took a ship from Bombay in December of '37, arriving in Southampton in the bleak and biting January of '38.

\* \* \*

I settled into life in Sussex very nicely, although after so many years in India I was bothered by the cold; my bones seemed to freeze solid in those icy blasts of air that catch one by surprise, crossing the road or turning a corner. Rufus, the dog, was a great success in my life, and I loved him and found companionship and congratulated myself on having found a pleasurable answer to my problem.

I took up hunting as well as polo and began to attend the Hunt Balls, which were rowdy and raucous affairs with young fellows bouncing about, shouting and sweating in their evening suits; harmless I suppose, and good fun, taken by and large. I could not help noticing the enormous change in social life in England since last I had been there. Young people were defying their parents and rushing off to Spain to back some ludicrous cause that had nothing to do with them anyway, girls were brash and forward now, and wore extraordinary frizzed-out hair-styles, movie-stars made more money than the Prime Minister and a king had abdicated for love. Hitler had turned Germany into a war-machine and I wondered what Rufus would think of the whole crazy thing if he could see it.

And then I saw *him* . . . in a very unlikely place . . . Across the room from me at a Hunt Ball! I dashed across the floor upsetting several couples engaged in performing a spirited canter called 'The Dashing White Sergeant' or some such rot, and came face to face with Rufus, only he was a girl! A girl, in uniform, with the same bland blue eyes, fair hair and friendly interested expression.

I stammered and stuttered and at last got out some semblance of a sentence demanding to know if her name was 'Milton'.

"No, I'm sorry, it's Boddington," she replied.

"Oh," I almost sobbed, "but you must be a relation."

"A relation of whom?"

"Rufus Milton."

"Ah . . . " she said knowingly, now accepting that I was not just a clever johnny making an inspired sort of pick-up. "Rufus Milton-Jones was my uncle, my mother's brother, but he was killed years and years ago in the war, I think, or just after it. Why, did you know him?"

"You look exactly like him," I replied, "exactly, it's phenomenal! What's your name, I mean your first name? Do you live near here? Is your mother still alive?"

She laughed at my eagerness, "Yes, my mother is still alive," she said. "Yes, I do live near here, and my first name is Cynthia."

I was trembling with excitement and continued to question her voraciously about her job. She was a corporal in the Women's Royal Army Corps. Was she married? She was not. Did she like riding? She did. Was she engaged to be married? She was not. She frowned at that. I was amazed at my own temerity.

I invited her to watch a polo match in which I was participating the next day, Sunday, and she agreed quite easily, much to my delight. Thus began my courtship of Cynthia Boddington.

It continued for a whole year—in fact, until the day the war broke out, the 3rd of September, 1939, when I asked her to marry me and she accepted. Cynthia was eighteen years younger than I was, and had been deeply in love with some half-baked poet (who had got his lot fighting with the Brigade in the Spanish Civil War) up until the time I picked her up at the Hunt Ball. I think she still hankered after the fellow, though she never discussed him openly. Sometimes she would refer to him indirectly, and I could hear a sort of yearning in her voice, and see a film spread over her eyes that secretly nearly sent me out of my mind.

I loved her with the same near-worship that I had felt for Rufus, but I was afraid that she might find out my fear of women and terror of the sexual embrace with any but whores. I had long conferences with Rufus, the dog, on the subject; I had never got further than holding hands and a gentle goodnight kiss after an evening out with Cynthia, even at the end of that whole year of courtship.

She seemed to accept my timidity in these matters as natural deference, but when war was declared and my regiment was immediately under orders, I was jolted into taking the final plunge and asking for her hand. After all, I was in my fortieth year, a Captain with prospects, not on the bread line, and in love.

Our marriage was solemnised in the little country church in Horsham according to her wishes—and attended by her mother, who was a thoroughly nice lady and heartily approved of the match—a handful of my fellow-officers and some of my polo-playing friends. We went to Brighton for the honeymoon.

After the usual quiet dinner of lobster and champagne we retired to our nuptial bed and to my everlasting shame, I was completely impotent. I hate even to describe the events (or shall I say non-events) of that night. Cynthia undressed in the bathroom and came to me, soft and yielding, in a pink nightie. She lay in my arms waiting: nothing, nothing happened. My bones were as dead as Caesar's, laid to rest for two thousand years, my hand would not reach out to touch the small, soft breasts and my manhood lay limply between my legs as though it had never belonged to me. Cynthia was devastated, but tried to hide the fact from me by excusing herself and pleading a headache; she took some aspirin and fell into a fitful sleep.

Two long nights later, I told her that I had urgent business to do with army matters which could not be postponed. I settled her in the local cinema and rushed headlong to find the nearest brothel, where I could prove to myself that I had not completely ceased to function.

I was enormously relieved when the two weeks of honeymoon were over and the pressing duties of wartime service began to occupy my life. We achieved a sort of temporary compromise with me bringing her to a climax manually and then satisfying myself later with a whore. I was still miserable and tortured by my failure but put it further and further back in my mind, telling myself that I *loved* Cynthia and that nothing mattered except that.

With prostitutes I was now violent to the point of brutality. I was quick and angry and I hated myself.

Cynthia and I never openly discussed my predicament. She did not know that I spent several hours a week in a brothel. When her leave was up she went back to camp, telling me that she had decided not to give up the Service.

I had been promoted almost immediately after war began and sent on a special course in tank tactics and mechanics;

nearly all officers in the Cavalry were deployed into other sections of warfare, as the horse had lost his place in the theatre of war, with the advent of the tank, the truck and the tommy-gun.

North Africa was where I spent most of my war. I liked it. I loved it, in fact. Silence, enormous skies of void blue, black nights of stars and sand, Arab children with fly-encrusted eyes, Wogs in filthy burnouses always pointing in the wrong direction —the physical race of North Africans has never left me with any illusions, like Indians have done . . .

Cynthia was stationed in Kent. She too had been promoted and wrote me most rewarding letters twice a week. Sometimes they were lyrical and ended with little poems and drawing of trees or flowers that she had seen and admired. I awaited her letters with apprehension and delight. Apprehension, because I dreaded a 'Dear Johnny', which would tell me that she had met someone more her own age who could give her the sort of love she had expected from me; and delight, because they were always so full and sweet, even though they contained no declarations of love. She finished her letters with 'As always, Cynthia'. I mustered all my words of tenderness for my return letters, though I knew they were scanty and paltry, they were all I had to give her.

And so we remained throughout the war. I was sent home on leave before the Italian invasion, and I brought her the most exotic gifts I could find; black lace underwear I had picked up in Tangiers, an inlaid jewel box from Morocco; inside this I put a filigree silver bracelet with moons and suns dangling. I made her wear the black underwear and put on the bracelet, I lay her on the bed, turned off the light and stripped her of all her finery. That is how I first penetrated my wife.

I returned to the Italian campaign a fulfilled man and a Colonel to boot, and finished the war in great spirits.

Immediately afterwards, I retired from the services and cast about me for something to do in civilian life. It was an awkward position in which I found myself, never having been a civilian before, and I decided finally that my direction lay in administration.

I took a year off with Cynthia and we lived quite comfortably in the cottage with Rufus, the dog, who was now a sprightly eight-year old. Perhaps it was the familiarity, perhaps the fact that we did not have any children, but I was soon back in my former rut of not being able to make love to my wife, and twice-weekly visits to a brothel. Cynthia stopped me from touching her intimately any more, telling me that she did not enjoy it. I was relieved that she did not seem to be distressed over the eventuality of our marriage; in fact, we were devoted to each other.

I saw the position at Kew advertised in *The Times* and applied, having first discussed the possibility of a move to London with Cynthia. She agreed wholeheartedly with the idea, and when I was accepted as one of the administrators. We found an ideal house in Ealing.

When Rufus died, I bought Cynthia a Boxer bitch which we called Lucy, and that is all the family we were. Cynthia took up writing poetry quite seriously after she had one of her efforts accepted by *The Observer*. I've never got along too well with the written word, especially poetry, but when I read her stuff, it seemed very outlandish, not like Cynthia at all, filled with very sensual images, that sort of thing; quite odd, really.

# Part Three

# 6

## Margaret Truro

THE FIRST THING I remember in my life is the back end of a cow seen by me from underneath. It was at my auntie Alice's. She was really my mother's aunt but we all called her 'Auntie' as well, and she had a dairy farm in Sussex. We used to go there for holidays. I remember being fixated about that cow's behind for quite a while, wondering why no one was angry with it for not wiping its bottom. And then there was that tasselled tail, huge cornered haunches and swollen udder; all *very* extraordinary. I remember walking along behind it with a big stick giving it a bit of a prod every few minutes to see if it would have any effect. The next thing I remember is my brother Benjy's new bike; how I *envied* him! How I *loved* him when he used to snuggle up to me in bed! How I loathed him when he picked a rose in the garden and gave it to my mother and she kissed him and hugged him and called him 'Darling' and didn't give him the smack that I knew *I* would have got for doing the same thing! I'm really telling you all this to show you how normal I am! A good, middle-class English upbringing I had, complete with anal frustration, oral deprivation, penis envy, father fixation, sibling rivalry (all the lovely words), deep discrimination against those of different race, creed and colour to say nothing of social position and money. In fact at twelve and thirteen I was the perfect product, ready to be polished into a diamond of the boring bourgeoisie, immutable and deadly for life. And then it happened. I got interfered with.

\*     \*     \*

It was probably the best thing that ever happened to me because out of it I became a person destined for other things. You could say I became a *person*, which is something I would never have achieved under the circumstances of my early life.

I had a friend at boarding school called Dolores Upton. Dolores was one of those fat-faced, squint-eyed girls who look naturally secretive and generally *are*, who don't belong to any clique. They range the field, accepting scraps of affection and confidences from lonely girls or new girls or girls who can't fit in like themselves. They do not seem to be unhappy with their lot but hardly anyone ever remembers them afterwards.

I liked Dolores because the very first day I was at the school when we had to wear our names pinned with safety pins and clearly marked on both our fronts and our backs, she did not saunter up and inspect mine with a scornful mouth and carefully unacknowledged eyes and make the usual mocking remark accompanied by titters and whispers, that so obviously cause distress to the name-bearer. I remember one girl called Doris Tinker who had a dreadful time while all the older girls repeated her name over and over running the two names together so that it became one lone sibilant, 'SSSStinker'. You can tell what sort of school it was.

Dolores did not even look at my name.

"Are you foreign?" she asked.

"No," I answered, aghast. "I'm English."

"Well, you look just like a girl I met in France last year and she was *French*."

"Well, I can't help that, I'm *English*."

"I'll show you around if you like. What's your name? I know all the secret places you can hide . . . It's a good thing to know in this joint," she added, glancing over her shoulder to see if one of the prefects might be listening.

I was flattered and at the same time offended. If I had known that Dolores was an outsider at that moment, I would never have become friends with her, but all I knew was that she was not a new girl like me and that anyone who showed interest in me at that moment would have been acceptable.

We found that we shared a cubicle also, so Dolores showed me around. She knew how you could get apples out of the orchard without anyone catching you; she knew where the fire-escapes were situated and how to get down them at night to creep out to the movies; she had access to money—which was forbidden; she was bold enough to buy cigarettes at the local tobacconists *and* to smoke them; I can even remember her sneaking down to the telephone-box on the corner and ringing up the headmistress pretending to be her own mother and asking permission to spend the weekend at home. She got it. She was one of that happy breed who never gets caught.

I was not altogether unaware of the danger of these escapades, but I too began to enjoy breaking rules and, though I chickened out of a few, I was Dolores's only true ally and friend in the school. The several times I was caught she covered up for me expertly. She was a good straight-faced liar but I am sure we were both suspected of being 'hard-nuts'.

There was something else that she did for me that I can never forget. I got my first period when I was eleven, and thought that I must be dying of a dreadful disease because my mother had never told me about menstruation. I was terrified and horrified by what I thought was some new sort of T.B. and hid the evidence from everyone. Dolores caught me trying to dispose of a pair of knickers and explained the whole process. She showed me what to do, laughed at my embarrassment, and we never discussed the problem again.

In the summer of my thirteenth birthday, I went to stay at her home. Dolores's father was an obscure liberal M.P. called Sir Giles Upton, and the invitation to her house came on writing paper that had a crest on it. Of course, this impressed my parents no end, so without much more ado I was dispatched complete with tennis racquet, jodhpurs, plimsolls, mac and wellingtons—all the accoutrements for an English summer holiday.

The Uptons' house was near Taunton and Dolores herself met me at the station. We smoked going home in the back of the local taxi and I was frightened that the driver might tell her mother and father.

"Oh, he'd never bother. He *knows* them," said Dolores airily, puffing away and blowing out lots of smoke. I know now that it was because she wasn't inhaling.

There was a long impressive drive of lime trees at the end of which was the house itself—a disappointment—not the sprawling romantic mansion I had expected, but a prosaic Tudor reproduction, overgrown garden, two monkey-puzzle trees in front and, out at the back, a lineless tennis court and rusty roller.

Dolores explained to me that the original house had been turned over to a Preparatory School for boys, and that this was only the estate agent's house being used by the Upton family to tide over 'hard times'.

Dolores's mother was a large, vague woman with enormous hands and feet and tiny head with features to match. She was fair and weasel-faced and seemed to be obsessive about how much milk we drank and nothing else. I could not believe that she was really Dolores's mother, and never felt at ease in her company. I don't think Dolores did either.

The father was a foxy-looking man in tweeds but I only saw him once as he spent most of his time up in London. The house revolved around Dolly's three brothers and her Uncle Ansell.

Ansell Upton had sideburns and a jolly manner and taught us to play gin-rummy the first evening I was there. I was not shy with the three brothers, having one of my own, and we all had a marvellous time, laughing and telling silly elephant jokes and vying with each other as to who could tell the most grotesque story about our various teachers at school.

The next day we went riding and Uncle Ansell led the way on a large grey gelding called Ambrose. He looked very grand on his mount and I was pleased when he fell back and gave me some compliments about my seat and how well I held my hands. I showed off a bit, cantering and then galloping; I even allowed my little black pony to jump a hedge or two, forgetting that I had not ridden all that year.

The next day I was in agony. My groin felt as if it had been pummelled with sticks and my legs then nailed on. I could hardly sit down, but once seated, could not get up. I told Dolores, who suggested rather half-heartedly that I speak to her mother. The thought of approaching Lady Upton with a sore bottom was absurd so I ended up going to Uncle Ansell. It was then that I was interfered with.

\* \* \*

The first time I was not sure that anything untoward had happened. Uncle Ansell was so thorough and tender and worried that the embrocation should be properly applied, I thought perhaps he was just being over-cautious for my welfare. But the second time there could be no mistake, even in my guileless state, that something other than medication was going on.

100

I told Dolores about it but she said not to worry, that Uncle Ansell often acted like that with *her* too. She told me that after a while I would get to like it, and not to tell anyone else as they would not understand.

The holiday continued happily enough, punctuated by visits to Uncle Ansell's room for treatment, sometimes with, sometimes without Dolly, until I was thoroughly indoctrinated and actually enjoying it as she had said, although neither of us took it at all seriously. It was just something we did for Uncle Ansell because he seemed to like it so much.

It was a pretty good summer weather-wise. The long days stretching out ahead of us took on a pattern—we rode, we swam, we motored into Taunton to the movies, we visited Uncle Ansell, and I wrote my dutiful letter home each week. I was astounded when it was suddenly time to go home. There was a tender scene of farewell with the other members of the family (except Lady Upton who, much to my relief, had disappeared for a short stay in Deauville) and a big box of my favourite chocolate-covered almonds to eat on the train, from Uncle Ansell.

When I got home everyone remarked on how much I had grown and developed, and my father must have told my mother that it was time she had a talk with me about 'various matters', because she arrived in my room on my second night home looking very strained around the eyes and playing her tape at the wrong speed. She gabbled on a bit about mothers and fathers and planting seeds and how boys were different from girls, how boys did bad things to girls if they let them, and then she stopped.

I must have looked bewildered and she certainly looked flustered, because she has this habit of scraping back her hair off her forehead when she's worried and she was doing it all the time.

After a while she touched her own breast and said, "You see, Margaret, when girls start to grow up they get these swellings on their chests, breasts, like you're getting now, and men want to touch them, but you mustn't let them. But I suppose they teach you all this at school," she ended hopefully.

"Oh," I said, touching my own small protuberances, "but Uncle Ansell said mine were perfect and would never get big and hanging like most women. He said that Diane de Poitiers, who was a lovely French lady, used to allow only ice-cold water to touch her breasts, and that that was why the King of France loved her. She never fed any of her babies either, but they were all healthy and that was why she stayed being the king's mistress until she was seventy. She was miles older than him too." I paused for breath, anxious to impart more of the picturesque tales that Uncle Ansell had amused us with, when I saw that my mother's mouth was hanging open.

"It's true," I continued, thinking that it was disbelief that sat on her face. "Uncle Ansell never tells lies."

My mother made a noisy swallow before she spoke again. "And did you let Uncle Ansell touch *your* breasts?"

"Of course, and he said that mine were much better than Dolores's. He said they had pinker nipples and stood up better," I said proudly.

A strange, strangulated sound came from my mother's throat and she sat immobile for a minute or two staring at me with fixed eyes.

"And this Uncle Ansell, what else did he do to you?" she said finally. Her voice had dropped to a whisper.

"Oh, lots of things," I answered defensively, "but Dolores said it was all right, and he's been doing things with *her* for a couple of years now and she's perfectly O.K." I used the same voice that I always used when I had been accused of something that I had seen my brother do two minutes before, and not be reprimanded.

The force of the slap my mother gave me I shall always remember. It was short and brutal and stunned me for an instant. By the time I had recovered myself, she had left the room and I heard her calling my father from the top landing and running down the stairs.

\*     \*     \*

Then there was silence. I sat like a stone, wondering what I could possibly have said that had drawn such a violent and precipitant reaction from her. I was sure that if my mother had met Uncle Ansell she would have liked him very much. He was fun; he knew lots of jokes and games and stories, and I knew that she always responded well to anyone who could make her laugh. As far as touching my breasts went, he had said that they were something to be proud of and to stand up straight and show them to the world, and never to slouch and fold your arms over them like Dolores did sometimes when we went to the swimming pool. I sat waiting and stupefied for what seemed like two years. Where were they? What was she saying to him? Maybe it was all right. Daddy had calmed her down and they were having a nice cup of tea.

I was still nursing my red cheek and perplexed when my father came into the room, his face a mask of white paralysed flesh.

Immediately I saw my father I knew that it was a very, very, very serious matter. I had only ever seen his face with that cemented aspect to it once before—when my brother Benjy got lost at a picnic near a lake and was missing for five hours. My father had demanded that they dredge the lake with that same look on his face.

"What's this, miss, that your mother's been telling me, that some boy has been interfering with you?" This was the first time I ever heard the expression 'interfering with' before, so I wasn't quite sure what it meant; I decided to put a bold face on.

"It isn't a boy, he's a man," I cried.

My father's neck seemed to bulge out of his collar in an odd way and his voice came out in a sort of squeak, like Benjy's does sometimes when he's been thwarted.

"Oh, is he just! Is he indeed!" He grabbed my arm. "You stupid little bitch! It'll be your own fault if he's got you pregnant. I don't understand you! Don't you realise what you've *done*?"

I was petrified. My father had never been so distraught and uncontrolled in my presence before. Oh yes, I had heard him scream at my mother from behind closed doors, and once he had clipped me very hard around the ear when I had called my mother 'silly cow', but otherwise with me he had always had a lovely protective and intimate manner—a sort of precious game we played that excluded everyone else. It had always made my mother mad as hell. Sometimes on Sunday mornings I used to climb into bed with him when my mother had gone down to make the breakfast and he would read me Rudyard Kipling books in a special tender voice reserved for me, carefully explaining the more difficult words and watching my reactions of delight when he adopted different voices for each and every character. My mother would always humph and bumph when she came back into the room and found us giggling and exchanging knowing looks over some secret that she didn't share. That was a sign for us to tickle her then you could see her face lose that left-out look. She would laugh and laugh with her mouth wide open and her belly bouncing. She's always been very ticklish, my mother.

And now this stranger father was shaking me and shouting at me, "Well, what happened? Come along, speak up! Did he force you? I'm losing patience with you, Margaret! What happened?"

My mother's taut face appeared from behind his apopleptic one and I stared at them both as though they had gone completely mad.

I was genuinely certain that nothing that had happened to me at the Upton house was anywhere near as horrific as this outburst, so what was there to say? That Uncle Ansell had touched me and I had touched him? That sometimes Dolores and I had both stroked him and how he had liked it? That he had caressed us expertly until we were quite ready and willing to be investigated, and this also he had done gently, so that neither of us was outraged or made to feel as though we were doing something dirty? When I look back on it I cannot help feeling that I have a lot to thank Uncle Ansell for.

Again my father's voice, scourging and furious, "What did he do to you, you stupid little fool? I shall smack you hard if you don't answer? What happened?"

Suddenly he collapsed. With a sort of muffled bellow he let go of my shoulders and threw himself down on my bed, covering up his eyes.

He made a lot of grating noises in his throat, dragging himself around on the bed and gnashing his teeth as though someone had shot him in the stomach, and then he lay still. My mother and I waited trembling for this spasm to pass and when it did, my father rose up cold and empty, without looking at me, and asked my mother to get him a glass of water.

He seemed to have lost interest in me altogether and sat there staring at the floor and muttering until finally he took out a cigarette and smoked it.

I tried to get some response by touching him on the arm and saying, "Daddy, it was nothing. He didn't do anything bad to me," but he shook me off without a glance and continued to stare into space. Of all the things he could have done, this was the most cruel. I felt humiliated and bereft, sort of like a fly that has been swatted and then left dying on the floor to be swept up the next morning with the rest of the rubbish. When my mother came back with the water he said, in a quiet controlled voice, "Well, Beth, if she won't tell us, there's nothing we can do," still ignoring me.

Of course, I started to howl as loud as I could so that there was nothing they could do with me but put me to bed and call the doctor. He arrived and carried out an examination that seemed to me far more unpleasant and offensive than anything Uncle Ansell had done, and finally pronounced that I was definitely not 'virgo intacta'.

None of them explained to me exactly what it was that had happened and the three of them left the room to discuss my malady elsewhere. My mother was in tears and I could only suppose that some overt demonstration of whatever malady I had would show itself in the next day or two. I stayed in bed and shuddered over the consequences of something that I had thought was no more important than having a few puffs of one of Dolores' cigarettes after lights-out in the loo at school.

Another silence. I was kept in my room for two days; my mother brought me sick-bed meals and even my brother was hushed and intimidated, sensing a situation. When at last I was allowed to emerge, my life had changed. I was withdrawn from boarding school (not a great hardship except for the fact that I was never to see Dolores again), and sent to a secondary school for girls that specialised in the Domestic Arts. My parents had decided that it was not in my interest to cause a scandal involving the Upton family, but each week I had to visit a child psychiatrist who endeavoured to gauge the extent of damage done to my unconscious by my experience.

The thing that hurt me most of all was that my father could hardly bear to be in the same room alone with me after the announcement of my changed condition by Dr. Savage. If he was speaking to me he now adopted an acid tone of perpetual rebuke and always directed his words at the top of my ear or my shoulder, my forehead, anywhere but my eyes. Once or twice I tried repeating the Sunday morning ritual of getting into bed with him but he always said that he wanted to read the papers and to get up and help my mother with the break-fast. Strangely enough, my relationship with *her* was now much less fraught. Sometimes I caught her looking at me with an expression somewhere between anguish and love, a sorry meaningful look meant to show her concern. I was unhappy, but there was no one else to really talk to but Dr. Cornish.

How can I describe Dr. Cornish? She was the psychiatrist chosen by my parents to unravel my knots. I cannot think how she had been recommended to them. Perhaps they had heard of her through some colleague of my father's who had an un-manageable child. She was tallish and broad-boned with a mass of greying, frizzy hair and a patrician nose, deep-set dark eyes, and a nice defined mouth. At first I thought I was going to hate her. She sat behind a massive table laden with books and papers, Kleenex and old chocolate wrappings, in a dilapidated swivel chair. The first thing she asked me was if I enjoyed school? She had a way of ending every question, *or* statement for that matter, with a long upward inflected 'Mmmm?' and until you were used to it, you felt that it demanded some vindicatory remark.

My first Thursday afternoon, the first of nearly two years of Thursday afternoons, I must have answered, "Not more than any other girl of my age" at least six times. Each time she would ask some question like, "And haven't you been having some trouble getting on with your mother, mmmm?" I would answer, "Not more than any other girl of my age." It was the same when she asked me about my dreaminess at school, my attitude towards by brother, my father, if I had pains with my period, even whether I liked pop music. She laughed at that, and told me that she had a daughter of about my age who played 'Can't buy me love' incessantly. I didn't believe her. She was not going to break down my defensive attitude. I felt as though everything and everyone I had ever known and trusted had betrayed me without cause, and that I had been left stranded on a solitary beach with no boats in sight.

I had started to sleep badly (a very unusual thing for me) and in fact I *did* stay in my room listening to pop programmes for hours on end. Before my disastrous visit to Dorset and on my thirteenth birthday, my parents had given me a guitar and *this* became my only consolation. I had had a recorder, so I understood the fingering of tunes, the pleasure of just waffling along picking out notes and singing soulful songs. It became an obsession. I had been rejected and I wasn't going to let them get to me again.

My brother Benjy, who was seven at the time, was always trying to get in, hovering around the door, calling me a 'moody pig' or throwing his arms around me to provoke me into wrestling with him, but I wasn't having any. Once when I came home from school late, he had got into my room and taken my guitar, and I found him out in the back garden bashing away at it with a large piece of wood. He threw it down and ran like a hare when he saw my face. There was a punch-up and it was only a week or two after this that I paid my first visit to Dr. Cornish.

\* \* \*

It was a long time before we got round to the subject of Uncle Ansell. I had been expecting it from the first session, and had prepared myself to answer "Not more than any other girl of my age" if necessary, or any other pert phrase that entered my head, but I had almost forgotten about his ominous existence by the time he finally came up.

It had been a different sort of session that day, with her doing most of the talking and me listening to stories of *her* daughter Margaret, my namesake (she called me Maggie to differentiate) who had evidently developed a singeing crush on some boy who taught swimming at the local pool. I had never really believed that this other Margaret was anything but a neat piece of fiction, but had always looked interested when she spoke of her, thinking perhaps this other Margaret was the perfect norm, that *she* was the one all good daughters should be like.

Anyway, for the first time since I had been making my Thursday afternoon visits, I could see that Dr. Cornish was actually not just thinking about the effect her words were having on me; she was genuinely worried.

I cannot remember what her exact words were, but they were something like this: "You see, Maggie, it's a very difficult thing to know just how much freedom a girl of her age should have. After all, neither of you are actual children. You have the bodies of proper women. In some countries you would already

107

be married and beginning to have babies of your own by now. To introduce a young girl to sex without damaging either her body or her mind (or both) is a very delicate matter. She is like a butterfly just out of its chrysalis, palpitating with the desire to get on with living, beautiful and vulnerable and perfect. But the wings are still wet; they have never been tried. It's a terrifying thought that those wings can be touched too roughly and all those radiant colours can come away on the finger-tips leaving just a transparent grey tissue behind. Now, if I was to forbid my Margaret to go out with this boy she would resent me bitterly. I'm sure this is the first time she's had an over-powering love for someone of the opposite sex, except, of course, her father, and even in that relationship I have been standing in the way."

"How do you mean, *you* have been standing in the way?" I asked.

"Well, every little girl has a feeling of ownership about her father, the man who was there when she was a baby, holding her, the large male figure who has dominated her life. And he, in turn, feels tremendously protective and tender towards this pretty little woman that he has helped to form. The mother stands between these two figures; her relationship with the father, the fact that she sleeps with him, stops the daughter from having sole rights to the father's love and so the girl unconsciously resents the mother for her intrusion—and vice versa sometimes—the mother may resent the daughter for the father's obvious preference and desire for the daughter."

"Do you think my mother resents me?"

"Mmmm—yes, probably. She *may*, unconsciously. But at the same time she cares about you and worries over you and loves you very deeply."

"She doesn't," I said abruptly, "she only cares about my brother Benjy, everybody knows that. Daddy loves me and Mummy loves Benjy."

"Then you *are* sure that your *Daddy* loves you?"

"Well, he *did*, before he found out about Uncle Ansell." I had spoken without a thought, and it was *me* who first brought up the dreaded name.

"And who is Uncle Ansell?" she asked predictably.

I shut up. What could I say? The man who touched my butterfly wings, Dolores's uncle, oh, yes, that would be very funny, "My friend Dolores's Uncle Ansell, the butterfly-wing toucher."

She waited but I wasn't going to say anything more, so she decided to go back to the father-and-daughter thing again.

"And do you feel that your father doesn't love you any more because of this Uncle Ansell? Why do you think that your father doesn't love you any more?"

But I had nothing to say about myself that I wanted *her* to hear that day, so I made do by switching the subject back to her Margaret.

"Do you think *your* Margaret doesn't love *you* any more?" I demanded brutally.

"No, I think that my Margaret loves me very much, but I think that she will be judging me in an adult way for the first time in her life quite soon now and I want to make sure that I don't lose her regard and trust."

"And how are you going to do that?" It was one of those peevish questions that you have been conned into asking but immediately resent.

"By not showing my disapproval at whatever she decides to do, and making sure that if she *does* do something that puts her out of her depth, she can always feel that there is a handy life-belt waiting to be thrown to her."

I looked at Dr. Cornish and I felt that horrible dry mountain rising up in my throat when I know I'm going to cry. If ever I'd felt like this before during our sessions I had always concentrated on her name—Mavis. Mavis Cornish. Mavis. It's such a terrible name. Mavis. Mavis and Margaret Cornish. Why should it make me want to cry because Mavis is going to throw Margaret a handy life-belt? How stupid! I got up to go, with tears just beginning to spill out of my eyes, and she had *seen*!

"See you next week, Maggie," she said quietly as she saw me through the door, and the awful thing was that I was actually looking forward to it.

The next visit we discussed *her* Margaret again, using her as a sounding board for my problems at school this time. The subject of Uncle Ansell still hung fire, a sort of ominous tinkling in the air like a glass mobile suspended and ready to shatter on my head. Neither of us was able to ignore it completely.

"Why do you think your parents took you away from boarding school, Maggie?"

"I don't know," I lied, "maybe they thought I was being naughty, or not doing enough work; maybe they thought I just wasn't clever enough."

"What subjects did you like doing best?"

I thought about the freezing mornings getting up with the smell of the paraffin heaters, prayers and prep., Dulcie Carruthers, the prefect on our dormitory trying to hurry us along and having laryngitis; Dolores showing me a five-pound note hidden in the frame of a large photo of Uncle Ansell on the dressing-table; putting blotting paper in our shoes before chapel on Sunday and waiting for it to draw the blood down to our feet and make us faint; a midnight feast in the dorm when Sue Prescott vomited on Betty Cosgrove's bed.

"I wasn't really mad about anything, but I suppose History and English weren't too bad. We had a mistress called Miss Percival who taught those subjects and who could really make you listen to everything she told you; most of the rest of the time I used to go into a sort of trance looking out of the window, seeing myself in fantastic situations, imagining that my mother or father had died, things like that. I wasn't bad at faking interest, either. I could look as though I was following every word and be thousands of miles away exploring underwater caves in my head."

I would have liked to continue "And I can do exactly the same thing with you, I can sit here and look vaguely intelligent and nod once in a while, while you rabbit on about things; your phoney Margaret and butterfly-wings and all that stuff; you might as well be tele-with-the-sound-switched-off most of the time—sort of mesmerising but unintelligible."

But Dr. Cornish was already in the middle of explaining how important it is in adolescence to have a fantasy world to escape into, that one must never feel guilty about it, and that nearly every sensitive teenager is subject to the wildest forms of self-dramatisation imaginable. I nodded sagely and looked off into the middle distance once more—there was no way I could ever get through to her that I was *unique*, that there were no words to describe the feeling of dreamy indifference I felt towards what I was doing or where I was going. Why try? I stared hard at the red velvet curtains, faded to pink in the middle where Dr. Cornish's hands had pulled them together nightly.

"—feel as though you are *unique* and that nobody understands you," her voice came through. "*Not so.* Not at all the case, my dear. It is an agonising time of your life, painful for those around you as well, who watch your unhappiness and can do nothing to alleviate it. Now, let's talk about the actual fantasies, mmmm? You said that you used to imagine that your parents were dead. How did you feel about that, mmmm?"

"How do you mean—how did I feel—"

"Well, were you very unhappy? Or did you feel relieved? How did their deaths affect you, mmmm?"

"Oh, I see." My eyes flew up to the pelmet where an old gold tassel hung down all alone. "Yes, well, mostly I imagined how sorry people would be for me, and then I used to think about how I would get to know lots of new people who were not like my parents and that I would turn into a different person if they were not there. I'd think about my mother's face all serene and dead and my father, too, not hearing him come home in the evening and shout to her that he was home. Sometimes I would even make myself cry about it and other times I would feel so free to be rid of them and sort of *new* and interesting."

"And did you feel ashamed afterwards about wanting to be rid of them?"

"I still feel awful about it sometimes, as though I'm an inhuman pig, a changeling, or something . . . but then we're sitting at the table eating, I look at them swallowing and chewing and he's saying, 'And it's little thanks I get for providing for this lot: eat, new clothes, ask for money continually, sulk, spend hours shut up in their rooms making wailing noises in the night—I don't know why I bother!' And then she says, 'Oh, you don't have to tell me about anything, I have doors slammed shut in my face, the radio turned up full blast, and bits and pieces of my clothes missing every day. It was a lucky day for you, miss, when you found that my things fitted you.' Of course, it's all directed at me and I loathe them both sitting there stuffing food down their faces and using me as some sort of a hate-object that is the only thing that brings them a bit closer together, except their horrible insurance policies. It is *love.* He has taken out one for *her* and she's taken out one for *him.* Ugh!!!!"

Dr. Cornish laughed quietly and, I thought, rather ruefully.

There was one of our usual silences. I had got quite used to them by now.

And then quite suddenly it burst out, surprising both myself and Dr. Cornish—the whole story of Uncle Ansell and Dolores and being 'interfered with', and the way it had really meant very little to me and seemingly *everything* to my father and mother. Words got jumbled up and fumbled over, my voice went faster and faster. It got higher and more urgent. I had to make somebody understand the misjudgements and injustices that I was enduring . . . and then I was just sobbing, sobbing and coughing and hiccuping and spluttering while Dr. Cornish held my head and made consoling noises and patted my back. I do not know how long I went on in this way, only that when it was over, my eyes were like two red carbuncles, I had a big bundle of soggy tissues bunched up in my fist, and I felt all calm and spent as though a great lump had been lifted out of my chest.

After that, Dr. Cornish and I were friends. Of course, there were times when I would say things like "I hate your genera-tion. They stink." and "Why don't you all leave me *alone*", but underneath I felt that she really cared about me, so it didn't matter too much.

When I was seventeen, no, sixteen and a half, she invited me to her home. I actually met the mythical Margaret who turned out to be a studious girl with thick ashen hair and pale pro-truding eyes. I even met the boy-friend, the swimming instruc-tor, who was at the university studying engineering. They seemed so sensible and juiceless that I had difficulty imagining them touching butterfly-wings, or kissing, or feeling any sensual urges at all.

Of course, at this time I was engulfed in a world of passionate encounters with phantom lovers. I would throw off my pyjamas in bed and stare down at my body trying to see it through the eyes of some imaginary lecher. At times he was a hideous scabrous wizened creature and at others, he was a beautiful princely youth with a lithe, white body and burning eyes. I touched myself all over to see how I would feel to some foreign hand. I learnt to masturbate, but not too often and I did not tell Dr. Cornish.

Real flesh and blood men and boys, I was extremely wary of, like the little fox on ice, frightened of getting its tail wet. I skittered along, head down, whenever I felt their eyes on me on buses or in the streets. My parents watched me, waiting for me to stay out late or smoke pot or get pregnant. They were convinced I was a bad lot, intended for the streets or scandal, anywhere other than a nice, middle-class suburb of Bristol. They were right. One Saturday, not long after my seventeenth birthday, I packed two small suitcases, took my guitar and got on the train for London. I even left the proverbial letter saying not to worry that I had gone for good, and that it was not their fault, that they were probably right about me, and goodbye.

\* \* \*

For the first two months in London, I lived in a Y.W.C.A. Hostel. It was run by a ferocious middle-aged lady called Miss Crump, who allowed no girl back into the establishment after eleven o'clock at night without having signed herself out beforehand and given a life-or-death reason for doing so. Even then, tell-tale signs of liquor, bleary eyes, rumpled blouses, were watched for by eagle spinster eyes and very few girls who were not completely inhibited had ever lasted out six months in the place . . . two months was my lot.

\* \* \*

I found a job in a coffee bar in Store Street where I got six pounds a week and two meals a day, which wasn't bad . . . and I was allowed to play the guitar and sing folk-songs three nights a week. What money I didn't spend on rent and taking guitar lessons went on having my hair tonged into a sort of Joan Baez wet seaweed look. She was my idol at the time.

I still shied away from boys, though I had two brief encounters. One with a boy down from Oxford, who was quite pimply and anxious and unmemorable, and the other with a Spanish boy called Manolo, who breathed very heavily and whispered hot, unintelligible words in my ear even when I was trying to serve him with cups of steaming expresso.

Manolo was difficult to ignore as he waited for me very night until the Sorrento Bar closed. He would stand in the doorway of the chemist next but one along, and then step out beside me as I passed. Sometimes I think that the English climate had affected his adenoids or his sinus tracts or something because you could always hear his breathing even if there was a lot of traffic about. He was a waiter at a restaurant off the Tottenham Court Road and though he was beautiful, with raven-black eyes, bushy sideburns and sharp white teeth, there was always a faint aroma of stale fat and over-boiled cabbage about him which he tried to cover by using one of those awful sweet-smelling Spanish eau de Colognes. He was fantastically insistent though, and finally I gave in one sleazy morning out of sheer apathy.

It happened because my room mate, Janice, had gone home for the weekend.

Janice was a bright, round-faced R.A.D.A. student who had been at the Y.W.C.A. with me. She had a boy-friend called Stewart, who looked so much like her that I sometimes suspected they must be brother and sister. Every Sunday like clockwork and with the same sort of precision, Janice would cook a proper roast in the landlady's kitchen, as *we* only possessed a gas ring ... baked potatoes, parsnips, greens, Yorkshire pud, the lot. We put fifteen shillings into the kitty per week to meet the cost (including Stewart) and every week he would turn up, round cheeks glowing, round spectacles winking, round mouth Oh-ing. In his hand he would grasp a round bottle of Mateus and standing behind him on the step would be some fairly un-attractive friend, generally drooling with hunger and hang-dog with hang-over. We would then have lunch sitting on the floor because there was no table to seat four, eat as much food as we could, and finish up going to the movies at one of the 'X' cinemas on the Tottenham Court Road. Janice always said it put her into a better mood for getting up on Monday morning. As I never got up any day before midday, I could not say.

Anyway, this Sunday Janice went home to Dorking. There was no Sunday roast, baked potatoes, frozen peas; nothing, no Stewart plus friend, just me, lying in a torpor of Sunday supplements. The doorbell rang at quarter to one, and I tottered out of bed thinking that perhaps Stewart had forgotten not to come. Instead of sensibly asking who was there from behind the closed door, I swung it open, and there was Manolo, my Spanish heavy-breather extraordinary, breathing heavily and trying to look winning with a bottle of Beaujolais in his hand. He had a battered record in the other.

I must say, he made a striking contrast to round, cosy Stewart. All angles and arrogance, he stood there, and before I could close my mouth and pull my dressing-gown together, he had whisked through the door and was heading purposefully towards the flat.

I don't know how he knew which was our door, but he waited until I had caught up with him and then swung round triumphantly holding both hands above his head.

"You see, Maggie, I am bringing you beautiful flamenco guitars to listen, and wine to drink! You like? Look, Juanito Verderama, the most best singing of flamenco!"

It was impossible to argue in the hall so I followed him into the flat and allowed him to close the door behind us, vaguely promising myself that I would give him a cup of coffee and then get rid of him with as little fuss as possible.

What ensued was very predictable and probably inevitable.

He took me to the accompaniment of a full contingent of flamenco sounds—heel-tapping, stamping, wailing, finger-snapping, olé-ing, and for good measure, the popping of the gas-ring, whose shilling was dwindling. What a fusion of two ways of life! The stamping and the popping.

It took me a long time to respond but at last I did, although part of me stood aside and jeered while our bodies met and laboured and fell apart, and met once more. A big Doubt was starting and I felt as though the roof would fall in, or my mother would arrive, or the landlady would hear us and call the police. Punishment for passion, pain for pleasure, something like that.

I was glad when he went home, pinching my cheek, his lips curling languorously, eyes blank and smoky. Smug and fat-cat sated.

I took myself back to bed for the rest of the day to huddle in sleep with my dread, and wake, sweating, in the early hours of the morning to hear Janice creep in.

Then I lay and stared up at the horrible Regency striped wallpaper with bouquets of flowers at six inch intervals, getting clearer and clearer as the day commenced; and I thought.

I thought about my mother and father sleeping side by side in their big, blue bed and the two water-bottles that she inserted so carefully every night, one on his side, one on hers. I thought about my brother growing a moustache and trying to get girls to sleep with him. I thought about Uncle Ansell and Dolores and I couldn't remember their faces. I felt my sore breasts and wondered why I had not taken this serious thing seriously before. Maybe *that* was the cause of all the trouble. Or maybe taking it *too* seriously was what *caused* all the trouble. Did anyone know? Who could tell even if they did? Or would? I suddenly wished I could talk to Dr. Cornish. Maybe I would go down to see her one weekend. I knew I never would. Then I wished I loved someone. Oh, I loved my brother Benjy, and even my parents, from a safe distance, but I wanted someone grown-up and unwarranted. Then I wished I could believe in a Cause, a Celebrated Cause—*Cause Célèbre*, the French call it—like Ban-the-Bomb, God, or starving India, but I couldn't, it was too remote. I was numb and dumb, daft and dateless, so I had a bit of a cry and began to think about my career.

\*　\*　\*

I hid all the next day, did not go to work, washed my hair in the bath, lay rinsing it under water until my lungs nearly burst, climbed out clean but still sagging with the Doubt, watched the telly, sat, ate, would not answer the phone, knew it was Manolo, did not want to talk, sat, made a decision.

Next morning at nine sharp, I started to make the rounds of the agents.

Resilience is all.

And I got work; singing in workman's clubs, Charity Balls, private parties, receptions, coffee bars. I was a sort of second-hand English Joan Baez without a 'Celebrated Cause', but making the right kind of noise and with the long, drippy seaweed look; my voice was improving and I was learning to handle an audience.

I was too busy to worry about my unemotional emotional life as none of the gigs paid very much and there were clothes to buy, agent's commission, a new guitar, fares, rent, keeping warm in the winter—the time of year I hate the most.

\*　\*　\*

I met Lew Hamlyn in May 1966 at the end of a gruesome winter, after a year and a half in London. He was the best known pop manager in London and owned six groups and as many solo singers, who were all crammed into the top end of the Charts. He was originally American, I think, and asked me to call him Eddie, and when he suggested that we take a trip to Spain I agreed without hesitation, partly because he seemed sort of estranged from people like myself, partly because I wanted to be in the proximity of a successful person, but mostly because I wanted the sun.

We spent the whole of June and July following the bull-fights, lying in the sun, making love, smoking pot and listening to music.

The first time I saw a bull-fight, I cried and cried, watching the poor bull turn round and round with the flickering capes pulling him, the sword twisting in his neck, his front legs shining with red blood and buckling under him, his muzzle dripping froth and more skeins of blood, and his poor stupid eyes that could not drag themselves away from the flimsy bits of pink cloth that surrounded him.

They say that the woman always identifies with the bull, and the man with the matador, but secretly, I think it is the most homosexual sport ever invented, the bull being the symbol of all things male, with its huge horns and balls and brute strength; it crashes into the ring like an express train, and is challenged by a smaller, flighty and subtler male symbol encased in tight shining colours. In the brief quarter of an hour that they meet, one must stab the other with horn or steel until he is dead, dragged from the ring for all to see; one small male symbol must fuck the other, brutish one, or die in the attempt, and that seems to me to be about as queer as you can get.

Back at our hotel after that first time I saw the fights, Eddie-Lew was so tender with me; he talked to me quietly and softly about life, and how it was, and why, and then he fixed me a joint and we smoked it together and danced to no music on the balcony overlooking the port of Malaga. We made love slowly and calmly, and I was happy and fulfilled for the first time since I could remember. And we listened to 'Sparticus' on one of his cassettes and it didn't seem sticky and sentimental any more. I felt as though I had a bond with a grown-up person for the first time in my life; it was lovely.

That was the pattern of those two months—a dream-time—I was beautifully passive to the situation—the smoking, the love-making, the bull-fights, the music—and could not look past him into the next day. No Doubts, I felt as though I had been stolen away from time and lay in a cocoon of sensual pleasure where only *he* could come.

I thought I was in love.

I thought I would have a baby and get married and live happily ever afterwards, but when we went back to London and I told him I was pregnant, he was a different person, a big operator, only interested in deals and going to lunch at Alvaro's and finding new singers. He put a hundred and fifty pounds into my hand and told me to go and do something about it and suddenly I was out of the cocoon and into the cold hard world again. So I did. I got rid of it one morning in Ealing and then I went back to Janice's flat and lay in bed for two days and bled and had more Doubts and got up to face the world.

But again, resilience is all!

# 7

## Francis Omerod

IT WAS IN September, 1966 (I had been at Kew for nineteen years and was considered one of the constant fixtures of the establishment) that the fellow Jackson came to see me. I remember driving home in a very bad mood that night, having missed my golf game. I had written out the recommendation for his scholarship reluctantly; I wished that I had kept his map to show some grounds for taking him on, and I had an uneasy feeling that I had made the decision for sentimental reasons. I resolved to keep an eagle eye on him. These fellows come over here and think they own the place if you let them.

Cynthia was surprised to see me home so early, but I did not bother to explain what had happened. For the past year or two she had been getting a glazed look in her eye whenever I tried to specify any of the finer points of administrative concerns. I had a vague suspicion that she was working out the *Times* crossword puzzle in her head, or deciding what to feed her Friday bridge party friends when I spoke about my labours at Kew. She could have been going over one of those deuced poems of hers for all I know. Anyway, I had stopped talking about my work to her.

The only time she asked me how it was going, was on Friday afternoons when she picked me up at the Gardens. I allowed her to use my car on Fridays. She would shop in the morning, and after one of those delicate epicurean delights which dieting ladies nibble at midday, she and three of her lady friends would sit and play serious bridge until five. After that, she would drive down to Kew to pick me up. It was a pleasant ritual established over the years and I looked forward to it, even though the poor girl had never quite mastered the art of changing gears correctly and was an inveterate clutch-hanger. It was the high spot of her week, so I did not have the heart

to reprimand her about the disastrous effect her driving would
have on my gear-box.

* * *

The Jackson fellow had been at Kew for about eight or nine
months when Cynthia arrived to pick me up on a particular
Friday afternoon in May. An oppressive heat had been with
us since Thursday morning; clouds bunched ominously low
above our heads and remained there, static. Fumes of cars,
pink and white chestnut blossoms, the dull red of lumbering
buses, seemed to hang in the air like unanswered prayers—
waiting for the rain that would carry them to the earth.

Friday dawned still sultrier. Things were moving in slow
motion, sounds seemed drawn out and half-hearted. We were
all awaiting the holocaust, because that's all one could do on
a day like that.

Cynthia arrived early. She said that no one could concentrate
on bridge and that they had all gone home to miss being caught
in the rain which was the inevitable end to two such days. At
about four-thirty the sky started to turn quite black and a dull
green light pervaded. I left Cynthia in the outer office while I
finished off a few letters. She sat watching the coming storm
from the window. It was just five o'clock when the first huge
drops began to hit the ground, and I heard Cynthia exclaiming,
"Good heavens!"

I put the last of my papers into my brief-case, told my
secretary, Miss Chambers, that she could go, and walked into
the outer office.

"What is it?"

"Who is that extraordinary person down there?" asked
Cynthia.

I looked down and saw the fellow Jackson prancing about
on the lawn below. He was doing handstands, turning cart-
wheels and jumping up and down shouting ridiculous things
like "Hello rain!" and "Yippee"; a few of the other lads were
holding up their arms and larking about as well, and there was
quite a lot of swearing going on. Jackson was obviously the
instigator. I thought he must have taken leave of his senses.
This was the second time I had seen him behaving in a peculiar
fashion. The first time was in the winter, in December, when I
had seen him cavorting with a girl right in the middle of the

Common. They had been playing in the snow and I slowed down to watch them as I drove past. (I remembered thinking at the time that these coloured fellows seem to attract females like flies), anyway, it looked harmless enough, so I drove on and had almost forgotten the incident; but now, with this new outburst of animal energy I began to wonder whether our coloured friend was not a bit of a mad-man, affected by changes in the weather like some people are by the moon.

"Oh, him," I said, "he's a half-caste fellow from the West Indies. He's really only here on sufferance; looks as though he's lost his head in this weather. We can't blame the heat. The fellow must be used to that coming from where he does."

But Cynthia was not listening to anything I said. She was staring down fascinated by the silly fellow's antics and I saw her lips parting and smiling and a little laugh came out of them which, I think she didn't know had happened. I suddenly felt extremely angry and leaned out of the window. "Clear off!" I shouted very loudly. "What the hell do you think you're up to, Jackson? Shut up and clear off!"

Some of the other young chaps looked up laughing and I heard them saying my nickname. "Watch out, it's old fuck-off Haemorrhoid," I heard. A few of them booed and whistled derisively and I was ashamed that Cynthia should see how unpopular I was. But again she did not seem to notice and continued to watch avidly while Jackson and his friends took cover. Hail-stones as big as pebbles began to rain down on them. Just desserts, I thought.

When they had gone out of our sight Cynthia turned away from the window with a sigh and her mouth twitched down at the corners. She hid her face from me quickly, slanting it back towards the window and crooking her head to one side as though listening to the hail clattering on the corrugated iron roof of a shed in the garden. But I knew that she was hiding tears.

"What's the matter, old girl?" I asked, rather wearily, snapping my brief-case shut and starting towards the door. "Has the storm upset your nerves?"

"No," she said, "it's nothing at all . . . just that sometimes I feel as though I have never been young . . ." I hardly heard her words, what with the claps of thunder and the drumming hail, but her bitter mouth bespoke worlds.

"Come along," I said hastily, "let's get cracking and try to miss the middle of the weekend exodus."

It is unlike Cynthia to whine or carry on about youth, missed chances, spilt milk, etc. She's not the type. I could see her mentally squaring her shoulders as she preceded me down the stairs and waited for me to back the car near to the doorway in which she stood, out of the pelting rain. She ran round to the driver's side and I squeezed over allowing her to do me this one small service of driving the car, which I knew she enjoyed so much.

We eased out on to the Fairfax Road at a minimal speed, the rain reducing visibility to about three yards. Most of the other traffic had pulled off the road to let the worst of the storm abate.

*I* saw the figure first, and had *I* been driving would certainly never have stopped, but Cynthia stepped on the brakes immediately.

"Poor creature," she said, pointing to the black shape, holding a soggy paper-bag over its head and hurrying along, only just distinguishable through the sheet of water.

"Get in!" she cried, leaning over to open the back door of the Rover. Before I could remonstrate, the drenched figure of a man bundled in out of the rain, discarding the paper-bag and sending a spray of water all over the back seat.

"Wow, Missus, thank you!" and there he was, the cranky half-caste fellow Jackson, grinning from ear to ear, streams of water running off him, his hair stuck down on his scalp like wavy black sticking plaster.

"Oh, it's you," I said, curtly, "what's the idea of all that bloody noise and carry-on right under my window?"

I did not introduce him to my wife.

"Well . . . er . . . we was just havin' . . . ah . . . a . . . I met a friend who . . ."

"Was that *you*?" Cynthia asked in a delighted voice. "Oh, you *did* look as though you were enjoying yourself. I envied you terribly."

I gave her a furious glance but she continued talking back over her shoulder without taking her eyes off the windscreen in front of her, as the wipers flew back and forth clearing the murk from the glass for that fraction of a second which allowed us to see where we were.

"Where do you come from?" she enquired, and without

waiting for an answer, "Francis says it's the West Indies, but there are thousands of islands out there, aren't there? Are you from Jamaica?"

"No, Missus, I'm from Hambro, but I bet you never have heard of *that* island. It very small, but we've got two good beaches and fantastic reefs. Good deep-sea fishing as well, Missus. Marlin, sail fish, giant tunas, sword fish," he added jauntily.

They were chatting away like two old friends in no time. Cynthia said, "Oh, by the way, I am Mrs. Omerod, not just Missus, and where are you heading for? I'm sorry, but I'm afraid I don't know your name."

"Matthew Jackson," he answered quickly, "Matthew Jackson . . . I live in Acton. Acton, near the Town Hall."

"Oh, that's lovely." Cynthia had now crossed Kew Bridge and we were moving with the great block of traffic edging its way towards the M1 roundabout. "We can pass through Acton on our way. We live in Ealing and that's just a bit further on."

"For God's sake, change down," I said to Cynthia who was crawling along in third gear.

"I'm sorry, darling. Oh, Mr. Jackson, are you here for a long time? I suppose you can't believe our climate."

He laughed that peculiar cracked-voice laugh that some of these fellows have. "Oh, I can believe it all right, it's easy to believe when you're covered in it!" He wiped drops of moisture from his chin onto his coat, a flimsy looking grey gaberdine, now wrinkled and shaped to his shoulders like a half sloughed-off snake skin.

All the windows of the car were tight shut and had steamed up considerably so that we seemed to be sitting in a plastic sandwich-box, surrounded by a deluge and with the sound of a thousand droning engines waiting to move three feet every five minutes. I could not understand Cynthia's obvious interest in the boy. She was making a fool of herself and he would probably have a whale of a time at her expense telling his mongrel friends about the wife of the administrator who had drivelled and footled on about the weather, etc.—how she envied him the freedom to disport himself on the lawn right under my very window.

"It would have been much better to go the Hanger Lane

way," I said tersely, and kept my eyes on the road for the rest of the journey.

Cynthia continued to make a fool of herself, asking him vivaciously about his impressions of London, his digs, and what had brought him over to study at Kew. He answered briskly enough; in fact, he was quite amusing about his experiences with landladies, one of whom had lost her false teeth and was waiting for some new ones on the National Health but in the meantime was completely incomprehensible when she talked.

Cynthia laughed uproariously at this and we nearly hit the car in front of us.

At last we arrived at the Uxbridge Road and Jackson emerged from the car and was swallowed up by a sudden rush of people getting off a bus.

"What a charming boy," said Cynthia. It seemed incredible that she could be unaware of my disapproval, but I looked at her flushed, pleased face and it was true . . she had no idea.

Cynthia is now a very attractive woman. Since I married her she has grown her hair longer, and it has darkened to a warm brown and become touched with grey, her face has fined down so that one can see her cheek bones; and her nose, which tends to have a slight hook in it, has much more character and distinction. Her figure is still slim and straight and she draws her hair back and does it in a sort of a bun halfway up the back of her head, I think they call it a 'chignon'. It gives her the look of a proud Roman matron. There is also some secret about her face which I cannot explain; it is as if she has discovered the answer to a mystery but will not let it out of her face. I do not know when this phenomenon happened but I had noticed it more and more over that last year.

I used to wonder whether she had taken a lover, and watched her carefully for any signs, but there were none—nothing in her behaviour to indicate clandestine meetings or guilty encounters; only her secret face to torment me.

When she had put the car in the garage and come inside I said, "Cynthia, I don't think you'd better come and collect me from the Gardens again on Fridays. You drove frightfully badly today and it makes me very nervous. All right, my dear? I don't want to upset you, but it *is* a fairly new Rover 2000."

She dropped her head so that I could not see her eyes but

replied amiably that she did not mind at all, that she had only done it because the traffic on a Friday night was so exhausting for me after a full week's work.

We did not speak about it again.

*     *     *

As the days went by, I was aware that Cynthia was becoming more and more reserved with me; sometimes we hardly spoke through the whole of a meal; just "pass the salt, please", and "I finished the crossword today", and "There's nothing on the box tonight." She did not seem distressed in any way, just preoccupied and dreamy—her secret face infuriatingly in evidence.

One Thursday afternoon in July I did not go to golf as usual. I had an enormous amount of paper work that had piled up on my desk. I decided to churn through the lot instead of trying to catch up at the tag-end of each day when my brain does not function as quickly as at other times.

I was driving home at about six, feeling the pleasant weariness of accomplishment, when I saw the back view of Cynthia about to enter a tea-shop on the Fairfax Road. Cynthia has a very distinctive walk, and her legs taper from rather large-muscled calves to a very fine Achilles tendon at the ankle. She was arm in arm with a man and they were talking earnestly to one another. I was about to honk, but thought better of it and decided to investigate instead. I parked the car several blocks away and walked back.

The tea-shop was one of those 'olde englishe' ones with bulging glass front, painted green, and wistaria crawled up the walls—a sign saying 'Afternoon Teas' swung on rusty hinges over the door. I faced the street as I approached, keeping my face averted, stopping as I reached the doorway where a lop-sided green blind pulled half-way down held an 'Open' sign in place. I squatted down and peered in under the green blind.

Cynthia was sitting facing the door but the man had his back to me. She looked happy and relaxed and was talking animatedly, smoothing her hair back and smiling. On the table in front of her was the folder in which I knew she kept her poems. Then suddenly my view was obscured as a fat woman carrying a baby and dragging a small boy, pulled open the door and practically stepped on me. She apologised profusely as though it was all her fault and I must have seemed very rude as I backed away hurriedly and ran down to the corner of the street in case Cynthia had glimpsed me, forgetting that I had parked my car in the opposite direction. I crossed the road and walked back to get it.

Then I drove back and placed the car in a strategic position so that I could watch the front of the shop and not be noticeable to anyone emerging.

They stayed inside for about half an hour, while I sat and observed, listening to the news, 'Sports Round-Up' and a few thumping pop-tunes. When Cynthia came out she looked a bit worried, consulted her watch and scanned the street for a taxi. A minute later the fellow Jackson appeared carrying her folder. (He must have been paying the bill.) He walked out into the road trying to find her a taxi. When he had whistled one down, he opened the door for her and stood holding her hand in a prolonged handshake. I could not see their expressions, but he held her folder tightly under his arm and they conversed. Then she leant over and kissed him on the cheek. The driver had shouted something over his shoulder; that they were holding things up, I suppose. Jackson slammed the door and she was lost to me in the traffic.

I sat on for a few more minutes and watched Jackson cross the road to catch his bus. I was dazed at the possibilities presenting themselves to me . . . Cynthia was having an affair with a boy half her age and coloured to boot; or she cared for him a great deal, otherwise she would never have entrusted him with her precious poems. In any case, if *I* had seen them wandering along the street arm in arm and her kissing him, so could many other people on the staff at Kew who would also recognise Jackson, and I was probably a laughing stock by now.

Angrily I threw the car into gear and sped home. I wanted to get there before Cynthia. No wonder she had looked worried as she emerged from the tea-shop. She thought that I would be home from golf (as I usually did) at about seven-thirty p.m. and was frightened lest the dinner was not on its way.

I was not sure if I had beaten her home as I put the car into the garage; there were no lights on in the house but then it was still only about ten past seven on a clear July evening. The Boxer, Lucy, who was getting very stiff on her pins, came out to meet me at the door so I knew that I was in first. She would have stayed in the kitchen had Cynthia been home. Lucy always waits about for her dinner, sniffing and slobbering and wriggling her stump of a tail when Cynthia is cooking; nothing can induce her to leave the delicious aromas of the kitchen under such circumstances.

I settled myself and changed my jacket, lit my pipe and had just picked up the *Evening Standard* when I heard her key in the front door, heard Lucy hurrying out to meet her, her nails clicking unevenly on the parquet floor.

"Goodness!" she said, "you're home!"

"Yes."

"Did you play well?"

"I didn't go."

"Oh!"

"No, I had some work to clear up at the office. I think I *did* mention it a few days ago, but you must have forgotten."

"I don't think so," she said, "I would have remembered."

"Well, what have *you* been doing with yourself?"

"Oh, I had tea with a friend. I've had a marvellous day actually. Don't laugh, but we went to Kew . . . just to look at the flowers. It's gorgeous!"

"I'm not laughing. It was a lovely day to do it. Who was the friend?"

She paused. "Oh, no one you'd know. Just someone who writes poetry too."

"I see."

This was the first time as far as I remember, that Cynthia had been devious, had even come near to lying to me. I felt sick. She must have been meeting the fellow for quite some time. It was obscene. The more I thought about it, the more disgusting it became. I sat pretending to read the paper, but my brain was surging about inside my skull; I was determined to do something about that scum Jackson, who had obviously used an assumed interest in poor gullible Cynthia's poetry to lure her into meeting him, and now she was besotted by him.

We ate pork chops in silence.

"What's the matter," she asked, "you haven't eaten anything at all. Do you feel ill?"

"No," I said, "I'm just not very hungry. I suppose it's because I haven't been out today."

"Yes," she said, "you're generally ravenous after golf."

"How is your poetry coming along?"

"I've been writing a lot lately. Oh, and I forgot to tell you —I'm to have another poem published. I only heard about it today. In *Queen* Magazine, of all places." She laughed as though it was a great joke.

"I must read it."

"But it won't be actually in print for a couple of months; they always set these things up months ahead of time."

"Haven't you got a copy of it?"

"Yes, I have." She got up to get the coffee and there was a note of genuine surprise in her voice, "I'll get it for you as soon as I've cleared away these things, and you shall read it." I had never asked to read any of her poems (specifically) before.

On summer nights we had coffee in the conservatory which faces the garden at the back. It is very pleasant and I have filled it with some of the more exotic flowers from Kew. I have staghorns draped around every pillar and great hanging baskets of Japanese hibiscus. Neither Cynthia nor myself cared to have a crowd of servants cluttering up the house, so Mrs. Balfour, the char, left at about four each afternoon and Cynthia always served dinner herself unless we had guests.

That night there was the stillness of a balmy summer evening in the air; the air was placid and fragrant in the conservatory and I could hear my own heart pumping steadily and the clatter of cups and saucers as Cynthia came though from the kitchen and placed the tray on the low marble table before me.

As she leant over to pour the coffee, I studied her face in repose, the calm mask, whose lip-corners turned up in secret indentures, whose blue eyes still gazed with expectancy at the world, whose rounded forehead hid what thoughts from my watchful eyes? I could not tell.

She gave me my coffee with brown sugar and cream as usual and I sipped appreciatively.

"Here," she said, handing me a typewritten piece of foolscap. "You probably won't like it."

I read:

Loose-hipped, in wondrous harmony,
We writhe and cling and slip apart,
Your sun-glazed skin,
A sun born with you is
The gift you give me.

The sea-tide rises in your eyes,
Your hands reach out for earth,
Your mouth for air,
We are together
With the cry of gulls.

Where will you fly to now,
My bird, my brother, my love?
The Gordian knot is cleft,
The die is cast.
Our pulses cease to coincide.

I re-read the poem, swallowing over and over; my own saliva tasted foreign and tinny in my mouth. Was this my Cynthia? What did it mean? Was she describing the sexual act with that filthy swine? 'Sun-glazed skin' seemed very suspicious. Was I sitting here, a doddering old cuckold being subtly tortured by my own wife? I was afraid to look up for fear that she might be watching me with condescending humour. I, who had not touched her body for ten years, suddenly felt an overpowering urge to defile her, to ravage and ravish her for letting herself be the pawn of that black bastard. I sat staring at the paper, unable to budge, but resolving with deadly sureness to have revenge.

I managed a very contrived laugh, "I suppose it's very good, my dear, but as you know, I'm not much of an expert about these things."

"Are you sure you're all right, Francis, you look terribly pale. What did you have for lunch?"

"Oh, for God's sake, woman, I'm perfectly all right!" I jerked up violently, knocking the coffee tray sideways. Without looking back I threw down her poem and marched up to my study where I closed and locked the door.

In the bottom drawer of my desk I keep my service revolver. I unlocked the drawer and took it out. I flicked the cartridge cases around to see that they were still functional and peered down the barrel. Not a bad weapon and still in serviceable condition. I loaded it, put the safety catch on, poured myself a stiff whisky to steady my hand, and sat down to try and work out some coherent plan of action.

It was obvious that neither my wife nor Jackson knew that I had discovered their furtive relationship, therefore I had to watch their movements carefully and find out where they consummated their trysts.

I decided not to go to Kew the next morning. If Cynthia used the telephone to ring her paramour, I would listen on the extension, and if she went out, I would follow her discreetly. I would carry my revolver with me and shoot the mongrel swine, Jackson, when I got the chance. Pictures of Cynthia, white and vulnerable, copulating with the black satyr, flashed incessantly across the screen of my brain, intruded like invaders, and interrupted any flow of thought that I tried to follow. I poured myself large whiskies and drank them without realising that they had disappeared. The fellow had to be put down, just like Lucy's mongrel puppy . . . you could never trust them . . . you never knew where you were with one of them . . . they were all scummm . . . horrible half-caste scum . . .

I took myself off to bed but lay all night tormented by night-mares not unlike the ones I had after the First War. Gaping mouths, empty eye-sockets, faceless, riddled and swollen corpses floated in a stagnant sea.

Cynthia came in to me once and brought me some aspirin, I vaguely remember that she said I had been groaning and grinding my teeth, but I pushed her away, and turned over to float through a monstrous world of gross phantom shapes and fornicating bodies on my other side.

The next morning, Friday, was Cynthia's bridge day. I had forgotten! I asked her whether she would postpone it as I was not going to the office, that I had had a bad night and was just going to potter about the house.

Of course she would postpone it; there was no question of having three talkative women in the house while I was not feeling well. She telephoned to each of her friends and can-celled the luncheon. Was there anything she could do? Was I hungry? Should she ring Dr. Gault? Could she ring my office and explain that I was not well?

I watched her machinations in a detached sort of way, marvelling at the incredible deceit of women. Here she was, looking quite agitated by my pretended illness, when she couldn't wait for me to be bundled into bed and kept there under strict doctor's orders, so that she would be free to meet her lover whenever she wished.

I dressed and had a soft boiled egg.

Cynthia fussed and hovered about me like a mother hen. I allowed her to do so passively, but observed her, lynx-like, for any signs of fright and guilt that she might show, perhaps guessing that her affair had been uncovered.

Nothing in her behaviour told me that she was worried about anyone but me. The char arrived and Cynthia enquired tenderly what I would like for lunch. She suggested kidneys, blanquette de veau, baby lamb chops, sole, all the things she knew I particularly enjoyed and said that she would go out and shop for them immediately.

This was the moment I had been waiting for.

She was getting out of the house to telephone him.

I said I would like sole.

As soon as she had left I hurried after her. The day was overcast and heavy and I kept back, hovering at each driveway in case she turned around, but she walked steadfastly forward—a blue shopping bag in her hand. She had wrapped a red scarf around her head so that she was easily spottable and I had no difficulty in keeping her in sight even when she turned into the crowded High Street. The fishmonger sold his wares from an open place near a telephone box.

I was expecting her to make straight for the box, but she walked by without hesitation and I positioned myself in the doorway of Boots to watch her. She took some time selecting her sole, or rather, my sole, and then continued up the High Street to the greengrocers. There she bought a melon, some tomatoes, a lettuce and a large bag of potatoes; next stop, United Dairies, where she was lost to my sight inside. She was there for five minutes and when she came out, headed home, past the telephone box without a glance. I had to scurry to get into our street before she turned the corner. As it was, I slouched along uncharacteristically, and did not dare enter our drive; instead I went in next door and climbed the fence at the back, so that she would not know I had been out.

When she arrived back I was sitting docilely in the conservatory reading the morning papers.

The day dragged on with no attempt by Cynthia to call anyone. We had our lunch—an excellent lemon sole with creamed potatoes and salad—and spoke hardly a word. Cynthia accepted my silence with her usual tranquillity while I seethed and forced the lunch down my throat.

In the afternoon Cynthia did the *Times* crossword puzzle and then retired to her room to work, she said, while I remained in my study and strained my ears for the click of the telephone signifying an outgoing call. Nothing.

At five-thirty I had my first drink of the day, a straight whisky, followed by two more. I had spent all day keeping myself in check, under control, while a rage burned my liver. I could not envisage any time past my moment of confrontation with Cynthia and the fellow Jackson. I fretted, began to mutter to myself and tramp about the room, trapped by my own passion for revenge.

At about seven o'clock, many whiskies later, the door-bell rang and I heard Cynthia going downstairs to see who it was. I squeezed myself into the corner window where I could just see the front porch; if whoever was waiting at the door stood back a bit, I could see *them* as well.

At first I could see nobody, but a few seconds after a second bellring, Jackson stepped back into view, Cynthia's folder was under his arm and a sort of schoolboy satchel in his hand. He was examining the blue clematis I have trained around the porch.

I rushed to the desk and picked up my gun; my rage had broken its bounds. The audacity of the bastard to come to my own house! I heard Cynthia opening the door and I flung myself into the hallway behind her.

Cynthia had just opened the door and I could see Jackson standing behind her on the doorstep.

"Get out of the way, Cynthia!" I shouted, raising the pistol and taking off the safety catch.

Cynthia turned around. I could see both faces registering total amazement.

"Get back!" I commanded again. "I'm going to put this black scum down like the dog he is. Get back!"

Cynthia gazed at me in stunned bewilderment, but did not move.

"What do you mean, Francis? What are you doing with that gun?" Her voice was light and breathless, but there was no hysteria in it. Jackson's eyes had widened too, but he showed no signs of fright either. The two of them were riveted to the spot, nailed to the ground.

I shot at Jackson and he fell backwards and sideways out of my vision; the folder fell and the satchel flew out of his hands, but I shot twice more at where he had been standing, exorcising his presence from my doorstep.

Cynthia rushed forward and snatched the gun out of my hand.

"Oh, my God, my God, what have you done?"

Once she had the gun she ran outside and threw it into the hedge. I stood in the hall, all my strength drained out of me. I could feel it flow down my back, down my arms and out of my fingertips, down my legs and into the floor. I felt very old and very tired.

"That'll teach the cur," I said to myself, but my voice sounded querulous and unconvincing even to my own ears.

Then I heard other voices outside, Cynthia's and Jackson's voices came up to me like sounds in the mood of songs. Hers was worried and placating and conciliatory, his, cracked and breathless and half-laughing.

I went and sat down in an armchair. I had killed him. It was no use either of them talking now. I had put Lucy's mongrel down for sucking my eggs. This one for touching my wife. There was no use them talking at all. My wife, who was not my wife, who was Rufus, my friend, but not my lover, Cynthia, who was my woman, but not my lover. Rufus was dead and so was the dog. The lover was dead, but not my wife . . .

I was aware of movement behind me but I did not turn around. They were going to pretend that he was not dead. But I knew better. I had killed him, hadn't I?

I went to sleep for I was very weary. It was curiously like the sleep that I had slept on Mignonne's bed at Madame Hermine's so many years ago, a little death that lasted as long as the mind decreed.

When I awoke in the chair, my legs remained asleep; I tried to move them but they remained useless and rigid. Cynthia came down the stairs carrying a suitcase. I pulled myself up with my arms and stood in front of her trying to flex the backs of my knees as I did so, pins and needles ran up and down my legs. I thought I might fall over if I attempted steps.

"I'm glad you're awake," she said quite normally, "I was hoping to talk to you before I went off." It was dark outside.

"Where are you going?"

She hesitated before speaking. "I shall be quite near. Was it really just plain, ridiculous jealousy, Francis?" picking her words like a gourmet picks hors-d'oeuvres.

"I don't know," I said truthfully. "Where is he? Have they taken him away? Did you call the police?"

"He insisted on catching a taxi home. Of *course* I didn't call anyone and nor will he."

"But he's dead, isn't he? Isn't he dead? I saw him dead."

"No, he's not dead. I told you, he's gone home. You opened up a nasty furrow right along his scalp. It bled a lot and I bandaged it; he's all right now."

I sat down in the chair again and covered my face with my hands.

"What will happen now?"

"There'll be no scandal; the people next door telephoned but I said that you had only been testing an old army gun. You'll go back to Kew; I'll go somewhere. You'll play golf, do your work and have a woman every month or so. The char will look after the house." She spoke coolly, with no show of any sort of emotion. She was like a nurse laying down the rules for a serious convalescence that would last for the rest of my life.

"That filthy poem. Do you love that fellow, Cynthia? Will you go to him now?" I blurted out.

"Oh, Francis, you have never known anything about me, have you? I am nearly *fifty*, Francis, nearly *fifty*. That boy is twenty-three. I am more than twice his age. Yes, I *do* love him in a curious way. He is a kind, alive, attractive boy who writes poetry and has an enormous drive and vision. My poem was written long before I met Jackson; it was my idea of child-birth, my idea of the child I have never had. Perhaps it *is* describing sex, but then I know a little more about sex than childbirth. Not much, but at least I've experienced it. The cycle of physical attraction, making love, pregnancy, childbirth and motherhood, *that* I shall never complete. My body still clamours, just as yours does, but only very occasionally now. Do you think I do not know when *you* have a woman? You are a different man when you come into the house. Freer, easier to get on with, interested in things. But there is no use talking about any of this now. We should have discussed it all years ago. It seems to me a most hypocritical and cowardly thing to try to shoot a boy who comes to the door unarmed, because you *think* he might be having an affair with a woman whom you care nothing for, have not touched for ten years, but who has looked after your house and been a sort of housekeeper-companion to you for over twenty years.

"So I am going away," she continued wearily, "I should have done so a long time ago; maybe I *will* go and stay with that boy, or be near him for a while. He makes me feel alive."

"But he's a half-black, uneducated creature from some backwash; these people don't think or live like us, Cynthia! You can't trust him. He's using you."

"For what? He's not asked me for anything. He has no idea that I am leaving you. And just because he is a half-caste I think he has twice as much right to understanding and attention. Try to imagine yourself born into a dilemma like that—anyway, there's no question of his needing me. I need *him*."

I looked at her impassive face, but I could not answer anything she said. Rufus stared back at me reprovingly and I bowed my head.

"I will give you some money."

"No, thank you." She was not being haughty but she wanted nothing more of me. "I have never touched any of the gratuities that Mother left me. They bring in a good income. I would rather be independent.

"Goodbye," she said. "I'll come back and pack up the rest of my belongings later."

I went back to Kew as she said. I played golf and the char looked after the house, just as she said, but I did not go near a woman again.

I drink more and I think I shall take a long cruise to the South Pacific when I retire.

Jackson did not go back to Kew, in fact, I have never seen him since he disappeared off my front porch, his satchel and Cynthia's poems flying out of his hands. I have heard about him, of course. Who hasn't?

# 8

## Maggie Truro

MEETING JACKSON IN the snow and talking to him in the pub is the most exciting thing that has happened to me since my dream-time in Spain with Lew Hamlyn. I feel a beautiful surge of energy sweep through me on the bus going home. I want to move and hurry up, shout and tingle. There's so much to *do*! I've been wasting time, letting myself get all bogged down in Doubts when all I have to think about is getting on with *life*, and stop allowing things to happen to me through sheer apathy. Start being like him and believing in something that has meaning.

I must have authority. I will make a life for myself that has no past and no future. The *now* is what matters. The *now* life where every moment is filled with new sensations and experiences and flavour. I want to be like him, like he was in the snow, sampling it with such abandon. I will go into a drive of doing! I determine as I sit on top of the bus.

\*     \*     \*

Ten telephone calls after I get home, I am booked at a small club in Brighton for five nights—"Twenty-five pounds for the week-nights," says the voice of Mr. Samuels, beefy and business-like all the way from Brighton, "Twenty-five pounds, and we don't pay your fares, of course."

"You're a beautiful man, Mr. Samuels," I say, "and generous to a fault. I'll be there ten sharp on Monday evening."

I skip around the room and eat two mandarins out of silver paper that Janice has bought early for Christmas. It's an *occasion*. You've got to do *something*.

\*     \*     \*

All Saturday I am busy sorting through my music, working

136

out what I'm going to sing. The snow melts on Saturday afternoon and Sunday morning dawns sunny with an ice-blue sky and the biting dry chill of champagne. I cannot stay indoors. I want to breathe the air, breathe life, the sky, and clean trafficless streets. Very early in the morning I wrap up and take the bus to the river opposite Chelsea Bridge. Gulls are sitting on the embankment primping and shuffling through their feathers as the sun begins to shine; some are squawking and squabbling over bread that a lone woman with a large boxer has thrown to them. The boxer becomes very agitated and rushes up and down the pavement, whimpering in his throat and dancing with excitement. I know just how he feels. I think about Jackson in his gumboots leaping in the snow and the world is incredibly wondrous. I feel jittery in my belly, a squirm of joy.

I cross the bridge and stop in the middle to see sinuous jade eddies whirl under my feet, hurrying bits of wood and rubbish—jam labels and discarded slippers, lost tennis balls and old fruit boxes, used french-letters, down to the sea.

Everything is moving in its own time, the moon will make the tides pull rubbish to the sea, and the sun will make children pull protesting parents out of bed for a walk in the park on this brilliant Sunday morning. Resolution: I must never have any Doubts again. It's all simple and patterned and orderly and wondrous, I think, as I cross that bridge. Life, I mean.

\* \* \*

The man coming towards me has his head down and is walking with the splayed, wide gait of the old, not seeing the day, not hearing the gulls, nor the river, not smelling the high-tide salt must of the river, a Not-on-Legs perambulating his way across the bridge like a chicken—to get to the other side.

We draw nearer to each other, and with a slowly intensifying feeling of shock I see that he is not old at all; that he is staggering slightly to keep himself balanced upright and not pitch forward. About five yards from me he seems to leave his legs behind and stretches himself out on the pavement like a dying samurai, sort of in slow motion. I rush in, glancing around me to see if anyone else is handy to the rescue and ready to shout for assistance, but the bridge is empty. It is too early for the

Sunday morning appetite-stimulating walkers and the lady with the boxer has disappeared.

Crouching beside him, I look down at the rat-tailed winter-dulled blonde hairs fluttering in the breeze. It is the only thing about him that is moving. Gingerly I turn him over holding both his shoulders and slipping my arm under his neck, and there, beneath me—not poised above me, rapt and panting, on the brink of coming, not brown and confident in the Spanish sun, not fiercely concentrated on the machinations of wheeling-dealing—there is the face of Lew Hamlyn, a new, bloated Lew Hamlyn, looking like a drunken baby with dirt on his cheeks and caked blood blocking one nostril. I nearly drop him in surprise.

"Eddie," I say, trying to loosen his collar, but it is one of those high-necked Russian affairs. "Eddie." He is breathing anyway. Short, shallow breaths through his mouth.

Slap the cheeks and wrists. Brings back the circulation. I remember from the First Aid class at that Domestic Science School in Bristol. I do it and he mutters a few words.

"Eddie."

Fused eyes open and for a second I see the criss-cross of tiny veins meet the brilliance of the day and fly back behind the chaffed red lids. He lets two tears out of the corners of his eyes in indignation.

"What the fuck are you doing?"

Eddie is himself again.

"You fell down on Chelsea Bridge, Eddie. I'm trying to revive you."

"Well, where am I now?"

"You're still there. Can you get up? What happened? Did someone hit you?"

Eddie wipes and covers his eyes from the glare, squinting up with one eye closed completely, he looks just like an angry fat baby.

"You look just like an angry fat baby."

Groaning from under dirty square fingers and spatulate thumbs, "Jesus, Maggie, where did you come from? I'm stoned out of my skull and not happy. Where do I live?"

"You used to live in Cheyne Walk."

"Yes, I still live there. That's where I live. I'm going there ... left my car somewhere ... having a sleep on it ... Hey, it's great to see you." He's dragging bits of himself together with great effort and little confidence, lying flat on his back. I put my handbag under his head.

A man on a bicycle stops. He has steel clips around each leg to hold the trouser-legs down. I'd forgotten men still wear bicycle clips.

"You all right, mate?" he says, walking stiffly forward with his head on one side in sympathy with Eddie's prostrate position.

"Oh, fine. Fine," says Eddie. "Just getting my breath back."

The man does not acknowledge me being there at all. He is one of those men who only speak directly to other men. I've noticed *them* before.

"Can I help you at all?" he says, squatting down beside us and again turning his face to mirror Eddie's.

"Just give me a hand-up."

The man and I quickly put Eddie on his feet and walk with him between us for a few paces like I've seen them do with footballers on telly after someone's done an awful foul on them. Then Eddie stands bracing himself on the railings and gagging on breaths of fresh air. I go back for my handbag and the man addresses me for the first time, still not looking at me, his eyes slanting up diagonally to gaze at nothing in the sky.

"He'll be all right now, miss. Got in a bit of a punch-up, did he?"

"I don't know. He just sort of keeled over."

"Yes, well, I expect he'll be all right then. You know him, do you?" I nod. "Then the best thing to do is to get a taxi and take him home, I should say."

"Put him to bed?"

"Yes, that would be the best thing. Get him off the streets. Looks as though he's had a rough night."

At last the man turns weary eyes on me. They are not unkind eyes, but they have seen everything and have stopped approving or disapproving of anything anymore. "You see," he says, "I'm a policeman, and I've just finished night duty so I don't want to have to go back to the station and report this. You say there wasn't a punch-up. Good. Now get your friend off the streets."

And the tired policeman climbs back on his bicycle and heads across the bridge without another glance.

"Fuzz," says Eddie, "Christ, I can smell 'em a mile off.

Lucky, 'cos I've got a pocketful of shit." Eddie's face has lost its baby look and is back in slablike planes and green-tinged around the edges.

"Caw—awse I've gaht a parcket-ful ahf shi—hi—hit," he sings, *basso-profundo*. "Hello, baby," he says.

\* \* \*

I don't know whether it's a fault or a blessing, but I've never been able to hold on to a hate for long, it sort of slips out of my mind and disperses into the air like smoke. And that's how I feel about Eddie. The *memory* of two weeks' hate after he put the hundred and fifty pounds into my hand and told me to go and get rid of the baby is there, but nothing else. I still like the look of him with his flat, pale, Polish face and chunky body, a juggernaut of a man, indomitable even in this depleted state.

"So what *happened* to you?"

"It was a bad, bad scene, baby," he says, and props himself up, back to the flowing river. "You look great . . . all smooth and pink and witty . . . Nice clean hair and straight eye-brows. Pink lemonade. Sunday school treat. Cool . . . Were you looking for me? How did you find me?"

"I was just walking across the bridge thinking what a funny old man was coming towards me and then it was *you*, and you fell down and stayed there. I wasn't *looking* for *you*."

"Sure, you were looking for me, so do what the good man said and get me off the street."

He's never asked me to his place before. It is like something out of *Playboy* Magazine, all hi-fi equipment, black leather and funny lights on poles that flash on and off in different colours and it smells of orgies. He slumps into the black leather and I make him a cup of coffee in the sterile kitchen.

After he's had the coffee, he disappears to wash the blood off his face and I shout through the door that I think I'd better be going. He comes bounding out of the bathroom still wiping his neck and grabs my arm.

"Hey, hey, hey, hey—stay, Maggie, I want to look at you. I want to chat you up. I want you. I feel great now. Honest. Listen, I saw you on the bridge and pulled that fainting act just so's you'd look after me. Believe me, baby. You don't? Well, you're right, but I *would* have, only I was really sick.

Don't go, baby. I hate this place all by myself, and I'd *have* to have a party and that would be very bad for me indeed, very bad." All the time he's chattering he's drawing me along the passage towards his bedroom. I know it but I don't try to stop him.

The contrast between his sitting-room and his bedroom is incredible. Natural-wood slatted windows down to the floor overlooking trees and the river, white walls, a plain peacock blue bedspread on a not large brass bed, an old polished floor, two washed sheepskins . . . a frugal room, almost monastic . . . nice.

Around the walls there are some pictures, a Lowry I recognise—immaculate mining town with tiny people, and there is a portrait of *him* in weird pastel colours against a blue background that makes him look half clown, half thug and very vulnerable. I look in the corner and see 'Griselda Grabowski' in skinny upright letters. Never heard of her; then there is a huge picture of a shambling, blurry knight-in-armour standing disconsolate against a windy sky, another of men leaping to put a basketball through the hoop, caught forever in a sixteenth of a second of striving muscles and distorted mouths, a large blue butterfly in a cork frame, and in the space between the windows, opposite the bed, there is the most sublime piece of sculpture I have ever seen. It is a woman, an exquisite, swaying Indian woman, no arms and cut from the knee, but with so much sensuous movement in her thrusting thigh and mounded belly, her tiny swerving waist and tilted head, that I am riveted. Her head and neck are decorated with bells and other intricate patterns of jewellery that flow down between her breasts, across one sinuous hip, to hold in place a small flowered sarong covering her loins in twin leaves. Her face is serene and smiling with antennae eye-brows and sightless almond eyes.

"That's Vriksaka from Gyaraspur," he says introducing her with pride. "She's the most expensive kept lady in town, but I can't resist her, so she's mine."

"How can you bear flesh women after her?"

"Well, I don't; not in this room anyway. This is my *sleeping* room. You're her first rival, so far. I don't bring girls into this room." He is serious suddenly and I feel at home.

Lying back on the bed, his arms folded under his head, he relaxes gratefully and there is a comfortable silence while I gaze at lovely Vriksaka from Gyaraspur and breathe in the secret grace of the room.

"Lie down," he says with his eyes shut. "Talk to me. Talk me asleep. Tell me a story. Tell me the story of you and dreams and days and things."

So I do; I take off my coat and I lie down beside him, not touching, and I begin.

I tell him all about Uncle Ansell and Dolores and being 'interfered with', Dr. Cornish and the other Margaret, running away, the Y.W.C.A. and Manolo, my Doubts that hang inside my head and imprison me in my bed for days on end. My tongue has never moved so freely and uncomplicatedly in my mouth before. I tell him about sitting in the hot-houses of Kew Gardens, about himself, and the 'dream-time' in Spain. I tell him about the ugliness of my abortion in the Ealing nursing home, with hordes of other haunted-eyed girls trying to be jaunty, the fear, and the aftermath of loss. I forget him, and talk about Jackson the Hybrid, and Friday in the snow, my elation and the wonder of this morning, sea-gulls, a sense of continuance in the bright blue day.

And then I am finished. His eyes are still shut. His face is placid, but he is not asleep. I examine this tranquil face minutely, the boxer's cheek-bones and overhanging brow, worry-lines, and the firm no-nonsense mouth. There is something vacant from his face though, it is like a sturdy house where no one has lived for many years . . . a house by the sea, vacant for the winter months, an off-season face.

I lean over and touch his forehead, trace the lines between his eyes and down the gullies of his cheeks. He starts for an instant and then moves his lips across to kiss my finger, but my finger will not linger and moves on down his rough chin, the soft skin underneath, the Adam's-apple rigid and round, right down to the base of his throat. Then I sit up and greet the smiling stone face of the lovely lady. Yes, he's right; she *is* a fitting mate for him.

Eddie raises himself up on his elbow and scrapes the hair back off his forehead like my mother used to do.

"She's the Tree Goddess, but the tree broke off. Tenth century. I found her in a flea-market in New Delhi. She's only a copy, poor girl, the real one's in the museum in Madhyn Bharat. I'd give my left ball to own the *original*." He lies back again holding his left wrist with his right hand, a habit I have noticed before; he always does it before he's got something important to say, something he's working out in his head.

"*You're* one, you know."

"One what?"

"An original. You're a little original planet floating about the Cosmos in and out of orbits like a celestial butterfly. And sometimes you get so far away from a sun that it's a cold, cold scene, and sometimes you fly in so close that you get singed round the edges." He laughs. "The wandering planet Maggie Truro, unique but ubiquitous, can seldom be seen with the unaided eye. If your eyes are keen you can sometimes catch the tenth and newest planet hovering on Chelsea Bridge or sitting in the steam of one of the hot-houses at Kew Gardens."

He takes my hand and holds it very tight, and we sit in silence looking out through his nice natural-wood windows, at the shining naked trees. I know he's trying to say he's sorry for singeing me round the edges.

"You have to be burnt out, burnt through and through completely to be a *star*," he says far away. "Burnt out and twinkling, that's what stars are. And they're not so pretty close to. Dead landscape. So you just stay being a lovely, original planet and maybe one day you'll find a nice, warm sun that you can orbit around and who won't burn you. It's not easy, but with you being so ubiquitous, maybe you'll have a good chance."

"What does 'ubiquitous' mean?"

"It means you can be everywhere at once, sort of omnipresent. I've felt you around about quite a lot."

"What's 'omnipresent'?"

"That's the same as ubiquitous, only better—more fitting for a new planet," he explains.

I'm beginning to feel as though I am climbing back into the same cocoon of warmth that he built around me once before, but which I know has all the desirability of going to the dentist, being given gas, and waking up with a terrible toothache.

"Maybe you'd rather be a big twinkly star, though."

"Well, big twinkly stars earn more bread than little original planets."

"Ah, but planets shine with a clear, steady light that never fails."

143

"Tell me, Eddie, why did you change your name to Lew Hamlyn?"

"Because I had a fink Polish name which sounded like I was trying to eat the world. Grabowski. How do you like that?"

"Eddie Grabowski. It's got a nice roll about it. It suits you. I think it's rather poetic."

"I told you you were an original." He touches my hair lightly with his fingertips. "You make me feel good . . . Did you ask that guy you met in Kew Gardens what 'hybrid' meant?"

"No. He told me before I could ask him but when I first heard it I thought it sounded like some sort of bird . . . a stork or a cassowary or something."

"A cuckoo," he says. "Coocoo! And how's your singing career shaping up."

"Well, that's not so great, but I'm opening in a club in Brighton tomorrow night, just for the week, so I'm doing *something* at least."

"What's it called? I might come down there and see you one of these nights."

"Aggie's Hearts and Flowers. It's run by a man called Samuels, but I've never been there, so I can't tell you where it is. Somewhere in the Lanes, I think."

He looks at me intently for a minute. "Well, girl, *shall* I come?"

His eyes are yellow in the sunlight, tobacco flecked and flinty, scouring out pretence, boring in on me like twin needles.

"Yes," I say faintly, "yes." And I get up to go, feeling a lurch of surprise that "No" has not come out of my mouth.

He grunts contentedly and goes back to his flat-out position, with arms under head and eyes shut. "I'm going to have a fantastic sleep now. Goodnight, sweetheart. Don't forget to shut the front door after you."

\* \* \*

Monday, the sky drizzles rain down like a nose on the second day of a cold. I sing. I practise all morning in my room, keeping the gas-ring burning, keeping my spirits soaring, keeping myself in one place, not expended, expectant, and in one place. It is hard, but I manage. I feel as though I had never had such a challenge before, such an obligation to justify my existence, such a time of breaking through the ice-age of my adolescence.

It's not such a big thing to sing, but it's essence to the person who's doing it. What can you do with your life if you're not having babies or looking pretty for photographers or saving peoples' lives in hospital or uncurling other womens' hair? Singing, you pour out your illusions, your hopes, your madness, your sex, your little inner flicker that makes you different and the same as they are, and they listen, approving of your exposure, gratified that someone is doing it for them, glad of the vicarious experience. They call it soul singing, and only a few people can do it without embarrassment or tremendous skill to cover their inadequacies or a million heartbreaks behind them.

That's what they wait for from Judy Garland, Ella, Pearl Bailey and Aretha Franklin, and that's what they pay the money for.

\*    \*    \*

Fourteen people paid money to see *me* at Aggie's Hearts and Flowers in Brighton that night and I give them their money's worth. I have purposely picked numbers that extend me . . . and I paint a purple flower on my cheek below the outside of my left eye, just to make me special.

I start with 'Summertime variations' which they receive courteously and then I swing into 'When you take me for a Buggy ride'; I stop caring what they think in the middle of this song and just belt and enjoy myself and do things I have never dared to do before except in the privacy of a practice room. Then 'Ode to Billie Joe', 'Surabaya Johnnie' in German which is a bit much for the clients of Aggie's Hearts and Flowers but to hell with them . . . I am going to finish with 'Till there was you' but they give me such a rousing hand for only fourteen souls, not counting Mr. Samuels, of course, that I sing 'Eleanor Rigby' and a song I picked up in Spain called 'Il Toro ena-morada della Luna' as well.

Afterwards Mr. Samuels buys me a drink and I win five shillings on the fruit machine. I actually leave before I lose it back which is very unusual for me. All the little superstitious games that I play with myself like whether my train ticket number divides by three, or if there's a nine in the number of the house I pass before I get to a job, wishing on the first evening star in the sky, ladybirds and tiny spiders, are paying off. I feel my voice come out like cream that night, smooth and rich and full of me.

I want Jackson to come on Friday night when there will be a few more people in the club, so I do not go down to Kew until Thursday afternoon.

I cannot find him. I wander around from green-house to green-house but there are only school parties and elderly gardeners on busmen's holidays. No Jackson. Freezing it is.

When it comes time for me to go I start to panic and search about for someone to give him a message. I cannot find a pen so I write on the envelope of an old letter from my mother, with an eye-brow pencil: " 'Aggie's Hearts and Flowers', 78 Byford Lane, Brighton. Come Friday night. Trains every hour on the hour. *Really* hope you can make it." And I signed it "Your Singing Friend, Maggie." I would like to write something scintillating but nothing springs into my silly skull, so I leave it at that and give it to a boy with steel-rimmed spectacles who is dressed like Jackson in overalls and gum-boots. He looks bewildered. I repeat three times that I would like him to give my note to 'Mr. Jackson' as soon as possible. I cannot remember Mr. Jackson's first name.

"He's sort of West Indian," I say, "with two-tone eyes, blue and brown."

The boy with steel-rimmed spectacles looks even more bewildered.

"Oh," he says, and I can see he's getting ready to dismiss me as a nut. "I only started here last week," he says, "I'm new, but I'll stick your note on the notice-board in the Locker Room. Is that all right?"

He is already beginning to move away, but I stop him once again.

"Well, if you see him around, don't forget to tell him it's there, *please*, because it's very, very important," I say, rather desperately. "Tall, a bit coloured, with blue and brown eyes!" I call after him as he hurries off down the path to the Wood Museum without looking back.

\* \* \*

146

All week long I have been rehearsing some new arrangements with Al, who plays the electric organ with the resident group at Aggie's, and it has been very exciting. "Oh God, let him come. Let him come and hear me and think that I am good. Let him like me a lot." And I suddenly realise that there is someone I hardly know whom I care about terribly, someone who has made things fall into place in my head, someone whom I desire earnestly to see again and whose good opinion I crave. "Is this love?" I think, watching the reflection of myself on the darkening carriage window while small spurts of water pulsate past the face looking back at me.

Is this the thing I keep singing about?

Friday arrives. All day I gear myself for the evening. Wash my hair, linger in the bath, titivate, tremble, try to ring up Kew Gardens and speak to Mr. Jackson, but am told that if I do not know the gentleman's first name, it will be impossible to locate him. When I leave the house I still do not know whether Jackson is coming or not.

The club is jammed with people when I come in, and when Mr. Samuels asks me if I will have something I drink a brandy very quickly to settle my mutinous stomach which is now threatening to expel everything I have put into it since breakfast. Still no Jackson.

Time comes for me to go on for my set, but I hang about in the Ladies Room, painting the daisy on my cheek with shaking fingers and getting it wrong twice, and putting on lower lashes that make me look too soulful and bereft, so I take them off again. At last I know I cannot fool about any more. I take a deep breath and belch what I hope is the last of my sick stomach and then I am ready to go.

As soon as Al slips into the introduction of the first number, its O.K., and I slog in with confidence. I can feel the audience come with me and support me and things start to happen. How easy it is when you bounce in on the right wave-length. It's like holding the end of a silk-worm thread. You musn't pull or stretch it or it breaks, but if you just hang on firmly to the golden thread, it skims out ahead of you like a gorgeous skein of light and you are safe and secure whatever you try.

Between numbers, I peer out into the sea of faces and several times I imagine I see Jackson's wide smile and clapping hands urging me on, but when it is over and I have gone through

147

everything we rehearsed, taken my bows and revelled in the approval of the audience, it is Al who comes forward and kisses my hands. I want Jackson.

I step down into the crowd and Mr. Samuels asks me if I'll have a drink with him, "To commemorate a memorable evening," he says, "and not the last, I hope." He heads me towards the five-deep bar. Someone yells out "Maggie", and I tug away from Mr. Samuels, expecting Jackson to appear like a paladin and rescue me from that hot wet hand on my shoulder.

It is Eddie . . . Eddie Grabowski, the indefatigable Pole . . . Lew Hamlyn has come all the way from London Town to see *me* . . . unbelievable, but true . . . but where is Jackson?

\* \* \*

Mr. Samuels is very excited when he learns who Eddie is, and behaves like he has personally hatched me out of an Easter Egg or found me in a Christmas cracker or something. I eke out the drinks still hoping that my friend will show.

Twenty minutes later I have to admit that the likelihood of Jackson turning up is very remote and I allow Eddie to take me to dinner. All the way through the oysters and Soave, he talks plans . . . I am going to sign up with him; I am going to cut a record, he knows a song-writer who was conceived just to write lyrics for me; I'm going to be groomed; I'm going to be a 'BIG STAR.'

"Dead landscape?" I say.

"Whoever told you that lie?" he says, looking at me sideways and slowly squeezing lemon juice onto a fat, grey oyster. "The man who said that was obviously suffering from large delusions or a mother of a hang-over. Out of sight," he sighs, sucking oyster juice.

With the steak he gets down to details. Tomorrow I am to come into his office and meet his lawyer to discuss terms; next week I will start lessons with a singing teacher who will give me some style and extend my vocal range; we will have dinner before Christmas with the song-writer, who will fall madly in love with me; I will cut the record in the New Year; it will be a hit, and I will do a promotional tour of the provinces and appear on hundreds of television programmes; he knows another guy who was conceived just to design clothes for me.

With the raspberries and cream he is anticipating a career in films. Maybe we could throw in some acting lessons with the singing ones; he knows a guy who was conceived to direct movies starring young, unknown girl-singers with talent; I could find my feet in films taking small parts in some other pictures he is packaging with other established clients from his stables.

We drink our coffee. I am feeling like a pre-packed turkey, trussed and ready for the oven. He is still moulding and refining my future like a happy boy building sandcastles, or perhaps more fittingly, like a master chef about to add the final touches to the trussed turkey, wrap it in tin-foil and pop it into the oven for a good four-hour roasting . . .

I feel suddenly utterly exhausted, deflated, that leaden four-o'clock-in-the-morning feeling; Eddie sees it, and suggests that he drive me back to London.

"That is if you're not still gonna go on waiting for your friend," he says. "He never showed, huh?" he adds, looking pleased.

I screw up my nose at him but for one horrible moment I think I am going to cry.

God, what if he *came*, and hated me so much that he left without saying anything? Paranoia is setting in.

In his bright green Jensen, with his trencherman's face discreetly outlined in the faint glow from the dashboard, he asks me to sing 'Surabaya Johnnie' again and I do, softly, while the oncoming car-lights flash past. The tiny hum of the engine is my only accompaniment.

When he kisses me goodnight outside the front door I know from his blunt dry lips on my cheek that I am 'business' to him from now onwards, and I am glad.

* * *

It is a full five months before I see Jackson again.

Five months so fraught and fantastic, frenetic, frightful, funny, in fact all the 'f's, that I am quite surprised to have survived them. When Lew Hamlyn takes over your life there's only one 'f' he won't hear of, and that's 'Failure' . . . no time to have Doubts, introspection or feelings of inadequacy . . . hardly even any time to have food . . . a steady diet of singing teachers, photographers, dentists, hair-dressers, song-writers and couturiers . . . that's what Eddie orders.

I never imagined that to launch a career you need so many *people*.

The song that is chosen for my debut is called 'I am waiting for my life to begin' and I like it a lot. It is written by a nice talented friend of Eddie's called Harry Sansom. I think he must be really demented to give it to *me* to introduce. It is the commercial lament of a young girl who has had a bust-up with her boy-friend in the winter and is waiting for her life to begin again in the spring . . . not very original . . . but the verse has a weird, persistent melody that gets embalmed in your brain, and then the chorus comes blazing out like a defiant challenge to the world. Any one of six top singers could have made it a hit.

It takes six sessions to get it right. Harry and Eddie have interminable discussions about backing and arrangement and when I finally get to hear the finished product I am amazed at the extra cello and harp accompaniment. It is a very disciplined piece of work.

They make me sing the verse very white, but I do six tapes of the chorus and they are eventually recorded together. This gives the effect of a great choir of mes, plugging out the title and making all the disc-jockeys jump for joy. It's one of those infuriating sort of one-line choruses that sticks in your throat like a wishbone for whole days, and you find yourself repeating the one stupid line over and over like a mechanical wound-up dolly.

It bounces straight into the Charts at Number thirty-five. The next week it is up to twenty and from there on in, it's only a question of whether it reaches the Number One spot or not.

"Eureka," says Eddie, and shoves me onto every television programme, promotional broadcast, interview, personal appearance and D.J.s how that I've ever heard of. It is instant exposure, instant fame and, quite naturally, a shock to my system.

I still wonder what has happened to my friend Jackson, but there is no time to go down to the Gardens and find out. I am on the merry-go-round, whirling to this appointment and that, singing my theme song continually until I become like Pavlov's dog, ready to open my mouth and belt it out everytime I hear them say 'Maggie Truro'.

By the beginning of April, I am beginning to loathe the song and despise myself everytime I repeat it. Of course, Eddie has been hustling Harry into writing another on similar lines to cash in on the success of the first. We have tried out five new songs, all perfect imitations of 'I am waiting for my life to begin', all less than the original. People begin to make dreadful jokes like, 'Well, has it happened yet?', 'Has it all begun again?' Is it possible to feel elated and depressed at the same time? No? Well, that's how I am.

I have a brief laughing affair with Harry, which we both go into knowing that it will be just *that*, a moment when two people go to bed together because they quite fancy each other and there is no one else to do it with, and they need it. No harm, no regrets, no illusions, no pain for pleasure; Fun. I must be growing up.

In May I tell Eddie that I have had it. I want a nice holiday away from the creeps, the merry-go-round, the promotion, the brouhaha, the boredom.

"Yes," he says. "Yes, yes," he says. "After you cut the next record, you will have a lovely holiday in Spain at the Marbella Club. Alfonso is a great chum of mine and I can get fantastic coverage in all the big magazines ... 'Maggie Truro begins life again at the Marbella Club'. How's that?"

"Horrible," I say. "I won't go!"

"O.K." he says, "you can have a holiday starting tomorrow, you obviously need it."

*　　*　　*

I love May. It is a real bombshell month. I mean everything is popping, promising months of summer with no electric blanket; it is all potential, ready for the explosion of buds and leaf clusters, ready for profusion and warm, languorous nights; people smell the air and look happier. I am, too. I call up this boy who makes my clothes and ask him for four new spring dresses. "Think of Boticelli," I say, "like that Venus coming out of the shell."

"She has no clothes at all," he says, "just some hair and a couple of hands."

"No, sorry, not her ... those three ladies that Paris is sizing up ... all flowing and spriggy."

"Hmmmm," he says, "it is either *about to begin* or it has all

*begun again.* I'd have to *see* you first to tell you which . . .
right?"

"Oh, shut up, and find some material to make me something
fantastic for the way I feel. There's no *reason.* It's just because
it's May and I feel so good I could jump out of my skin. I'm
on holiday," I add.

"I see," he says. "It's about to begin. *Got* the picture."

Actually, one of the nicest things about having made one hit
record is that you *can* call up a boy and ask him to make you
*four* dresses, and he doesn't start straight in about the bread.
Also, that you can go to the theatre, take a taxi when you
wish, see a movie at the Curzon without queueing, buy
expensive perfume, and not write too many lies about your
financial state to your parents . . . these are some of the *good*
things, and, of course, now I have a pad of my own . . a whole
two rooms with kitchen and bathroom. A small, compact
penthouse situated on the top of a red-stone house in Albemarle
Street. I can see part of Green Park and the tops of the trees in
Berkeley Square. How about *that?* That's luxury and much
appreciated.

*    *    *

For a whole day I laze in bed, wallowing between silk sheets,
and not because I am hiding out with my Doubts. I laze
because I am fundamentally lazy. It is Thursday, a threatening
Thursday with huge banks of clouds crowding into every
corner of the sky until it looks as though they must burst it . . .
They seem to be jostling each other for elbow room. In the late
afternoon I climb out on my narrow terrace (from which I can
see Green Park and the tops of trees in Berkeley Square) and I
wait for thunder, lightning, the release of a tempest . . . but
nothing happens. I watch hundreds of accountants, hair-
dressers, errand-boys, pimps, tourists, bowler-hats, berets, hair,
and great round swooping ladies' hats, hurrying for their buses,
their undergrounds, their parked cars and their taxis, all fearful
of being caught in the storm. I feel omnipotent and wonderfully
relaxed sitting above their heads, knowing that at the first
thunder-clap I can walk into my cosy bedroom and snuggle
back in bed and just listen to the rain beat down outside.

Darkness descends, but no rain; I sleep.

The next morning, despite the ever-present and lowering

clouds, I take myself down to Kew Gardens with a book, some sandwiches and two apples. Chestnuts are in bloom, pink and white flowers stand as steady as candles on Christmas trees; I walk underneath them, under their leek-green verdancy. Not a leaf stirs. The air is warm and heavy with unspilled moisture and I swim through, admiring the white stars on the oriental azalea tree, the lush grass ready for the crush of mothers' and childrens' and lovers' bodies, the yellow beak of a black-bird.

I do not go to any green-houses because I know they will be closed until one p.m. Instead I sit in the rose-garden behind my big Victorian dome with the Queen's beasts in front, and I open my book.

I swear I am actually reading and minding my own business, when I hear a strange but familiar sound. I look up and there he is, not twenty paces from me . . . Jackson . . . head down, humming his little Sunday song, raking manure in under the rose bushes. Beside him stands a large wooden wheelbarrow full of it.

Nothing could have made the day more beautiful, not even if all the clouds had suddenly scurried out of the sky and left it limpid and blue, not even if a great, big rainbow had dropped down above my head and a heavenly choir had been piped in singing 'Somewhere over it'. It could hardly have been planned better if George Cukor had been directing.

I stand up rather shakily, walk over to him taking small Japanese steps, and put my hand on his arm. I can smell the good undergrowth sweat of him immediately. He stops humming and his mouth opens, first in surprise and then in a laugh of genuine pleasure, which is the best sound I have heard this year. He drops his rake and picks me up, "Maggie! Little Maggie Forgot-your-name! Where the hell have you been?"

I can feel all the juices in me move, but I cannot say anything.

"I came to that place in Brighton, but it was on the Saturday night and you'd finished on Friday . . . didn't get your note until Saturday morning. Why did you never come back? I looked out for you." There is no doubting the fact that he is pleased to see me, almost as pleased as I am to see him.

He sits down and takes my hands and looks into my eyes and then he inspects me thoroughly.

"Hey," he says dismayed, "you've changed. You smell rich . . . Did you get married?"

"I *am* rich," I say, "I'm rich, single, and Number Seven in the Charts."

"I forgot your second name," he says. "All I could remember was Maggie. You didn't sign anything but 'Maggie' on that note, you crazy girl."

"Well, I forgot your *first* name, so I couldn't telephone you because there are evidently at least three other Mr. Jacksons on these premises. I *did try*."

"O.K.," he says, "we'll make a deal. I'll tell you my first name and you can tell me your second."

"Truro."

"Jesus, how could I forget a lovely name like that . . . Truro . . . Tru . . . row . . . very good. It's in my head forever now, thank you, Miss Trurow. Oh, and mine's Matthew, but you can call me Jackson for short."

He gets up and starts raking in the manure again, slowly and methodically, talking over his shoulder, but giving most of his attention back to the soil and the rose trees. He squeezes a few green-flies off the new leaf formations and mutters "Bastards" in the middle of telling me about the new hot-house he's helping to build.

He goes away and gets another wheelbarrow full, and while he is gone I cannot help but keep my eyes on the spot where he disappeared, terrified that he will not return. When he does, it is from the other direction and he comes up behind me.

"Excuse me, madam," he says in Best British Official voice, "would you mind removing your ass from this hallowed grass. The last female ass to be lowered onto this spot was that of our gracious lady Queen, and I'm sure you realise that we keep this place marked out for special bottoms . . . Oh! Oh!" he strikes his head in grand theatrical fashion, "*Now* I recognise you, madam. Are you not Dame Maggie Truro, the celebrated mouth-organist? Oh, madam, all I can say is that your ass is welcome to any grass it can find in these gardens . . ."

He eats both my sandwiches and one of my apples, but I'm not hungry, and he's the one who's doing all the work, so I don't mind, and later—three wheelbarrows later, in fact— after I have told him all about the record and Eddie, and the last five hectic months, after we have drunk two bottles of Coke apiece (he has brought them back with one of his other loads), the light begins to turn quite green and everything seems to take on an unnaturally intense colour like Technicolour. It is just after four o'clock.

"Here she comes," says Jackson. "Here comes the best hailstorm in the history of Kew, ever since the Hookers planted their first petunia. Listen," he says anxiously, "meet me tonight, eight o'clock, outside the big movie-house at Marble Arch. I'll be *there* unless I'm struck by lightning . . . Remember eight o'clock, Marble Arch, *Matthew* Jackson meets Maggie *Truro* . . . You dig?" He pinches my waist, and pushes me towards the Main Gate. "Now *run!*" he says. "*Run* before this big mother drowns you."

I walk a little way and then turn round to find him smiling and admiring my legs.

"Wow," he says. "What's my name?"

"Arnold," I say. "Where are we going?"

"Out," he says.

And the two of us stand there grinning away at each other like a couple of crazy Cheshire cats.

"Something lovely always happens when I see you," I say.

"Same deal," he says.

"Goodbye."

"Run," he says.

I mince off down the broad path that leads past the Orangery, not hurrying myself; I feel dainty as a cat. I only look round when I have reached the far end, and he is still watching after me. He does a little bow, clicks his boots together, and disappears at a canter dragging his wheelbarrow behind him. That is the moment when I am sure I am in love.

\* \* \*

At nine o'clock that night we are still wandering around rain-drenched streets, under trees whose leaves still drop with accumulated wetness, breathing air that has been cleansed and lightened by the downpour . . . smelling humid earth and exhaust fumes. Down Park Lane, across Hyde Park Corner, St. George's Hospital, Belgrave Square, across Sloane Street, to the Chelsea Pensioners and then to the river . . . and we talk, he talks about his grandmother. "She was about sixty before she had a change of life," he says. He talks about one of the administrators at Kew who had bawled him out for jumping about under his window that afternoon just as the storm starts. "I was feeling so great to see you again," he says. This old administrator cat's wife has stopped in the torrential rain to give him a lift. "The most genuinely beautiful middle-aged lady I ever met," he says. The administrator himself has clammed up tight in the car, and by the time he gets out, hate waves are being generated at one inch frequencies. "I don't know whether it was because I was chatting up his missus or what," he says.

Sometimes we have to shout when the noise of traffic is too deafening, sometimes break off in the middle of a sentence to cross the road. By the time we get to the river, I have been through my mother and father and the horrible Domestic Science School, Uncle Ansell as well. He is just beginning to tell me about a Canadian who lives on Hambro Island in a house he built himself, and who is Jackson's most admired friend now that his grandfather is dead.

My stomach is making horrible growling noises from no lunch, no dinner. I tell him that I am likely to faint unless we eat soon, which is only the truth, after all, and soon he has led me into a small clean café on the Battersea side of the river. He orders double hamburgers for us both. Hamburger and hot strong tea is the best restorative for an aching hunger that I have ever encountered.

\* \* \*

Ambling back, replete, across the bridge, I suddenly realise that this is the exact spot where Eddie fell down, and this is where I had my first ecstasy, *right here*, looking down off this very bridge. And now I am here again with Jackson, the instigator of the whole movement.

I am in love with him. I love everything about him . . . the way his lips move when he speaks, what he says, his hands that squeeze bugs off rose-bushes and have palms as hard as boards from all that digging and raking; the way he holds his head, his pointed ears that hug his skull so neatly.

Just across the bridge we come to a fence, a high fence made of welded iron bars set at about nine inch intervals and held together by three horizontal bars. It has a gate, cleverly concealed because it does not break the continuity of the bars, but the gate is firmly locked and padlocked.

In two giant steps, he is on top of the fence, facing the river, his boots at my eye level, each boot just fitting between the spears that finish off the bars of the fence. He jumps down from there into the grass on the other side. I heard him land on both feet like a cat, but I cannot see him any more.

"Come on," he says, "I'll show you something I found on my first trip around London Town."

Intrepidly I climb up the fence the way I see him do it, and then he is there again, waiting on the other side and looking up at me.

I teeter on the top, terrified that if I jump I will be impaled on one of the spikes.

"Jump," he whispers, "I'll catch you."

So I do, my hands on his shoulders. Both of us go tumbling down the little slope towards high-tide . . . the Thames, my friend, the pretty river.

I land up on top of him on the wet grass and we lie there laughing and looking up at the mellow May night-sky, pink now, and purged of all its clouds. I feel his longing fingers on my waist as he lifts me up. "Come," he says, giving me a small hug before he moves off to the left and down nearer the water.

He stops under a huge tree, overhanging the river and silhouetted by the bridge which looms up behind it. "Look at this," he says.

"What?" I say.

"This tree. Isn't it fantastic! It's a fig tree, growing right under Chelsea Bridge! It's got to be the biggest, oldest fig tree in London."

He reaches up and picks a leaf. "Here," he says. I touch the three-tongued furry leaf to my lips. It has a peculiar individual sort of smell like new musk and tomato leaves mixed up.

"I'm in love with you," I say, because I can't help it.

He puts his hand under my hair at the nape of my neck and holds my head, slowly pulling it towards him until my lips are against his neck. I open them and touch his skin with my tongue. He reacts almost as though he has had an electric shock. With great urgency he lifts me, his hands under my buttocks and holds the whole of my body against him. He is shaking. Then he lays me down on the grass under the fig tree, unbuttons my blouse, unzips my skirt; I help him with my pants and his shirt, and he comes inside me with a searing, beautiful pain that hurts and makes me feel whole at the same time. It seems to me that everything he does is *right*, the *only* way it could ever be done, the way he moves inside me and cups my breasts and does not lie too heavy on my chest. I have no other sensation but his mouth and his tongue, his hands, and him, the core of him inside me. He owns all my five senses and I feel as though I could live inside him forever . . . Wasn't it Jupiter who put the embryo of one of his children into a pouch in his thigh, and brought him out perfectly formed nine months later? . . . Well, I feel as though I could live quite happily in Jackson's thigh and he would bring me out to see the world whenever he wanted me.

So this is what it's all about! This is the fulfilment of all the dancing, the beat, the singing, the dreams, the sighing, the beating hearts, the blood, the babies, the Dr. Cornish talks on sex, butterfly-wings, the urges, the hates, the loves. Love, I love you, love.

And then the moment when all the concentric circles that wax and wane in one's subconscious come together in a pin-point of unbearable delight, a death and a birth of the senses, too immense to hold on to . . . and then it is over . . . I can see the lit-up upstairs part of buses, the people in them, above me. They are passing over the bridge. I can hear the traffic move as the lights change on the corner. I can see the splotches of dark leaves behind the outlines of his head. I reach out my hand to feel his face and I know he is smiling.

\* \* \*

We sit with our feet dangling, watching the empty barges and the loaded ones, the blasting pleasure-boats and the police launches going up and down the river; the enormous chimneys of Battersea Power Station are bright in the sky and one of them pours out a funnel of cream-coloured smoke that hangs in the air like a word-bubble in a cartoon. We sit, and I tell him about the day after we had played in the snow, about how I had come down here and seen the sea-gulls, and how Eddie had fallen down on the bridge. He listens with his head on one side and his eyes on the water. He has a way of listening that is totally absorbed and flattering—as though nothing is so important as the fact that he should understand perfectly what I am saying.

158

It is a sort of deference which I have only seen in himself and, perhaps, Dr. Cornish. A gentle deference, lost in the world of constant contrapuntal noise and trivia, where nobody really *hears* anything unless they are high, or it means money in the bank to them.

When I have finished, he strokes my hair, and talks seriously about himself. How he is dedicated to making his island self-supporting. How he has been writing poetry and thoughts in some notebooks which he will show me soon and see what I think. How he would like me to be his woman. Lovely things that I have been waiting all my life to hear out of someone's mouth. Not since my childhood have I believed in anyone so thoroughly. Without using a lot of relentless clichés, in a strange language of our own, using images and caresses and silences and a few words, we manage to convey to each other that there is nothing temporary in our new relationship, that we are more interested in each other than in anyone else in the world, that we delight each other fantastically. In fact, that we are un-ashamedly, stupendous lovers, and that we will undoubtedly remain together until we wish to be apart.

As I lie in the snug bliss of bed reviewing and reliving the marvels of our evening, deep in the dim recesses of my con-sciousness there forms slowly but irrevocably, the intuition that tonight has somehow been a crucial and deciding moment in my destiny.

# Part Four

## 9

### Eddie Grabowski

I LIKE SHIT. But it's got to be good shit. Someone brought me
some great shit from Colombia, South America, once, that was
yellow, as yellow as a light marigold, but two pokes of it and I
was crowding the moon. I never touch anything stronger
though, having had one bad experience dropping acid. A
couple of earth-quaking quiffs of cocaine and a few goes of
speed when I really need it, are my lot. But shit, I like.

The greatest thing in the world is to take about ten good
pokes of some superb shit, so that you're flying but not stoned
out of your skull, and then watch a bull fight—Ordonez or
Paco Camino or Diego Puerta—the classics—and man, it's real
poetry. You can really *see* it, it's one big moment of truth. Or
make love. Same deal, only you have to do all the work yourself. Which, on pot, is sometimes not so hot.

Or just listen to some real groovey music. Bach, Brubeck,
Beethoven, Bartok, Beatles. You name it—I like it. My taste
is so catholic I'm practically the Pope.

Me and this chick went round Spain following the bull-
fights for two whole months once doing all our things. The
fights, hitting it in the sack, pot, and I had brought one of those
tape affairs with hundreds of cassettes. So that's all we did, and
a little sun thrown in here and there. When I came back,
people asked if I'd been in the hospital, my eyes were so bugged
out with good things.

Me, I'm a funny sort of guy. Now that I've made it it's all a
heap of bones, man. Nothing that I see really turns me on any
more. I've tried all the kinky stuff and all the sincere stuff and
it's all no use to me.

I may as well start at the beginning instead of the end, but I
warn you, the story's a drag, a hundred per cent pin-point
borzoi from start to finish, so it's on your own head if you read

on from here. Right? Fatigue duty . . . Fall in! AttenSHUN!
Quick MARCH! Onetwoonetwoonetwo!

*　　*　　*

To Jacob and Ethel Grabowski of Hazleton, Pennsylvania
on April 8th, 1939, one son, Edward Dashiell (after my father's
favourite writer, Dashiell Hammett) Grabowski.

My father was a miner in the Pennsylvania coal mines in
Hazleton, named the 'All-American town' several years ago
by a group of genuine experts, folks, and we lived on the wrong
side of the tracks.

It was my grandfather who had come over from the old
country, from Poland. He came over at about the turn of the
century when the Atlantic must have been red hot with traffic
from Ireland, Poland, Germany, Italy, Serbo-Croatia, how do
I know? Anywhere where a hungry over-populated pogromed
bunch of idiots could scrape together enough to squeeze them
on to those tubs that were only fit to carry cattle.

So my old man's old man got here with nothing but the lousy
clothes he stood up in, and he went to work in the mines like
all the other mugs, the Irish and the Italians and the Pennsylvania Dutch and us Poles. It was pretty rough so I've heard,
with shootings and muggings, looting after fires in the general
stores, starving kids, racial violence and hatred; just like the
situation is in my country right at this moment with black
people.

Well, when I was born, work in the mines was beginning to
fall off, and after the war the mines were left idle altogether,
or at least the great majority of them, and my father got himself
a job in a sports goods store. He got maybe twenty-five to
thirty-five dollars a week depending on what his sales percentage worked out at, so we were not what you'd call rolling
in hay.

We lived in a wooden house with white lace curtains, and my
father built a cellar which is where my mother spent most of
her time. She never let any of us go sit in the front room, which
she kept looking like a spotless show-room in a furniture store,
in case any of the neighbours decided to pop in.

My mother baked our own bread and made slivovitz and
Polish sausage and dill pickles. Unlike my father she had been

164

born in the old country and could not get rid of any of the old habits. She was always telling me, "Eddie, you should be vorking, Eddie, hang around golfink place no good, Eddie, shoot the pool, no good, Eddie, no good people Eddie, no good, no good, no good." And that's exactly what I wanted to be— 'No-good-Eddie'.

From the age of twelve, even before I took Katy Wypoff around the back of the barn on Mr. Wypoff's farm for dairy cows, I knew that I was never going to live in Hazleton, Pennsylvania, for the rest of my life.

So I did everything my mother told me not to do—I hung around the Country Club and caddied for the big shots. I listened to the sons of the mine-owners, the Llewellyns and the McGraws, the Kingsleys and the Pagets, make their bets and speak their piece. They were a gamey lot on the whole, not very intelligent, but snobby, and determined, in fact, bred, to keep hold of that load of bread which their daddies and grandaddies had amassed by burying the faces of the poor in those old coal mines.

Then I had two friends . . . Richie Reisenweaver and Chic Cherry. Richie was Penn. Dutch (which is German) only four foot six inches tall, with a big round face, huge shoulders because he worked on the weights, and a heart about the size of the Empire State Building. He was crazy about big girls, the bigger the better, and would pursue them relentlessly until they gave in from exhaustion or just plain curiosity.

Chic was a bean-pole black boy from Scranton, who had the greatest sense of humour I have ever come across and who had buddied up with Richie because the two of them were such a weird couple that they could get in anywhere—a big tall, skinny black cat and a squat pink one with fat muscles and tiny hands and feet . . . they could get away with murder because people couldn't stop from laughing. I played pool with them and we were not a bad team. We would get hold of some sucker and one of us out of three was bound to take him, it didn't matter which one, because we always split the bread.

We would ride up to Scranton in our hot-rod; we had worked over a 1936 Caddy convertible until our eyes watered and our fingers were black for months stealing parts from garages, begging bits and pieces from other hot-rod buffs, until finally we came up with a real fang motor, capable of 110–20 on a good day and fantastic acceleration. We would go to the Trotting Races in Scranton and try to pin a few winners, or swing round the clubs raising hell wherever we went. That was back in '55 and '56 when I was just breaking out of High School.

That was when life was one big fat hash cake that I couldn't swallow enough of, and I never got guts-ache, no matter how fast and furious I ate. The only thing that ever bugged me out of my mind was not having bread, and that was when I decided to dedicate myself to getting some.

I had no idea how to begin to collect the stuff, but me and Richie and Chic had always messed around with skiffle boards, guitars, and Chic was a wizard on the drums, so we formed a group, The Hot Rods we called ourselves and played at High School dances and barbecues for a few bucks a night. There must have been a million groups like us, since Elvis had appeared and shook up the nation, and I would lay odds that a good percentage of them were called The Hot Rods, but we persevered and raked in enough to keep us moving for a whole year. Of course, we had the added advantage of Chic being six foot five inches tall, myself about five ten and Richie four six. This meant that when we lined up we looked like something out of Barnum and Bailey. We worked out a comedy routine where Richie and Chic played touch football but could never find each other; we would improvise mad scenes and they always went down the best, probably because we enjoyed them ourselves and they were spontaneous. We always ended up with big Chic climbing on to little Richie's shoulders, and me trying to climb up on Chic's, never quite succeeding. Little Richie would puff and blow down below, and then dump us just as I was about to stand on Chic's head. We were a wow with the routine, but they never went out of their minds about our musical efforts.

We invited a representative from one of the big hotels in the Poconos, which is the smartest mountain resort place in Pennsylvania with skiing in the winter, hunting, golf, drag races in the summer—you name it, they got it. They book some real big names there in the summer to come and entertain and they pay them big money too. Anyway, this guy comes to see our act and books us up for six weeks at the end of the summer season. "Give us more of the comedy, work it into your numbers, cut out the big sound, it's just noise you're making; and you've got yourselves the beginnings of a real cute act, guys," he said.

We bought ourselves outfits; levis, leather zip-ups, and black cowboy boots with red and white markings. We all wore our hair duck-tailed; at least, Richie and I did, Chic couldn't make the tail on account of his kinky solid cap of hair, so he wore *his* cut in a way-out peak in front that was crazy. Oh, we were the berries. Really. We changed our name to Jet Pack.

That summer in the Poconos was a gas. We played three shows a night and had Monday nights off. The comedy routines had gotten wilder and wilder until the management told us to tone them down after Richie found an enormous blonde sitting ringside and jumped bang into her lap in the chase between Chic and Richie in the touch football part.

It was not that the broad complained. She really dug Richie and palled up with him afterwards like he was Frank Sinatra or someone, but some of the square old customers had complained about us using language and all, and one lady told the maitre D that she was going to report Chic for 'throwing his hips around in a disgusting manner'. I wonder what was going on in her little brain while he was doing it?

We weren't supposed to mix with the guests outside working hours but we managed to get ourselves some very cool-looking chicks and took off to Scranton to stay with Richie's Mom every Monday night. Chic bought himself a motor cycle, a B.S.A., but Richie and me stuck to our old Caddy. By the end of the summer I had saved three hundred dollars; Richie took a job as a bell-hop at the hotel so's he could stay near his big momma, and Chic went back to hanging around the pool rooms of Scranton. The Jet Pack packed up.

I had to decide what to do with myself after that summer, so I stayed at home for a while, just goofing off and wandering about trying to think about how to make a million without really working. Ma would get on my back and ride me about not going to college or not taking a job in a bank or some such, but I knew that that was not for me. I hitched a ride up to New York about the middle of December 1956 just to see what it was all about, and got myself a job in Macy's for the Christmas rush.

Macy's is about the worst place in the world to be at Christmas, especially if you have a yen for the good things in life, like privacy and quiet and doing what feels right at the moment it feels right.

I got to hate people that Christmas at Macy's. To have seen the shoving shrieking hysterical mob dragging their poor unsuspecting kids to see a phoney old Santa Claus, and those little no-neck monsters being bribed into goodness for the price of a few lousy toys and a couple of sacks of candy, has put me off the family scene for life. I am a strict follower of H. J. Mencken who said, quite rightly, that to be a bachelor is sensible, stable and sanitary.

Not that I have been sensible, stable and sanitary all my life.

I stayed on for the White Sales which were nearly as bad as Christmas. This time there was a mob of thrifty housewives counting their pennies. It was really scary to watch those sewn-up mugs all day; most of them put all their sexual drive into stretching the buck—it doesn't make for pretty faces.

Three months of Macy's and my call-up papers, forwarded from Hazleton by Mom's straggly hand, did not seem like the disaster that they would normally have been; and three months after that, I was inducted, given a half-inch crew-cut that exposed the back of my neck for the first time in years, and was on my way to Fort McPherson, Atlanta, Ga., the headquarters of the Third Army, for training preparatory to overseas duty.

Ah . . . the Army—that fairy-land of horror and delight, the place where anything can happen if you've got the right formula, the con-man's paradise, the rebel's come-uppance, the intellectual's despair, home of the sadist and his brother, the boy who likes to be whipped. I firmly believe that the Army as we know it today was invented by an under-sized father-fixated deviate trying to prove to his buddies that the impossible can only be achieved by taking away a man's identity, pushing a weapon into his hand and waiting till he gets so mad that he will attack anything he's turned loose on, including his own, provided they happen to be in the wrong place at the right time.

Very early on I decided that the jumping-to, shiney-shoes, ass-licking YesSIR! side of the business was not for me, so I bore my first fatigue and K.P. with a detached philosophical air and an eye fixed unswervingly on the future, I bided my time and kept my nose clean until I could safely apply to be switched to entertainments. In my application I built the Jet Pack into a group who could easily have shared top-billing with Elvis, and myself into a budding Billy Rose who had not only master-minded a record-breaking season throughout the Eastern seaboard states, but who could fulminate the stage given a plugged-in guitar; a guy who sat in on sessions with Buddy Rich at Birdland and handed out useful tips, and whose natural talent for organisation was limitless. I managed to convey that the Army had snatched me away on the brink of a fantastic debut in New York and that even so, I was not going to be a dog-in-the-manger about my talent, but allow them to make full use of me during my two-year stint, just as long so they were nice to me.

*    *    *

Nothing happened. Not one nibble. No four-star general came searching to give me news that Bob Hope had just lost his liaison officer and would I mind being promoted and jump into his place; there were no frantic phone-calls for Private Edward D. Grabowski 24681/OJ/126 demanding his presence at Headquarters owing to the non-arrival of the lead guitarist/drummer/spoon-player who should have been accompanying Doris Day. Nothing. The movies lied. Direct action was required. I set out to find and collect any droppings of talent that might be lying about in my own platoon, and I was lucky.

That first group I formed consisted of an Italian bugler camed Cecchetti, playing trumpet, and Ossie Witherspoon, an elegant black neophyte from Mississipi, who clung to his clarinet like it would open the door to banks, fannies and liquor stores (all of which it *did* several years later), Egg Henry, trombonist from Wichita, myself on drums and Sockie Wein-traub, a body builder from Brooklyn who played bass and was also our vocalist. We were keen, we worked, but would have gotten nowhere, except to play fill-ins at local hops, if we hadn't had a genius in our midst.

Ossie Witherspoon led us musically through mine-craters and barbed-wire, through rubbish dumps and sniper-infested jungles, out into huge landscapes of invention where anything is possible. He led, and we followed breathless and stumbling, choked with the opposite of indifference, and the times he was not with us, we stank. We were dragged along in the wake of his discovery—his discoveries—panting to keep up, practising, eating, sleeping and digesting his gifts; none of us could really hope to compete with those hurrying ephemeral fingers. He was like a May-fly who has only one day to live and wants to get it all in. He was the most compulsive musician I have ever met.

*　　*　　*

In six months I knew that we were good. Not *very* good, but good, and getting better. Army life receded into a grey round of duties that ceased to interfere with the tremulous colour of our sessions. I listened to the roars of appreciation after an Ossie solo and I knew I had got it made. We were in demand, and even old thick Sockie Weintraub, whose chief reason for being with us was to lay chicks, was inspired into mediocrity instead of just plain badness.

Ossie—close-faced, obsessive, Southern black-dandy Ossie— the pivot on which our success oscillated, I cultivated and nurtured like he was my second skin . . . maybe my first. He liked to drink gin and coca-cola after a session; said it cooled his throat. I've seen him put away five or six of them without a word . . . but afterwards they just spilled out of him. He would sit with his legs wide apart leaning way back in his chair until it rasped and creaked with every change of weight; sometimes he would talk and talk until the words became a drawling drunken vowel with chewing sounds, the only indication that words were being spoken, sometimes he would throw back his head while in his lap his fingers played out some cadenza on an imaginary clarinet and a few grunts were all that could be heard of what I am sure was a show-stopping solo, plucking away at all the drillion molecules in his brain.

I was not envious of his talent like Cecchetti, the bugler turned trumpeter. He played a good trumpet, but aggressive, like he was trying to drown the rest of us out, but even *he* could not withstand the total absorption of Ossie in flight, and had to follow along like the rest of us. It bugged him that Ossie was a black man, I knew that; and he didn't love what he was doing with the music enough to forget it all the time. Still, he was not stupid, and so he put up with the itch and only scratched when he thought no one was looking.

Egg Henry, the trombonist, was thirty, five years older than any of us, a regular sergeant, with a high-domed bald head like

170

Phil Silvers that had earned him his name. He was mild-mannered and courteous by nature, as different from the popular conception of a sergeant as caramel is from granite. He always mediated in any argument that broke out among us.

Seven months after my induction into the army, our platoon was sent to Germany, to Dusseldorf, and there we had our first glimpse of how the other folks live—the ones who *don't* live in the home of the free and the land of the brave . . . the 'orrible 'un, the British call them . . . Krautie and the funky frauleins.

I was happy; Ossie was out of his mind with delight, Egg Henry took it in his stride . . . he had seen it before; Cecchetti went on a three-day blinder on our first leave and didn't show up at practice for a week. The only one who was not happy was Sockie Weintraub, who kept muttering about seven million Jews, and looking belligerent every time we passed a middle-aged man in the street. We worked consistently for the first six weeks playing at every opportunity; camps, social clubs—we fraternised anywhere to try and familiarise the United States Army of Occupation with our boast that we were the best group throughout the Armed Forces.

And it paid off. I overheard men discussing Ossie and comparing him respectfully with Charlie 'Bird' Parker. I heard them refer to the 'Grabowski Group' as the best thing that had happened in local entertainment since Louis Armstrong had made a tour sometime previously. We were in demand again wherever we went, and I found we could always pick up a few bucks on the side for playing privately at some officer's wingding.

\* \* \*

In July 1959 we were flown over to England to play at a ball held in Barbara Hutton's old house in Regent's Park and then for a tour round the U.S. bases in the country. I had always thought London would be a cold, bombed-up place with Sherlock Holmes characters popping out of the fog and saying 'Gad' or 'Veddy pleased tomeechyew', a place where plumbing failed and the women wore tweedy skirts and medically-inspired stockings to keep their varicose veins in position. I was not at all prepared for the warmth of that summer, the hottest in living memory, the colour, the style, the craziness, which I met on that trip. I fell in love twice; once with the whole ambience of London, and once with an incredible chick called Griselda Harvey-Smith.

Griselda had periwinkle-blue shark's eyes, freckles and an austere kind of face that you see in old Victorian prints, but when she smiled, it was like having a secret encounter up a blind alley. She had red hair and a pointed chin and I found her the most exciting, enticing and intriguing woman I had ever seen.

The first time I caught sight of her she was sitting in the medieval section of the National Gallery gazing at a fresco of 'Episodes in the Life of St. John' with a concentration that can only be described as penetrating. It was a picture of what looked like Christ, but must have been St. John, being boiled to death in a giant egg-cup, while a man with a shepherd's crook and halo pushed a small boy into a rubbish-tin—at least that's what it looked like to me. The faces of the people were all flat and expressionless and I could not think what hidden fascination the picture held for her. It was like a badly-drawn medieval comic strip. Come to think of it, maybe that's why she liked it.

I was twenty, raw-boned and eager to make a million bucks, anxious to accumulate a little culture on the way, a G.I. Joe with nowhere to go on a Saturday afternoon, and besides, the National Gallery is free.

I stood beside her in front of the fresco and made some derogatory comments and waited for her to bite. She did; turning her head sharply towards me she gave a succinct little speech on the merits of eleventh-century art. So I was in like Flynn, and we did the rest of the gallery together.

Griselda lived at a place called the World's End, a fitting habitat for one so way-out as she. She had one enormous room dominated by a studio window twenty feet tall and a narrow staircase leading up to a kind of gallery on which she slept. Her paintings were great sprawling affairs of blocked colour. They seemed formless and incomplete to me but I admired them enthusiastically and was willing to agree with anything her taste dictated as long as she would invite me up that narrow staircase to share her lumpy mattress.

* * *

Griselda was used to the attentions of young nobodies like

me, and at first she hardly seemed to have registered my continual presence. She flew about town in a souped-up Jaguar sports car, was always dropping in at various seedy painters' pads to drink white wine and discuss subjects far beyond the range of my experience, like 'The Tibetan Book of the Dead', and Labour Party, and 'Reich's Orgone Box'. I was out of my depth and rushed back to rehearsals with a kind of relief that there would be people whose language I could understand and whose motives I could gauge.

But I could not keep away from her. During the week I was in London I saw her every day. Love-making could happen at any hour of the day or night with Griselda; you just had to be ready when the fancy took her. I remember one day she was standing in front of her easel daubing energetically and uttering small cries of disgust when things didn't come out exactly how she wanted; I was lying on the rug leafing through a magazine on deep-sea fishing which I'd found on the floor. Suddenly a mouth fastened on to mine and there she was beside me, all limp and soft and mewing like a lost kitten.

I went back to Germany with two things on my mind. One was to manage Ossie Witherspoon after my discharge from the Army, the other was to return to London and alkalise the potent acid of Miss Harvey-Smith's attraction which ate into my person with such vigour.

\*    \*    \*

By this time I had been in the Army one year and three months, and had nine months more time to serve. I was a corporal in the Quartermasters, which made life easy; our sergeant was Egg Henry, a sweet guy to handle, and I had added a pianist to the group who was a very good musician and had studied at the Juliard College of Music in New York. He was Class, and the only member of the group, except for Cecchetti, who could read and write music.

It was then that I decided to form another group that could cover for any of us who had special duty or could not make the schedule for some reason. Understudies. Men came to *me* this time, lugging their instruments, for auditions, keen to have my approval, anxious that I should use them.

I tried out all the guys *with our original group* to see how they would adapt to Ossie's improvisational style. I discovered a flautist who enjoyed playing with Ossie so much that he practically paid me to let him sit in on sessions. I found a new vocalist who had a Joe Williams voice that could be heard without a mike from one side of the Grand Canyon to the other and back again. I could change places with a drummer who spent every minute of the day, when he was not parading and drilling, polishing his equipment or stuffing his face in the mess hall, labouring lovingly over his skins like he could see his mother's face with every stroke. He wasn't very bright, Joey Wainwright, but he had rhythms in his head that were intricate, glorious abandonments.

\* \* \*

So now I had two groups . . . Or one big group if we all got together. I was determined to get Ossie's sound on record and made my plans accordingly.

We had discussed what we would do with ourselves after our discharge and I had persuaded Ossie that when I started a company for cutting discs he would record for me immediately; we would call it Hamlyn Enterprises and I would be his manager in business deals and get a twenty-five per cent cut of his gross income. In exchange I would figure out how to present his talent to the world, how to get the best price for what he was selling, and how to invest the money that he made so that those hungry tax-men did not get their hot little hands around too much of it, after all that sweat.

And all the time I was hustling and grafting for Eddie, I was thinking about Griselda—aching, shameful school-boy pining that got in the way of my big plans.

\* \* \*

I wrote her twice and sometimes three times a week, pouring out uncharacteristic sentiments on paper, which I am sure she skimmed through at breakfast, one eye on *The Times* obituary column and the other veering towards her latest vast canvas of pale chunky colours.

In return, I received a few scrappy scrawls, mostly un-decipherable but studded with 'darlings' and 'supers' and 'loves' and 'agonies'. I called her house long-distance once or twice but was discouraged when there was no reply at three o'clock in the morning. Too many disquieting images and painful pictures of where she might be came into my mind to try calling again.

I had thirty days furlough coming to me and I counted off each day on the Reingold Beer calendar with a fervour which made each cross a high spot in my day.

I continued to underline the date of my arrival in London in every letter, fearful that she would forget and go off skiing in Switzerland or skin-diving in the Red Sea. With Griselda, anything was possible.

\* \* \*

We were married at the Kensington Registry Office as soon as I could get permission from my Commanding Officer. She was twenty-six, I found out when she signed the ledger. The witnesses were two taxi-cab drivers who were anxious to be on their way, and only waited until I had handed out the tips. They wished us a speedy good-luck before they put their 'For Hire' signs up and were swallowed back into the traffic.

I looked at the strange face of my bride, with her flat blue shark's eyes, and I wondered what I had gotten myself into. I did not know her or understand her. I did not even know if I liked her, but I know I had to have her.

Holding my hand she led me into an empty pub at eleven-thirty in the morning and they brought out a bottle of un-chilled champagne. She handed me mine and said, "To Happiness."

"To Happiness," I answered, and felt a constriction around my heart in that dark dank place, so ravaged with human encounter and yet so bleak and old-beer-smelly in the morning.

We went back to Griselda's studio and she set up a fresh canvas, sat me in an old wicker chair and started to paint my portrait. She would not let me move for an hour, and blocked in the outlines of my face with bold strokes of pale lime and stone, against background of deep blue curtain. I watched her darting back and forth, mixing her oils, taking measures with her thumb, screwing up her eyes in concentration. I, me, Eddie, the new husband was forgotten. The huge studio window of sky behind her changed from grey and white to sombre black. And then, when I could not see her face any more, she sighed at last, set down her brushes and poured us two enormous brandy snifters.

"I'm going to sign this one Griselda Grabowski! Have you ever heard of such a monstrous name?" She laughed with her head back and drank her brandy in two gulps. She had forgotten me again it seemed, so I held my glass to her lips and said, "I'm not thirsty. You drink it."

"Well, it *is* a dreadful name, darling, you must admit," drinking. I saw her throat move up and down swallowing. I did not say anything. She had a child's neck.

"Still, it's better than Harvey-Smith."

"Stop sulking," she ordered, clinging to me suddenly.

She smelt of fresh oil paint and 'Fleur de Rocailles', a heady, secretive scent she always used; I have never smelt it since without feeling an extraordinary nostalgia for something that I never owned and always wanted . . . it was not just *her*, *or* the scent, it was a thing that she carried round with her, an aura, charisma, an essence, I don't know what you'd call it, but nobody can touch it, and people who have it wield a terrible power over others, without even knowing it. It burns other people up and sends them mad.

We made up the fire downstairs and I asked her if I could bring her bed down from the gallery. Somehow I could not face the narrow staircase up to that precarious balcony where she normally slept. How many men had picked their way up those wonky steps?

Wife-like, she put away the unfinished portrait and hung our clothes—her brown velvet suit and my dress uniform, dark blue coat and sky-blue trousers—elegantly, over her easel.

She cried out "Oh, love!" when I went inside her and took my head between her hands and I could see her eyes turn shining purple in the firelight, searching my face with the desperate melting look of love and union. Those were the only moments when I felt I knew her, could understand her, give her what she wanted, and I rode her like a king that night, while our empty clothes stood guard over us, and the fire died.

Next day, she got up and wandered around humming and combing knots out of love-tangled red hair; she disappeared up to her nest on the balcony.

"Eddie!"

"Mmmmmm?"

"Why did you *insist* on getting married?"

I lay there fusty in the morning light and I didn't know what to answer. I couldn't confirm anything to that disembodied voice.

"Eddie? But *why*?"

It came down from above me like a conscience voice in dreams. "Why were you so anxious to stand up in front of that ludicrous little man and mouth all those drab words?"

Silence.

"I mean, I'm not *complaining*, but it just doesn't add up with the rest of you." Then her voice was muffled, as she pulled some clothing over her head. "You know, I'm six years older than you."

"Well, maybe I'm just a simple country boy who wants to put you back on the straight and narrow." I shouted too loudly for the distance.

"You'll never do that!" laughing.

*　　*　　*

"Do you play chess?" she said conversationally breezing down the stairs in lavender wool, that made her hair look redder and her freckles stand out. "I've promised to go and play with old Blyford Edwardes this morning; you know, the painter. He's dying of Parkinson's Disease, the shakey kind, and it's about the only pleasure left to him, so I can't let him down, poor man. Do you want to come?"

"No," I said, staring up into the rafters.

*　　*　　*

And that was the pattern of my thirty-day marriage, because that's how long it lasted . . . until my leave was up. She continued to zoom about Chelsea in her car, popping in and out of the houses of an awful assortment of dead-beats; aging diesel-dykes, Italian painters, crummy photographers, drunken Celtic bards roaring obscenities, camp interior-decorators—she was the darling of the whole flatulent Chelsea scene; and I continued to wander around London drinking in pubs, drinking in atmosphere, waiting for her to come home. One morning, when I opened the *Daily Express* I found a picture of her in the gossip column, smiling from under an enormous mushroom hat and announcing that she had decided to reveal her marriage to Corporal Edward D. Grabowski of the U.S. Forces stationed in Germany. It said that her father had been Rear Admiral Sir Iain Harvey-Smith, V.C. and that he had died after the war, and that the family came from Norfolk.

All this was news to me. Griselda had told me only that her parents were dead, and I had never imagined her in any background other than her beloved Chelsea. I tried to pin her down but I could only do *that* in bed, and not with words.

Only once, the day before I left, did she stop gallivanting and stay home with me. She had bought a game pie from Fortnum and Mason's and we sat on the floor and drank champagne with it and I told her my plans for Ossie and the record company. She was gay and coquettish and caressed my hair, told me how clever I was, listened to stories of Sockie Weintraub busting his gut training to be Mr. Universe and then cursing the route marches that sweated off the extra poundage he was so carefully storing. She listened to stories of Ossie and the excitement of sessions, how the boys had shaved off half of Cecchetti's moustache when he was stoned out of his skull. We worked out that I had three months, seven days and some hours left to serve, and that after that, I would come back and we would start our life together, find a place to live, that she would keep on the studio and paint, and that I would launch myself into the world of recordings and music-making for the masses.

We had a great night. She was an uninhibited girl, Griselda, and that night she was abandon, explosive and resourceful, full of pride in her own body and glad of me, glad of me.

I never told her that I had found out on my first visit to London that work permits were given only to Americans who had *married* British citizens . . .

"I *had* to marry you to get a permit to work in England!" I *should* have yelled back that morning nonchalantly, picking my nose. She would have loved that. Well, maybe not *loved* it, but she wouldn't have minded if I'd brazened it out and told her that my 'big plans' included a company registered in England —a change of name—and a bona fide *work permit*. I had solved at least one of those problems by marrying Griselda and I folded that marriage certificate away carefully and with a feeling of genuine accomplishment.

The fascination of Griselda would surely diminish once she had 'dwindled into a wife' and I would be a proud possessor of a genuine permit as soon as the request and the certificate had been examined. Hallelujah! I was on my way.

I had chosen 'Hamlyn' as the new name of my company— and myself—after Hannibal Hamlyn of Maine . . . I just liked the name . . . (Pied Piper) . . . *Hamlyn Enterprises*. It had authority . . . sensitivity and authority. That's what the watch-words were to be.

I went back to Germany the next morning mentally confident, spiritually hopeful and physically shagged out.

\* \* \*

Owing to the circumstances I never finished my term, my full two-year stretch in the army. Ten days before my time was up, at midnight, I was lying in my bunk mentally listing the numbers for Ossie's first record, when Egg Henry came and shook me telling me to get up and get dressed—Captain Shelby wanted to speak to me.

He would give me no clue as to what it was all about, so I jumped into fatigues and flew across the compound to the captain's residence. He stood in the centre of his living room in a short tartan robe with a chunky glass of cut crystal weighing down his right arm. He offered me a bourbon and told me to sit, while he walked stiff-legged over to the bar to fix it. He was one of those regular officers with 'ARMY' printed all over their thick iron-grey crew-cuts, armoured faces and rigid no-assed backs.

"I've just received some bad news for you, son," he said, "seems as though your wife has had some sort of accident and they want you over there right away."

I sat still, because I knew he hadn't finished.

"I've called Transport; you can catch a flight at 0400 hours this morning . . . you'll be landed in Oxford at 0630; she's in a hospital, some place called Banbury. You'll be given a car at the airport."

I took the whisky and held it in my hand. He had poured

three fingers over a half-dozen ice-cubes. It looked very strong.

I did not know how my voice would come out when I asked, "Do you have any idea how serious it is, sir?" The voice was normal, amazingly controlled, I thought; but everything, including Captain Shelby's throat-clearing and harsh mid-western accent seemed to have moved into science-fiction; not true, any of it.

"Seems like some . . . er . . . kind of freak . . . er . . . mis-happening, corporal," he said, selecting his words like an election candidate. "Seems like she was asleep in the passenger seat of a car . . . er . . . the driver jammed the brakes on and somehow—don't ask me how it happened, because I don't know—somehow the jerk . . . broke her neck . . . It's *very* serious," he added, bobbing his head down to take a quick suck on his Scotch. "How long will it take you to get your stuff together?"

"Fifteen minutes, sir," I said, half-rising and looking about for somewhere to unload my drink. My throat felt like a dust-bowl but I knew I wouldn't be able to swallow. I was imagining Griselda's narrow little neck which I could encompass with four fingers and a thumb. The neck with baby tendrils sprouting at the nape and the two tendons that stood out, leaving a small straight hollow down the middle, and reminding me of a boy's who used to sit in the desk in front of me at school. Noellie Pardon, his name was.

"Finish your drink before you get going, corporal; and you'd better have a meal before the flight. I'd stay with you myself but I have a lot of paperwork to finish up. Sergeant Henry will look after you and see to the details . . . It's a tough break, son . . . I wish there was something we could do . . . Your discharge comes through in a few weeks' time, doesn't it? Well, you'll be given compassionate leave until then, so this is probably your last day of service . . . not much compensa-tion, I know, but about all I can offer you at this moment." He swallowed down the last of his drink and called to Egg Henry, who must have been hanging about in the hall anticipating a summons.

"Have a drink, sergeant! Keep Corporal Grabowski com-pany. If you hit any snags you can call me on the private number and I'll see to it."

"Goodbye, Corporal Grabowski," he said, shaking my hand

and patting me on the arm, "and good luck!" He left the room and I felt as though I had been given a formal farewell by the entire U.S. Army.

Egg Henry scuffed about the room fingering his bald pate and flicking me worried nervous glances like I was going to blow my mind or something, but I was hardly aware of him except as an interrupter of my anguish. And it *was* anguish that I felt, a peculiar passive anguish that kept my body like a stone, while my mind conjured graphic pictures of Griselda's snapping neck, the stretching moment of terror between waking and sleep when she realised that something irrevocable had happened. I was filled with a terrifying awareness of Griselda's pain, a correlation of mutual pain which I never thought could have existed in me. I actually *felt* that I held her experience inside me, and there was nothing I could do about it except accept it and hope that somehow it might alleviate some of her pain through my own.

The only person I woke up was Ossie. I told him what had happened and asked him to meet me in London the day after his discharge. I gave him the telephone number of Griselda's studio.

\* \* \*

She died at six o'clock the next morning, about a half-hour before I got there. I saw the doctor who handled emergency cases but there was nothing I could say.

I saw the frightened guy who had been driving the car. His name was Nigel Something-or-other, and he explained to me in a very threatened, fearful blame-denying voice how he had met Griselda at Gerald Something-or-other's and gone on for a drink at Moira-Something-or-other's where Griselda's car had broken down, or wouldn't start, he couldn't remember which . . . so . . . she had asked whether he'd give her a lift home, and as he lived in *London* and it was on his *way* . . . well, obviously, it was the least he could do . . . They set off at about midnight . . . When they were coming into Banbury (she had dozed off), a large, white dog rushed out in front of the wheels and he stood on the brakes . . . he heard an awful clicking noise from the passenger seat, choking sounds and then a horrible rattle. He reached over to hold her head up and found that it was lolling sideways in an unnatural position . . . and then he found that she was not breathing and had tried to apply the kiss of life . . . she responded a little . . . he had driven as fast as he could to the nearest hospital . . . it was a ghastly, ghastly thing, but not his fault . . . "That great, fucking dog, that great, fucking dog," he kept saying before he broke down and wept. Poor Nigel Something-or-other. There was nothing *I* could say.

* * *

An old lady came up to me at the funeral and told me she had been Griselda's 'Nanny'; she said how tragic it was; that Griselda had told her that she would be needed to look after the new member of the family—that she would have been proud to do so.

I went back to the hospital in Banbury and asked the doctor. "Yes," he said, "the autopsy proved that Mrs. Grabowski was three months and some weeks pregnant."

I felt sick. I knew that somewhere deep inside, I was pleased that she was dead. I was glad that I would not have the responsibility of a wife and child. I could not help it, but families were not included in my plans.

Two days after the funeral I received confirmation of permission to work throughout the British Isles.

* * *

I had a period of self-revulsion which did not go away until Ossie arrived in London. I set up Hamlyn Enterprises and decided to change my first name as well. I chose Lew because it was bland and at the same time had a sporty ring to it, like Lew Hoad, and so Lew Hamlyn of Hamlyn Enterprises was born out of the anguish of Griselda's death, Eddie Grabowski's revulsion at himself and the large ambition that goaded me on regardless of event.

* * *

In the next period of my life, everything I touched succeeded. Ossie's first three albums are still classics, collectors' pieces, and they set me on the map incisively and forever; if I did nothing else I would be remembered in the world of modern music as 'the discoverer of Ossie Witherspoon'.

But I was insatiable for work, to earn money, to build an empire. Within two years of its inauguration, Hamlyn Enterprises was promoting most of the talent that recorded in England—the new talent that is. I was the tireless patron of the young, the new, the controversial, the way-out—and it paid off.

I opened record shops and branched out into merchandising. If I thought a record should go, I bought ten thousand copies myself and shot it into the Charts myself. I made a few mistakes, but mostly they sold like hot-cakes after an initial push.

And that is how I made my first million, children, and after the first million, it's easy, as any good economist will tell you.

But when you've done it, when you've made your pile and you sit back and look at yourself, you suddenly find that it's a heap of bones, so I avoid self-examination, if I can. Hamlyn Enterprises rolls on and me with it. You can't beat the system, you've got to go along with it and I *have*, all the way.

I told you that the story was a one hundred per cent pinpoint borzoi, a big white dog that runs out under a speeding car and the whole world changes.

Nothing in my life changed, except the amount of money I owned, since the big white dog, until I met Matthew Jackson of Hambro Island and if it hadn't been for him I expect things would have gone on getting more boring and less exciting every year.

# 10

## *Lew Hamlyn*

ABOUT ONCE A MONTH I have a real wild night. It generally
starts off early in the morning when I take a sauna bath. I sit in
my little, hot, pine-smelling cell for two hours, dripping sweat
and meditating, and then every fifteen minutes or so I go stand
under the shower and allow icy jets of water to rain down on
my skull and chase the cobwebs. By ten o'clock I am a fit,
dehydrated, clean ball of fire, greedy for anything that comes
my way and avid for a drink. I start with cold lager; that
takes me up to cocktail time when I switch to martinis—long
on the vodka and short—very short—on vermouth. In fact,
sometimes I just pass the vermouth bottle over the shaker a few
times and say a small prayer. A pitcher of martinis later, I do
not remember much of what happens.

Once I ended up in a cat-house in Manchester. Another
time it was the Channel Ferry to Dieppe. They are expensive
days, those lost ones, but they are safety valves, and I do not
resent a penny of the money I spend on them. For the rest of
the month I am an industrious, imaginative, block-busting
dynamo, goading his employees to ever greater productive
energy, having an occasional cop-out evening on shit, but mostly
a well-behaved citizen.

The wild night, before the morning I landed up on Chelsea
Bridge, had been a lulu. I can vaguely remember a group of
hop-heads and gannets dragging me out of a party, and all of
us piling into my car, and some cat pulling me out of the
driving seat and taking over as chauffeur. I recall going up a
lot of stairs that smelled of old lavender-ladies and cats, into an
apartment full of camp writers and friends, middle-aged lady
writers and friends, and other freaks with friends. I was the only
one who didn't seem to *have* a friend, so naturally I got into a
fight. Someone threw me out, I remember that well enough,

because I fell down all the stairs and finished up in a heap with some empty milk bottles at the bottom. Then I went and had a little rest in the car, but the bastard who drove us there must have taken the keys because they were gone. That's when I started in to try and walk home.

The next thing I remember was someone slapping my hands and taking healthy swipes at my face. I opened my eyes and *there* was this little chick I had been to Spain with—a sweet, crazy little chick who had got herself knocked up and tried to boff me into marrying her.

Mr. Fuzz himself rode up on a bicycle and I pulled myself together on the count of ten, aware that my pockets were bulging with stuff that one of the hop-heads had shoved me before the party.

I was very glad that the chick looked so cool and respectable-like on a Sunday morning, so we grabbed a cab back to my pad and I got my eye-balls mobile again after a cup of coffee.

I found that she was the nicest chick I had talked to for a long, long time.

I sent her home before I was tempted to change the whole scene into another small forgettable lay, and slept until six that evening. When I woke up she was still on my mind and I decided to do something about her; professionally, that is. I get these hunches about people once in a while. Sometimes it pays off, sometimes not, but when the hunching is there, it's always worth a try.

I got my secretary to find out where Aggie's Hearts and Flowers was in Brighton (that's a hell of a name to forget), and the next Friday night, I drove down to find out for myself if she had the qualifications I was looking for.

The club was on the borderline between squalid and cute; a long narrow room at street level, with a raised dais at one end for the performer, a bar, fruit machines, pink hearts and purple flowers painted all over the walls, and as many tables and chairs as they could squeeze into fifteen by thirty foot. Upstairs, there were two roulette wheels and a couple of black-jack tables presided over by some bored women in imitation bunny outfits. A hell of a place to rumble talent, but I've seen worse on my travels. "Betting limit—five bob, dear," said a cold croupier as I laid out my ten bob on the seventeen.

I waited until I heard Maggie begin before I went downstairs. I always do. It's no good letting them register the presence of a notable manager before they start; it tightens their throats and they try too hard.

*　　*　　*

Her voice lashed out over their heads like a stock-whip and fell around their ears like confetti. I never thought the girl had it in her. She belted and purred and spat and crooned and the Brighton bullies shouted for more.

I could tell she was singing for someone special, because after every number she tried to pierce the darkness with her eyes, searching out someone—a face that would make the whole thing hang together. I wondered if it was me.

She was wearing a purple daisy painted on her right cheek-bone and an orange mini. Her hair looked dark red under the lights, her skin white-on-white, and with those huge, black-fringed searching eyes, she certainly made an electrifying impact.

I had already decided to sign her.

*　　*　　*

Girl singers are hard to manage. They demand maximum effort, what with images and clothes and the right sort of song to project their special thing—their special emotional climate which must communicate its mood to the public . . . like, for instance, Lulu is always a bouncy, tough, sexy, little fun chick with a golden heart underneath it all; Dionne Warwick is an impeccable black one, whose flawless musicianship shows through a wounded soul; Blossom Dearie is a little singing bird who has made her nest in your lap, and so on.

Maggie Truro was an amalgamation of intensity and little-girl-lost—little girl searching—little girl hiding big feelings—a lady-bug with soul.

But little lady-bugs with soul are not so rare. There was the mother of them all, Judy Garland, who flashed her little lady-bug soul at the audience for years, in fact, ever since 'Some-where over the Rainbow.' There is Pet Clark, another little lady-bug if ever I saw one, and countless other would-be lady-bugs perched around on bushes all waiting to be told that their house is on fire. But this girl has a strange white voice, no vibrato, a pure, untouched-by-human-hand voice, no gift wrappings.

"Now, if I can distil that small, raw voice out of all the copying and junk that inevitably surround it, if I can capture its unselfconscious presence on record, then I've got a proposition . . ." That's what I was thinking as I watched her take two encores at Aggie's and decline to sing a third, probably because she had gone through all her material.

\*     \*     \*

She sang to me going home, but only because I asked her to. I wanted to get an undiluted dose of that small, raw voice again before I rang Harry Sansom the next morning and told him what sort of a song he should write for her, what sort of a song would project her. Of course, he would *meet* her for himself, but I like to give my people an idea of the direction they are going—not a road map, just an idea of the *direction*.

\*     \*     \*

"Have you got any little-lady-bug-with-soul songs, Harry?" I asked him next morning, "Kind of like Pet Clark, only harsher, younger, ballsier and been-stood-up-by-the-guy songs . . . or, maybe never-even-met-the-guy kind of song? Definitely not Minnie Mouse. Don't say yes if you haven't . . . I know *you*, you bastard, you'll scrape the words off some dug-in number called, 'I want you ten times a day' and call it 'I'm weeping for you in the kitchen'.

"Listen, Harry, I want it *original* . . . this chick has got a good thing going for her . . . she doesn't care . . . or maybe she does? . . . I dunno; anyway, I like her. Dig? You can meet her any time, probably on Wednesday?" I waited for Harry to make his usual objections; like he's "tied up for two years writing a great, new concerto"; like he's "flipped out and wants to give the whole thing up and disappear to Pakistan with Tariq Ali"; like he is "taking a course in Orgonomy and is leaving for Oslo on the next boat"; like "his best friend has just run off with his life savings and he has got to go to Greece for a couple of months to recuperate". He's always full of the most incredible excuses for not working, is my friend, Harry.

He gave me a new one that day—that his mother had been

arrested for shop-lifting in Cheboygan, Wisconsin, and he had to fly back to give her a character reference.

"That's the worst I've ever heard, Harry; who's writing your material these days? I'll meet you in the bar at the Aretusa at six-thirty tomorrow, before all the naffs get there. I'll ask the girl as well."

He's really a very reliable guy. I knew he'd be there.

\*　　\*　　\*

We had eaten all the olives and two platefuls of almonds before she arrived the next night. Eight o'clock, it was. She wore a turd-coloured dress with Indian beads hanging in a big 'V' around the neck, square-toed brown boots that zipped up inside the calf, and a long khaki mac, ex-Army and Navy Stores, thrown over her shoulders.

She walked in like she was at least a stockholder in the establishment, ordered a Campari soda, and sat on the high stool as though she meant to stay about two and a half minutes.

"This is Maggie Truro. Maggie, Harry Sansom."

Harry did his thing with her hand. I mean, he's picked up this Italian way of taking a woman's hand and holding it up as though he's going to kiss it and then doing a small bow over it instead. Kind of a put-on, but that's the way Harry is. It was only then that I saw how nervous she was. So did Harry.

"Did you get lost?" I said, "Harry and I are bloated with fat green olives, and wondering. How did the lesson go?"

"O God, she made me realise just how little I know. It was awful! I nearly didn't come at *all*. Are you really sure you want me to cut a record?" She gulped her drink like Griselda used to, in two big gulps. I had a strange moment, looking at her thin little neck swallowing down the Campari . . . a sudden apprehension for her . . . a reflex that told me if she hung around with us something might snap that pretty little neck just like Griselda's had snapped. But I kept my mouth shut. I didn't say, "Piss off out of here, little girl, and stay away from us eaters. Us eaters will take out your vitals, heart, liver, lights and all, and eat them one by one." I kept my mouth shut and let Harry give her a big rush. Harry did all the talking and I shut my mouth.

\*　　\*　　\*

" 'I am waiting for my life to begin'," said Harry, after we had dropped her off at her pad off the Tottenham Court Road. "I'll call it that: 'I am waiting for my life to begin'." He stayed seated in the back of the car after she got out and sang "I . . . yam . . . waiting-for-my-life-to-begin . . ." to different tunes, until he found one that suited, and by the time we got back to Chelsea, he had some lines as well.

"I can see the leaves from my window,
Bursting out of branches to the sky,
I can see my face in the window,
Lovers' lips meeting in my eye,
And I am . . . waiting for my life to begin
        waiting till I find
          myself in love again
      da da da da dadada
      dah dada . . .

Kind of like that, eh, Lew? That's the type of song you want to launch your little lady . . . because that's what she's doing, baby, that's what that little chick is waiting for—and if it's a *hit* . . . well, you can go on from there, right through her life, until I rewrite '*Non, rien de rien, Non, Je ne regrette rien*' (he sang) for Maggie Truro instead of Edith Piaf. How's about that for an idea, eh, Lew? You could sign her up for a fifty-year contract and do twenty-seven albums called 'The continuing saga of Maggie Truro'."

I could only see the top of Harry's head because he was stretched out on the back seat. It's hard to know what Harry thinks even if you're looking straight at him, because one of his eyes is independent and is looking out towards a distant horizon over your shoulder. But he has non-stop imagination and a good nose for people . . . I ask him for his opinion about nearly everybody.

"She's a sweet, nervous, little pussy who's waiting for her life to begin . . . and I wouldn't mind helping her start a few chapters," said Harry. "I'd have to hear her *sing* before I can tell you if she's *got* it or not," he added.

*    *    *

We sweated over that record, Harry and me. I got Johnny

Parsons (the best) to do the arrangement and we had six full sessions to get it right. I knew it would be a hit, but I also knew it would not stick around the Charts for very long. It was catchy and commercial, but did not have much staying power.

I gave it, and her, enormous promotion. I had her on every television programme from 'Crackerjack' to 'Late Night Line-up' and on every regional network in the British Isles. When I gauged that both she and the song had reached saturation point, I gave her a holiday, while Harry and I worked out the next step in her progress towards prominence in the pop world.

We decided on an L.P. featuring 'I am waiting for my life to begin', plus two or three Sansom originals and about six other re-hashes and new arrangements of old songs. I had already thought up the cover and title.

The cover would be made up like a huge, old-fashioned postcard, one of those early Edwardian affairs with pouter-pigeon ladies, penny-farthing bicycles, boaters and precious curls ... then mixed up with these there would be pictures of Maggie, in bloomers with a hockey stick, Maggie, asleep in the arms of a statue like Charlie Chaplin, Maggie chained outside 10 Downing Street, Maggie, lying naked on an immense bear-skin stroking its snout. It would be called 'Yours, Truro' ... corny and tasteful, an unbeatable combination.

We started serious work in the beginning of July, after I had had *my* holiday and Harry Sansom had had time to exhaust all his excuses and create.

One hot Friday night somewhere around the middle of July, I was lying on the floor listening to Sibelius—David Oistrach playing the concerto for violin (Opus 49), I remember it was; I had had one or two joints, but I was not really high. Well, Oistrach and me were poised and flying, wheeling and floating like hawks in the middle of a particularly fabulous part of the 'adagio di molto' passage, when I became aware of a great pounding on the front door. I was just high enough not to hurry or to feel furious. I carefully removed my earphones, switched off the machine and padded down the stairs wrapping a towel around my waist as I went.

There was Maggie Truro, a plaster-white faced, frantic Maggie Truro, who dragged me by the arm out into the street. A taxi was waiting outside with the meter still ticking over. I noticed that it read twenty-four shillings and sixpence. On the back seat a guy was stretched out and there was a bandage around his head.

She would not tell me anything until she had paid off the taxi-driver, who would not help us get the guy out of the back of the car, in fact, the bastard refused to move out of his seat. I opened the kerbside door. I took the guy's shoulders and heaved him out while Maggie waited on the pavement to help me take the weight of him once I had got him there. It was just as well that she *was* there, because my towel fell off with the effort of lifting him and I was in danger of being arrested for indecent exposure.

Between us we carried him into the house and laid him on the sofa in the living-room. He was very heavy.

When I got to look at him in the light I saw that he was a spade; well, not exactly a spade, but somewhere in that direction, and the bandage he wore was soaked with blood. Blood had run down the side of his neck into his sweater. He was hanging on to a small satchel with a tatty-looking folder sticking out of it, but his eyes were shut. I tried to take the satchel away from him but he still clung onto it although I could see that he was not fully conscious.

Maggie was fluttering about, getting a cloth from the bathroom to wipe the blood off his head, pouring some brandies, taking off his shoes.

"This is my friend Jackson. He's just been shot, I think, but he's not going to die . . ." she flashed at me on her way to the kitchen for glasses. I've never bought a proper bar . . . just keep the bottles lined up on the floor.

"Where did you find him?"

"Well, I was waiting at his house in Acton; outside it, as a matter of fact. He lives in one room and the landlady won't let him have female visitors inside the room. Anyway, I was waiting there at eight, he told me to be there at eight. A taxi drew up and he said 'Get in' in a funny voice. I did, and got a terrible fright because I could see he'd been hurt. He told me that he was taking a lady her poetry back after he'd read it, and her husband appeared out of nowhere and started shooting a revolver at him. Luckily the first shot creased his skull and sent him flying. The poor lady tried to patch him up, but she was so worried that he might go to the police, that he pretended it was nothing, hardly a scratch, and let her get him a taxi. The blood did not stop, and by the time he got to me, he was fainting. He must get some professional attention. The last thing he said to me before he passed out was that I mustn't take him to a public hospital." Breathless she was, but still controlled.

"So you brought him *here*?"

"I thought of you, because you know hundreds of people and you've got so many contacts . . . surely you know a friendly doctor who'll come and have a look at him, and sew up his head without asking lots of questions."

She was being very calm and sensible but I could tell by the grating in her voice that she was only just keeping herself together.

I picked up the telephone.

"O.K., sweetheart," I said, using my best Humphrey Bogart lisp, "I'll see that your Clyde gets his holes filled in. Not all his holes—only the ones that hurt. But remember, baby, I'm doing this for *you*. For *you*, baby, and when remembrance day comes round, I hope you'll be ready to deliver." I leered at her and rolled my eyeballs up.

She laughed, not very convincingly, but good enough to get by. She had hardly taken her eyes off the guy's face since we put him on the sofa.

\*     \*     \*

I called Abel Mee, M.B., B.SC., who is a great buddy of mine and who lives fifty yards down the road. Abel Mee is the most confidence-inspiring name for a doctor, I've ever heard.

"Hi, Abel, it's me."

"Who's me?"

"You."

"Ha Ha, Hamlyn."

"Uh huh. Listen, Abel, would you drop what you're doing, or whoever it is, and come on down here. Bring all your gloop. I have a small emergency on my hands. O.K.? Good boy. Won't take you more than three minutes, I'd say, knowing your speed."

Maggie handed me a brandy. She had poured a large one for herself as well.

"No thank you, baby. I'm going to have a long glass of water to brisk me up."

I went up to put on some clothes before Abel came. He would probably get a whole wrong idea of the scene if he found me in the buff.

*   *   *

"A crease in the left temporal lobe," said Abel, "a bullet wound which would have caused instantaneous death had it been a quarter of an inch further to the right. Your friend has an agreeably thick skull and is, therefore, in no serious danger. Twelve stitches and an injection of Pentathol I have given him. Don't move him. I'll come back tomorrow and have a look at the head. He'll probably have delayed shock and concussion. Nothing to worry about."

Abel is one of those drawling, relaxed Englishmen with impeccable manners who are schooled in the art of public decorum, but who are like jack rabbits in private. I have heard Abel described as 'The Harley Street stud'.

He went home, however, having given Maggie a long, probing perusal, but not having asked anything more complicated than whether either one of *us* had shot him. We both said no and Maggie added, quite truthfully, that neither of us had been present when it happened. "It was some sort of silly accident," she said, "I think one of his friends was playing around with a gun that he had no licence for. That's why Jackson didn't want to go to a hospital."

"I see," said Abel, smiling in his lugubrious way. "People can be such fools with guns."

*   *   *

Maggie insisted on sleeping the night, so as to be there when her friend woke up; I gave her some sheets and a blanket and she made herself up a bed on the other sofa. She covered the guy up, and I took the satchel out of his arms. I was very curious to see what was inside that bag. I have always had a fascination for little bulging bags that people hang on to even when they're unconscious.

Maggie and I talked for a while, mostly about her L.P. She had cut three tracks which I liked, and one which I thought was a load of dog's dollops. I didn't want to upset her any more that night, so I just said that the backing had gotten fouled up and that we would have to re-record. I sat on the floor until I could see her eyes closing, and then I surreptitiously took the prize upstairs so that I could examine its contents in peace.

*　　*　　*

I went through the folder first. It was filled with a whole pile of loose-leaf papers with poetry written on them. I read a few and they were quite sexy, not scintillating, but sweet and prettily written . . . some of them were signed 'Cynthia Boddington'; not a very sexy name, I thought.

Besides the folder, the satchel contained note-books.

There were seven fat ones in all and I spent the rest of the night reading them. When the noisy, early-morning birds started up and light began to filter through the blinds, trucks began to roar, I went into the bathroom to lie in a steaming tub to finish them.

*　　*　　*

They were all marked quite clearly, according to dates, and inside the hard cover of the first one, written in a rounded unformed hand,

> Matthew Jackson,
> Hambro Island. West Indies.
> Northern Hemisphere.
> The World. 7th of April, 1956.

The words had been scored deep, written over at least three times to make sure that they could never be erased, and there were little drawings of dolphins and seahorses dotted about. On the first page there was an indian-ink sketch of a nasturtium with leaves. 'Tropaelum majur' was neatly printed above. Underneath the same rounded child-like hand had written, 'If you bite the tip off the spur of a tropaelum majur and suck, you get there before the bee.'

The succeeding pages were also covered with the likenesses of flowers and plants, but I noticed that as the drawings grew smaller, so the comments grew longer. By the end of the first note-book, pictures had disappeared almost altogether.

About halfway through, there was an erotic poem called 'Ode to Black Lily' which was extremely beautiful and simple, and another poem called 'You and me, Baby Doc Bates, we're here!' A shout of exultation in being. They were all written in a totally unaffected manner, just what the boy thought and saw. I found them terrific. There was one called 'Joanna Windy-Belly's Bunions', and 'Brodie's Revenge', a story about a man who used secret farting as a terrible form of punishment on the boy who was forced to sleep in the same room with him; both were hilarious.

The second book was devoted to the building of an air-strip and a story called 'Sidney's Great Tree-felling Exploit', about a man who tried to blow up a tree with dynamite but who only succeeded in making a huge hole in the ground which immediately filled up with water and became a bottomless lake. 'Ode to Black Lily' (Opus II), and a description of a boy reef-fishing with an Indian surveyor who had a desperate fear of being eaten by a shark. 'Artocarpus altilis' (the Breadfruit Tree) was a poem in praise of his grandmother's cooking, and there was a dissertation (illustrated) on the migratory habits of 'Bobolinks', some sort of bird from Canada.

It was all told with such truth and reality that I found it impossible to put the books down or to disbelieve a word.

In the third and fourth books I could sense a certain awareness of the world outside creeping in—he had been to Jamaica and taken ship as a merchant seaman. There was a new type of poem, filled with loneliness, and called 'The Voyage of the Maruja' about a vessel which plies between Miami, Galveston, Panama and Kingston, and a poem which showed that he had started coming up against discrimination. This was it.

> You ask me, *Who* are you?
> *What* are you? *Why* are you?
> You never speak it with your breath,
> You breathe it through your eyes,
> I can only show you—
> But now you will not look.
> I will tattoo my pedigree on my arm
> If it's so important to you—
> Or my number, if you'll do the same.

*   *   *

On the next page:

> Making love one day
> With a girl they callin May-May
> Makin love one day
> With a girl that's
> Known as May-May
> A little bit of May-May
> Down by the railway

And she said:

> Baby, don't bite me,
> Don't do that to me honey
> I never had a man treat me this way
> Oh, Oh, Oh, no, no, dou-dou, darlin,
> With the cause-result
> You're makin me weak, so weak
> Stop, Sparrow, stop!
> (Song of the Sparrow)          (Trinidad 1962)

\* \* \*

There were also some quotations from Shakespeare:

> But in a sieve I'll thither sail,
> And like a rat without a tail
> I'll do, I'll do, and I'll do.

headed a group of poems, and

> "Men have died from time to time, and worms have eaten
> them, but not for love"

preceded 'Ode to Black Lily' (Opus III) Black Lily had married
Brodie while he was away at sea.

Book four was devoted to an analysis of himself as the half-
caste and the conflicting attitudes of people towards him in
each of the ports he had visited on his voyage. He was learning
at first hand about 'nigger' and 'black mother-fucker' and
'whitey', the big, unspecific, indelible hates that have grown
up and ruled mens' lives. In Galveston *Texas* he was a 'jigger-
boo' and no one looked further than that; he received a very
painful kick from the kindly-looking proprietor of a drug store,

who walked back into his store dusting his hands and exclaiming to the rest of his customers in an amazed voice, "Well, how do you like that black bum sittin' hisself down in here an' orderin' a shake, cool as y'r Auntie Abigail."

In Kingston, where he was paid off, he bought himself a new suit, the first he had ever owned, but immediately noticed that black people treated him with the scarcely concealed contempt they reserve for a 'jumped-up' white boy.

He grappled the problem without bitterness but with a great curiosity, and finally came to a conclusion at the end of the book that, since neither black nor white people could accept him completely, he must be the originator of a new sect of people called 'hybrids' (Elliot Brodie's word), *he* had written in brackets. "I am a hybrid."

"An *identity*," he wrote, "which stops me having to feel that I continually make excuses for my own existence—Hybrids will probably take a long time to make themselves felt, but we *must inevitably* be acceptable to all thinking mankind one day."

Book five commenced with a poem called 'I am the proof' which took up the theme of his 'hybridism' and pursued it with relentless logicality. It was a good poem and the thought suddenly came into my head that perhaps it could be set to music—a Brecht-Weill kind of song with a steel-band backing reggae beat instead of the thirties staccato thump.

It would be a great gimmick to produce a long-player which had a proper controversial theme like this one promised to be. I looked back over the other poems and decided that there was enough material to cover several L.P.s and I still had three more books to read. A strange excitement began to ferment in my brain and I stopped reading to smoke a joint and try to inject a little lucidity and less aggression into my thoughts.

For a while I lay on my bed staring at Vriksaka of Gyaspur. I think I expected her to open her sweet, stone mouth and pour out a few answers. I was wondering what sort of voice this Jackson had, who lay downstairs on my sofa. I knew what his childhood had been like. I probably knew more about him than I knew about Harry or Maggie, or my secretary—people I saw every day—but I had never heard him speak.

I was tempted to go down and take another look at him to remind myself what he was like, but I resisted, anticipating Maggie's waking and discovering that his satchel was missing.

I lay and pondered on what was the best way to present this future leader of the misfits. It would *really* be interesting if he had a good voice.

I thought about all the long-haired, protesting, young guys with their gear and their shit, their beads and their vanity, who sang their little songs and made their bread. I knew that mostly they were nice, lower-middle class lads; but what were they really trying to say? What were they protesting against? If you analysed one of their lyrics, it was generally a protest against work . . . or a plea to let them fuck when and where and who they wanted . . . or an exploitation of one of their hash-fantasies . . . or a song in praise of loving or shit or peace . . . but all so vague; a nebulous strumming and thumping that kept the idiots twitching and me with my pockets full.

It would be fascinating to assist the rise of a guy who had a genuine beef and a solution that meant dynamite in places like Rhodesia and South Africa, where his mere existence was a crime—intermarriage being a punishable offence in those countries.

My limbs began to tremble as I lay there while the first light of dawn crept spider-still across roofs and rivers, and through webs of television aerials. I felt an anticipatory pulse throughout my body, a strange, new, pleased sense of occasion and a delight at being alive—to pull the strings and plug in the electricity.

\* \* \*

At ten o'clock in the morning, refreshed from my bath, I was up and making coffee. I felt no evil effects from my sleepless night, only a drought thirst and a draught-horse hunger. I squeezed oranges into three large glasses and gulped down the overflow. I threw slices of brown bread into the toaster and sizzled bacon on the skillet; I broke ten eggs into the mixer, a dash of salt and pepper, and set it whirring. Then I put two egg-shells in the coffee percolator like my mother always did, poured the egg mixture and a blob of butter into a brass-bottomed saucepan, lit the gas, and sat back to wait for breakfast.

Maggie arrived, looking delicious, with her face still full of sleep.

"Mmmmm," she said, "what a lovely smell!"

"How's your friend?" I said. I had repacked his little bag and put it down behind the kitchen door.

"He's still asleep."

She got a wooden spoon and started stirring the scrambled eggs and when the toast popped up she was ready with the butter.

"Domestic Science School," she said, "is better than Girton. I'm not much good at talking in the morning."

We put everything on a tray and carried it through to the terrace that faced the garden at the back of the house. As we walked through the living-room, Jackson woke up.

He did not just wake up. He jumped up, his eyes wide open, trying in one second of illumination to assess me, the room, where his satchel was, where *he* was, the sun, the whole dream of us. His face was an exclamation point, his fingers crept carefully up his skull to feel the new stitches and his eyes, which were extraordinary in the bright, bright light of July, asked Maggie for an explanation.

Maggie introduced us and explained.

He had slightly blood-shot blue eyes surrounded by a brown boundary, and they looked down on me with a curious intensity that could have been caused by the drug. I was being scrutinised with the open curiosity a child uses, although beneath that regard I could detect a very adult vigilance. He asked Maggie where she had put his bag. "It's by the kitchen door," I answered for her.

We did not say much while we ate. All of us tucked in, munching toast and gulping coffee like ravening beasts; we had to satisfy our stomachs before we made any real contact. Maggie went back to the kitchen, made some more toast and brought out the rest of the coffee, and his satchel. We slackened the momentum of eating and sat back.

Now it was my turn to examine *him*, but I did so covertly, while I asked him questions for which I already knew the answers—like where he came from, how long had he been in England, what was he doing here, etc.

He was a tall, robust-looking guy, well-built, with hair that started away from his forehead, wide cheekbones, skin coffee-coloured. His lips were well-defined and slightly protruding; front teeth were spaced and large, but the thing you could not get away from was those strange two-tone eyes. His voice was deep, sing-song, and he said 'out' like a Canadian, never sounded the 'g' in 'ing' and said 'som' for 'sum'. I liked him immediately.

I could see that Maggie not only liked him, but was unable to exist without him. She unconsciously mirrored all his movements. She radiated great golden skeins of love through the space between them and even when her back was to him, you felt that her eyes had inverted themselves to watch him through the back of her skull.

And so the three of us sat, on that brilliant Saturday morning, Maggie basking in her love and the sun, Jackson contemplating his Kewless future with philosophical humour, me, still holding my excitement and my sense of occasion inside me alongside my undigested breakfast.

I had no desire to be anywhere else in the world at that moment.

"I read all your stuff last night," I said, because the time had arrived to discuss serious things, to give ourselves a direction, to consolidate the coincidences.

"Yes," he said. It was not a question. All the birds that had been chirping and bouncing for crumbs, seemed to have flown into other gardens, so that their noise came from far away. He was neither surprised nor annoyed, and we sat in an undiminishing silence waiting for me to speak again.

"I'd like to do something about it."

"Have you thought about it already, or did that just come off the top of your head?" he asked, smiling straight into my eyes and rubbing his sore scalp.

"I thought about it while I was reading, I thought about it while we were making breakfast and I'm thinking about it now," I said, giving him his direct gaze straight back through his pupils. Zap. Zap. Zap.

"O.K.," he said, leaning way back in his chair and expanding his chest. "I'm willing, if you are."

Our first contract was as simple as that.

\*　　\*　　\*

For the remainder of that Saturday we sat on the terrace and discussed his work. Maggie went out and bought us some sandwiches and sausages from the pub on the corner at lunchtime, and we exchanged ideas, debated strategies, felt out the workings of each others' minds, sipped lagers and champed sausages between our teeth, while birds sang and insects mated and London moved around us. Abel Mee dropped in to have a look at Jackson's head and declared his amazement at the rapidity of his patient's recovery and, late in the afternoon, my answering service rang to ask how long I was going to remain incommunicado, for Heaven's sake, as some people had called as many times as twenty times and were getting desperate.

"To hell with them. Tell them I've gone to Hong Kong for the weekend," I said and hung up.

* * *

From there on in, I dropped everything I was doing with other singers and devoted all my energy and imagination to Jackson. I had enough assistants and ambitious young lions to take care of my other clients, Maggie included, and this was something *special* . . . since Ossie's time, I had not experienced the same boundless belief and exuberance. I had another original on my hands, and I was going to exploit the situation with as much drive and attention as I could muster. Besides, it gave me more of a charge than shit, or fucking, or eating, or sleeping . . . and that's the only other kicks I know about.

Jackson, the man, was a different proposition than anyone I had ever handled. There was always something happening wherever the guy was. He could not help creating reactions, actions, moods, laughter, love, anger, envy, joy, excitement. Perhaps that is the operative word . . . excitement . . . he was so substantially alive, that it jazzed everyone else up and made them remember the time they spent with him forever.

His was a genius of 'diuturnity'. At least that's how some critic described him in one of the Sunday papers. They grub up these obscure words from their *Roget's Thesaurus* and it takes no college graduates to find out what they actually mean. And that's how the Jackson Cult began. If some old fud with a gun hadn't tried to do away with him, he would probably be digging little holes in the ground and planting beans on his island right now. But that's not the way it turned out.

From that day onwards we worked together. I had decided to move very cautiously at first . . . not put him in front of a live audience with no experience . . . to try recording after recording until we got exactly what we were looking for . . . a saleable product that had a sledgehammer kick. A new Hybrid image that gave them a whole acre of nuts to chew on, before the next walloper hit them between the eyes.

Jackson with his work, was fastidious and intuitive and quite tireless. He could do a ten-hour session without sleep and not show a red eye or a white tongue. He pursued perfection in form and simplicity like a ratter on the scent of an army of mice, and even when I was satisfied, he would demand extra sessions, tiny changes of intonation, a swannee—A river whistle, mosquito noises, kettle drums, french horns, or the sound of an inner tube losing air. Crazy, but they worked.

I suggested that he use his poem that started 'You ask me who are you' as a demo adding a verse, and I got Harry to help with the music.

Harry came to the house armed with his usual quiverful of excuses, ready to greet and reject yet another hopeful untalented; he was just as surprised as I was when Jackson picked up a guitar and strung off a few chords like Manitas de Plata. He told us that he had once lived with a guy who was crazy about the guitar and that he had learnt out of self-defence. He and Harry became bosom buddies in one day.

But Jackson could be as blunt and immovable as a ten-ton truck with locked brakes if he disagreed with me on something. Like the time I wanted to introduce black-and-white heart-shaped buttons for fans, he just gave me an unconditional no and said that he would not have anyone sticking any little buttons on themselves for his sake. "If you want to kill something dead," he said, "the surest way is to stick a pin through it, put a label on it and hang it on the wall behind glass."

I got the message, although, by that time, I had stopped arguing with him over details. In the beginning it was very different.

It was inevitable that two such volatile characters as ourselves should do battle, and we did, grand slanging matches, punch-ups, angers and furies that lasted through long sessions while musicians and recording engineers sat smoking and smirking and finally gave up listening to play poker. I admit that there were certain things that got between my *idea* of Jackson and the real man. One of these was the fact that for quite a while I could not accept that he was a true phenomenon, that he was not a self-seeker, that he spent nine-tenths of his money *importing earth* on to his mangy little island, for Chrissake. He really meant every word he said, and he could say no with such uncompromising sureness.

I could not believe that anyone connected with the pop world in the capacity of 'performer' could be anything but a cypher. I suppose I had been associating with too much drek.

*       *       *

Our first effort was a single. We used the demo, and I worked out later that approximately five hundred and eighty-five man hours were spent on its production. The 'A' side was his poem and we called it 'If you'll do the same'. The verse was new:

> Black Queen, White Knight,
> Sitting in your squares,
> White Queen, Black Knight,
> Forming into pairs.
> The bishops flirt across the board
> Diagonals in a row,
> Castle and pawn, rising dawn,
> How does your garden grow?
>
> You ask me, Who are you?
> What are you? Why are you?
> You do not speak it with your breath,
> You breathe it through your eyes.
> I can only show you—
> But now you will not look.
> I will tattoo my pedigree on my arm
> If it's so important to you,
> Or my number, if you'll do the same.
>             if you'll do the same.

*       *       *

Harry wrote an incredible tune for the song. It was sombre and funny at the same time . . . an ironical tune, full of quirky stops and half-tones, and it fitted Jackson's style of delivery

203

perfectly. As a performer Jackson was extraordinary. He had no precedents, but his voice had an edge to it that resembled Aznavour's. He talked rather than sang some lines. He shouted full-throated. He swooped on words like Bob Dylan, but was at all times unpredictable and himself.

I was astounded by his boldness, his infallible sense of the correct phrasing, his timing. I let him choose the flip side of the record, stipulating only that it had to have a more up-beat theme.

It was called 'Chelsea Fig'. A concoction of mad lyrics about a fig tree that grows under Chelsea Bridge, has shaded the greatest assortment of lovers in its three hundred years and is now waiting with relish for next spring to come.

Both sides became hits.

The Pop world jumped on him with the avidity of starving monkeys and I feared that he might be carried away by the deluge. He was the biggest thing since the Beatles, but I insisted that he made no public appearances until his first long-player was ready three months later.

I designed the jacket of that record and I still get a charge every time I see it. I got a guy I know who does photographs of insects and microscopic flora and fauna for textbooks (a blow-up expert) to take some shots of Jackson's eyeball in colour. The front cover was a huge blue and brown eyeball staring out, and written in white fluorescent letters in the centre of the pupil was 'Hybrid', made to look like the light shining from a reflection in the actual eye. On the back, there were five more smaller blow-ups of eyes, in squares—green, blue, tobacco-brown, black and grey eyes. There was no blurb, just a short statement.

"This record is dedicated to all the other hybrids of the world. It is meant to justify my own existence and to give me and millions like me, an identity which is not an apology. I do not acknowledge that the sins of the father will be visited upon the children, nor the children's children. I believe in love with no guilt. The only way that this planet can survive."

I had only ten thousand pressed, but these were snapped up before they reached the stores, so I stopped chickening after that and went ahead with a million more; when the million was sold out only a few weeks later, I pressed a million more and so on and so on, until 'Hybrid' topped the four million mark and out-sold 'Sergeant Pepper'. The word was on everyone's lips, the songs were in everyone's heads, and Jackson was an overnight millionaire.

Personally, I think it was the most imaginative, highly polished piece of work he ever accomplished, but there are many people who would argue with that statement, I guess. Anyway, it took off like a jumbo jet and that's what mattered most.

Of course, there were violent reactions. Naturally, it was banned in South Africa, Rhodesia, Pakistan, Turkey, Greece, Argentina and Australia, and newspapers had to cope with a barrage of letters from protesting parents, racialists, W.A.S.P.s, Black Power groups, 'Keep Britain White' and John Birch Societies; it was the one time the extremists of both colours got together . . . in their condemnation of Jackson.

I took the Albert Hall for his first public appearance, but there was such pandemonium, fists flying, women shrieking, pepper bombs and maniacs brandishing sticks and knuckle-dusters, that we called the whole thing off and I banned personal confrontations with the public after that.

In fact, I had to hire a troop of body-guards to protect Jackson wherever he went.

To the young people on the campuses throughout colleges in the United States and in British Universities, he was living proof of the basic rightness of integration and it was in those places that he became the Cult, the Speaker, Two-Tone Hybrid and Leader of 'The New-Chosen'.

\* \* \*

He employed a firm of accountants to sort out his enormous tax commitment in Britain and when he had enough capital, he formed a company which bought six tankers to run a non-stop service between the mainland of Florida and Hambro Island transporting cargoes of earth to subsidise the meagre soil of the island. He left the distribution of the stuff to his father, Sidney.

For us at the centre of the holocaust, life became more and more constricted, but *we* had inaugurated the monster and we had to live with it. Jackson bought the house next to mine and we built a connecting passage so that he would not be exposed to the hundreds of sightseers and fans who hung around the pavement to gawp and wait for any surprise appearances. His secretary was a Mrs. Cynthia Omerod (née Boddington) who was loyal, charming and infinitely patient and who showered motherly affection on us all. It was explained to me later that it was *her* husband who had creased Jackson's skull for him and only *then* did I remember the poems in the folder signed Cynthia Boddington; the sexy sonnets.

Maggie lived in the house too. She made some more records and she and Mrs. Omerod took it in turns to clear up and do the cooking. We were a peculiarly isolated group, isolated by fame which believe me, can be tougher than the penitentiary.

Within a year of his initial success, Jackson became a living legend and, of course, there was the usual rash of imitators who called themselves 'Half-breed' and 'Mr. Grey' and 'Mulatto Membrane', but none of them got anywhere near his originality, his truth, or his natural instinct for capturing the imagination of the public.

Denigrators lined up to take cracks at him, but he had always expected them, so they faised him not at all; in fact, he enjoyed reading their swipes at his work, especially as each new recording went to the top of the charts the day it was released. Attacks on his personal life he was not so keen on, and when they involved Maggie, he became quite apoplectic.

He installed a gym in his basement, fruit machines for Maggie in the hall, a library and an enormous chessboard set into the floor, whose pieces were two feet tall. He cared for his own garden at the back of the house until someone shot a barrelful of buck-shot at him from out of one of the houses overlooking his. He quit after that.

I received a daily mail of about fifty abusive letters myself, so I don't know how many *he* got. It is remarkable how people, who are ordinary, surface-respectable and respected citizens, sit down in a frenzy of destroyed hopes and self-disgust, and work out all their frustrations writing letters filled with every form of violence, perversion and lust of which the human mind is capable. Still, I suppose it's better than saving it up until they commit mayhem.

On the other side of the coin, there was adoration; the spontaneous combustion of people who had wanted a figurehead and had at last found one. He could not help but inspire a terrific fascination; people wanted to know everything about this new idol—what he wore at home, ate, chewed, spat, smelt like, whether he wore contact lenses to make his eyes two-tone, if he was queer, how he wrote his work, what he slept in and who with, whether his snored, what he telephone number was, how many times he crapped a day . . . poor Jackson—he took it all like a man, but when he could not get outside, I could see the pressure begin to wilt him around the edges.

Maggie devised incredible disguises for him to escape from the house without a pursuing mob—blonde wigs, workman's overalls, nun's outfits, white dentist's jackets, jebbellahs, moustaches of all colours, and hats . . . she had a room that looked like a Wardrobe in a Film Studio where they are making seven different productions at once.

We had plenty of laughs and Jackson would sometimes clown about wearing such horrible conglomerations of false teeth, padded bellies and costumes that even the most uninterested bystander would have followed him out of sheer curiosity.

I watched over him with extreme vigilance.

My reasons are not very hard to imagine.

Firstly, I owned twenty-five per cent of his gross and that was not bird-droppings, baby; secondly, I never knew what was going to happen next. Thirdly, I was fascinated by the man himself. A gladiator had entered the arena with the nonchalance of Manolete. He was not a stupid man. I think he knew exactly what he was risking and what he was forfeiting . . . I watched him because you always watch the unfolding of a mantle, the red flag flouted in the face of a bull, the charges and the passes, the close shaves and the gorings . . . excitement gives you fluxes of adrenalin and stops you getting old.

# Part Five

Part Five

# 11

## Matthew Jackson

I KNOW NOW that I am on a journey. It is not a journey that goes over earth or through air or across water. It probably travels about the distance of a good knock-out punch. It is a journey into the centre of me. Maybe this journey began the night I went down to Snipe's Bay with old Doc Bates, the night Lily had her baby and Doc talked about the half-caste stuff, maybe it was Elliot Brodie who started me off . . . or maybe it started at the moment of my conception . . . Anyway, I'm on it, and already its led me into a position where I'm near enough being a prisoner of what I've said and done to be uncomfortable. I cannot look at my *self* in the world clearly yet, but I feel that what I am putting out is being picked up by some people and made part of *their* particular journeys, and that is good. That is important. Inside myself, I have felt sometimes stupid at provoking such hot gusts of disapproval and such sea-cradles of love . . . I have been through whole armies of varying emotions by myself about people's reactions to what I am saying. But *that* is not going to change anything, so I have stopped wasting my energy on excessive reactions and started trying to figure out more about the *me* and the *them* behind the reactions.

I know that more than anything I want to be able to tell them. I want to be able to tell them not just through words, but music and colours and experiences and trees and food and eyes. And I want to grow things. I want to make an atmosphere where people can *really* see what's important and not just tinsel surface shit that satisfies all the conditioned needs which this society has trumped up to keep itself afloat. I want my journey to take me anywhere just so long as I don't betray myself into stagnancy and repetition.

All this last year I have had a gnawing in my brain, a nibbling on the fishing line that joins up what I *feel* with what

I *know*; not a giant tug of a runaway grouper, just tiddlers and jacks whisking around making a nuisance . . . Then, bang, one morning the big strike—I woke up and knew that I had to go home. I had to get home to Hambro, back to the roots and the beginning of the journey. Had to get out of the big city, the house on Cheyne Walk, out of those used-up airs and graces, out of merchandising and telephone talk, radio so bright and Hahaha, television in the night-time like sinking into nothingness, studios, dead air and no vibrations; looking at my hands I can see they haven't done anything for too long, feel dry and porous, sponge hands. Time to move.

No one in the world so pleased as Maggie when I told her time to move. Singing and trilling round the house, giggling with Cynthia in the kitchen, swearing and shouting at her old fruit-machines, grinning all the time when it rained and sleeted. I grabbed her and wrassled her till she cried out in that put-on Jamaica accent she picked up somewhere, "Stop, stop! man, I faintin' from all dis lovin'."

My Grandma May, last thing she said to me was never let any little bird suss that she got in under your skin, otherwise she might try to peck her way out; but not my Maggie. She is gentle, my girl. She is a gentle, headstrong, vulnerable, tough, sweet girl. She is easily hurt and is often screwing herself up with worries about things she can't control . . . like once, before a concert in Hyde Park which Lew had arranged for me to do, we had to sit in the back of the car for an hour and a half while police cleared a way through the crowd. Kids rocked the car, smashed a window, batted on the roof, stared and shouted, screamed and smeared kisses on every piece of available glass. Poor Maggie . . . she locked her eyes up so tight that tears came out the ends of them . . . she hung on to my hand and whimpered like a little girl who thinks that if she shuts her eyes she's invisible . . . so long as she keeps her eyes shut all the spookies and duppies and bad bogeymen in the world can not harm her, because she's not really *there*.

And that is my Maggie, frightened and loving, but proud and telling me she has no past and no loyalty to anyone but me.

I want her to be with me but she has to make up her own mind about where she is, where she is going. No use pushing and pulling people. Specially the ones who keep us warm in the night.

\* \* \*

I told Lew that I was going home for a holiday. He was worried, but he lent me his Lear jet to make the trip. It is his newest toy so it was quite a gesture.

He wanted to come with me at first, bring the whole circus —bodyguards, Cynthia, secretaries and Harry Sansom. But I said *wait*—no use rushing all those people into an area smaller than the West End. I wanted to see what was happening with Sidney and the soil distribution first, and I was right, because the moment I looked down out of the sky I saw that Sidney had been messing up. I asked the pilot to circle the island a few times, take a good look.

New tarmac and hangar on the air-strip, a big fancy hotel sticking up like a sore thumb, big green golf-course spotted with white bunkers, two new lakes in the middle, but no fields under cultivation, no new road down the middle of the island to Snipe's Bay . . . looked like everything stopped where the golf-course ended. I couldn't believe it.

Ever since I made the first record and earned the bread to start importing soil to Hambro I had been waiting for this moment; to look down on my island and see it flourishing with bananas and pineapples, corn—*crops*, worthy of the name . . . It is the dream of my childhood, my grandfather's dream, maybe even my grandfather's father's dream too. It means more to me than the fame and the excitement of being able to create the songs and say what I want. I don't know exactly why my songs make the impression they do, but I *do* know why this dream of covering the island with earth is so important to me. It is to be the re-creation of Utopia, a self-supporting microcosm of what the world should be. There will be no segregational ideas here. No money. There will be enough food so that all can share. It will be a joy to help in sowing and harvest. Writers and musicians and painters will want to come and live here. There will be no passports or papers to fill out. There will be a state of beautiful anarchy. It *can* work on an island as small as this, but only if the island is not dependent on the outside world for food and necessities. Only if none of us gets the greedy bug.

I found a passage in Sir Thomas More's Second book of *Utopia*. He says:

'I can perceive nothing but a certain conspiracy of rich men procuring their own commodities under the name and title of the 'Commonwealth'. They invent and devise all means and crafts, first how to keep safely, without fear of losing what they have unjustly gathered together, and next how to hire and abuse the work and labour of the poor for as little money as may be. How different in Utopia, where the desire for money with the use thereof is utterly secluded and banished! How great a heap of cares is cut away! Yea, poverty itself, which only seemed to lack money if money were gone, it also would decrease and vanish away.'

I love the man who wrote that. I understand him. He is fighting city hall. So am I. He is the sort of man I want to be, not a philanthropist spraying out his money through a gilt hose, not a politician backed by organisations run by the 'rich men' More talks about, not a performer only concerned with keeping his image lovable and cuddly for the public. I want to build a lasting Utopia in the place I know best.

So when I looked down out of Lew Hamlyn's Lear Jet and saw the big status-symbol golf-course, the four and a half star hotel, the silly lakes that do nothing except set off the status-symbol golf-course, I would cheerfully have dropped Sidney into one of those lakes wearing nothing but cement boots and a big smile.

But when we got down on the ground and they all came swinging out to meet us I could only feel a big joy to see everyone again . . . Grandma May and Libby all dressed up and all the kids grown a couple of feet each and new ones bobbing about and Sidney sporting a new-grown moustache and covered with rings. It was great—knowing all the familiar faces that were a part of my breathing.

Sidney was walking on eggs when he brought up a guy who looked like an ad for after-shave lotion—tough blue eyes and big capped smile. He got a grip on my hand that meant business. "Welcome to Hambro!" he said like he owned it.

I had met this type before—two rungs up from a mobster, a front man if ever I saw one, confident that he has the backing of a powerful syndicate behind him, unscrupulous but smooth Santa-Claus-looking—ready to use the ingenuous man as his weapon at every opportunity, deadly, and too big for this island. "Jesus," I thought, "what has Sidney got us into?"

"Mr. Rawlings owns half shares with us in the Hambro

Excelsior Hotel and in the Casino. He got the designer of the golf-course to come out and he is our partner in business, man. He is big backra here, but I know he is real cool too. No sweat, sar!" Sidney said, and I knew why there were no fields under cultivation, no new road down to Snipe's Bay and why Sidney had been so silent about exactly what he had been doing with soil distribution. I knew why he had only sent telegrams back to my enquiries, "Everything under control", "Soil consignments taken care of" and "Hambro economy excellent".

Mr. Rawlings must have been a very busy man.

As soon as Sidney had said his piece, Rawlings stepped in and started one of those flattery speeches which are intended to put you in your place. What he meant was, "You lucky half-breed son of a bitch—you hitched yourself on to something that made you a few bucks and now Big Daddy Rawlings has stepped in to take over the gravy." What he said was, "Well, son, you really did it, didn't you. You really made it. You put this place on the map, and this is only the *start*. Wait till you see what we do with this island, son." And again, "You really *did* it. You really did it, son."

The only way to handle someone like Rawlings is to keep the head, to wait for the right time and place, the correct moment for action, and then act only when the campaign is prepared. Mine wasn't, so I shut my mouth and took Maggie's arm, got hold of Grandma May and walked away.

Next thing, old Quincey Mortimer turned up babbling and batting his way through the crowd, using a microphone like a hammer on people's heads; Quincey Mortimer, the crimpy-haired, buck-toothed brother of Lily from Snipe's Bay. But this Quincey had filled out into a sort of seal-shape and his hair had stopped being crimpy and was standing out in a big Afro-halo round his head. I never knew anyone change so much.

We did a few words into his microphone as he told me he had started the Hambro Broadcasting Station, and was running it with a partner.

I kidded him about a bit, and we had a few laughs remembering the batterings we used to give each other in the old days. He told me that Lily was married to Brodie now, but I already knew that. He said she had five kids.

I was disappointed that Elliot Brodie was not at the airport. As Sidney, Maggie, Grandma May and Rawlings climbed into the long black Cadillac which *had* to be Mr. Rawlings' personal import, I gave Quincey a dig in his fat belly.

"That's a pile of rum and bananas you've got stashed away, Quincey!"

For an instant, the whole wide welcoming mask fell off and behind it I looked into two little hate-holes. He put his hand carefully over the microphone, "You cunt," he said quietly but distinctly, and turned away to finish a lively wind-up of our arrival into the mike.

I could not speak for a little while when I got into the car. I sat and looked out of the window, making mental notes of all the changes that had happened to the familiar road since the last time I travelled it.

I don't remember saying anything until we reached the Hambro Excelsior Hotel except that Sidney and I would take a trip around the island the next day and make a tally of every ton of earth and where it had been put.

The hotel was worse than I expected and better to look at. It was a huge grey cement flower growing up out of my island. Impressive and sterile, it loomed over me. My immediate instinct was to blow it up.

There were crowds of well-heeled tourists standing about waiting to be introduced on the steps leading to the entrance, and Rawlings led me up like the prize entry in a dog show.

Halfway up those stairs I stopped. I felt a mouth-drying spasm of uncontrollable anger.

I turned on Sidney and let fly.

"What the hell *is* this, Sidney? I'm not doing no goddam promotional tour for your friend Rawlings or anyone else—I'm coming home to see *you* and Grandma May, Libby and Doc Bates . . . *us* . . . Call them *off*, Sidney, or I'm going back to London."

*He* had stuck me in this shit, betrayed me into this scene, pushed me into the ludicrous position of being Rawlings' pawn in my own backyard. I wanted to smash his teeth down his neck. He was my own father and I had trusted him.

He didn't answer. He didn't do anything; just stood there looking unhappy and bewildered. He kept turning sad eyes to Rawlings for support. Maybe he thought Rawlings would flick his fingers and I would come to heel like the good dog show entry that I was supposed to be.

I left them standing, went back to the car, put Maggie in the back with Grandma May, got in beside the driver and told him to go to the old house.

Sidney ran after the car waving his arms. I shouted, "I'll be back to see *you* tomorrow!" and left him too.

\* \* \*

I did not want to go into the house straight away. I showed Maggie round the trees, letting the smells and the feel of bark pull me back into a womb of well-being. With Maggie I walked under the old mango trees that dangled half-ripe fruit like green Easter eggs. I showed her a wild pink franjipani that I had brought back from Venezuela when I was a merchant seaman, and which now stood fifteen feet high. I took her to the hidden place under the oldest Spanish elm, the place where five of my cousins and I had sworn to call ourselves The Wolf Pack, and have council meetings every full moon. I lay down with her under that tree and knew that I was really *home* for the first time.

We could hear Grandma May's voice coming from the house. She was getting everybody moving, fussing about, arranging where we were going to sleep, fixing for the dinner. I closed my eyes and tried to work out what I was going to do about Rawlings and the big cement flower.

One thing was certain—I would stay here until it *was* worked out. I had started a train of events which had led to Sidney putting himself into the hands of a group of 'rich men' who would not leave the gold-mine until the seam was exploited. Then, and only then, would they take their money and run. The big cement flower was the gold mine; the big cement flower that housed the Casino and the luxury that made the golf-course possible. If we got control of the gold-mine, the 'rich men' would lose interest . . . if we did not, the gold-mine would have to go.

I felt Maggie lying there beside me, felt the sympathy and love without her touching me, and I began to tell her some of the things that were in my head. Speaking the words, it fell into place . . . I knew what I wanted. I wanted to stay here and finish what I had started. Finish the journey into myself. Grow things, grow old, die. Stop being a Symbol and a Cult.

*Be* a hybrid, but stop telling everyone about it. Just live it. Living. It's a dream in your head.

\* \* \*

We lay and I held her and we made plans for the life we would lead here. I think we must have dozed off because the next thing I remember is that one of my cousins arrived to fit in another piece of the crazy jigsaw that made up the picture of what had happened on this island since I left.

His name was Martin, and he was one of the cousins who had sworn, under this very tree, to be 'Grey Brother' in the Wolf Pack. He was the son of my uncle Hector, Sidney's brother. Hector's wife, Ida, had died when Martin was seven and I was five, so Grandma May had always treated us as brothers. I remember we had shared the use of an underwater gun which Brodie had donated to the family when he first arrived on Hambro. The first time I beat him in a fight was when I was ten, but all the boys in the family knew that he was a bad one to cross, so I never fought him after that.

He squatted down, chewed some grass, and gave Maggie the fish-eyes, waiting for her to go away. Wanted to talk serious talk with me, he said. I insisted that she stay, so he turned an attack on her that would have earned him a couple of belts from Grandma May's skyrocket stick even on that very day, if she had heard him.

Then it all came out, the whole putrid shit was mouthed out, black militant jargon about the original pure black man who inhabited the earth, the mad scientist called Yacub who worked on producing a 'white devil with the blue eyes of death'. That was me—it was staring out of my eye, he said. He worked himself up into a frenzy of hate and abuse against me and Maggie, and even the white blood in his own veins. It was a terrifying performance but I'd heard it all before. Not from *him*, but from every indoctrinated black reactionary to come out of one of the ghettos of Watts or Harlem or Cape Town. I can understand *them*, but Martin came from Hambro. It was hard to think that he had not been persecuted all his life, but I was his cousin and had lived in the same house until he was nineteen, so I *knew* that none of these ideas had been stuck into his head before the arrival of the Rawlings syndicate.

He accused me of using the whole cult of hybridisation to further my own interests in the hotel-casino urbanisation of the island, and for *that* I could not blame him. *I* would have felt exactly the same if I had seen my island being commandeered by a bunch of high-powered musclemen. How was he to know that Sidney was not taking direct instructions from *me*? That Rawlings was not *my* choice? That I was not owned by the syndicate myself?

Suddenly the whole madness of the situation hit me. Instead of making my Utopia, my microcosm of how the world should be, I had indirectly created a microcosm of exactly what the world really *was*. I had a batch of foreign businessmen ready to exploit the tourist potential and tax-free trendiness of 'Jackson's island in the sun' on one side, and a bunch of fanatical black militants led by my own cousin just waiting to jump in and cause havoc on the other; me, sitting in the middle like a fried egg.

Now I understood why Quincey Mortimer had called me cunt at the airstrip.

I stood up and started walking around in circles cursing myself for allowing this situation to develop; I had to clear the sheet and start to get things into shape, find out how deep both sides were committed. Work. Plan. Graft.

And then suddenly Maggie was on her feet and yelling, shrieking out "Shut up! Shut up!" and a whole string of incomprehensible words, sobbing and crying like a hysterical child. She ranted and wept until the weeping turned into terrible laughter while I held her and tried to stop up the laughter and enfold her into myself to keep her from the hurt of it.

I rocked her in my arms like a baby and crooned in her ear. I had never felt such an overpowering sense of being part of another person before, or another person being part of me.

"Take off your clothes and let's go for a swim, missus," I whispered in her ear. "Come and lie in the sea with me."

I picked her up and carried her through the coconut-palms down to the sea behind the house.

We took off our clothes and walked into the water hand in hand.

She came to me in the sea and I felt her breasts, soft and undulating with the motion of the waters, rise and fall on my chest. Everything about her had the blossom and the fullness of what I had looked for all my life. She was honey and clove and sweetmeat in the shade. She made me whole again.

*　　*　　*

Doc Bates had not changed. His hairs may have been finer and whiter, but they still stood straight up and at right angles from his scalp like thousands of microscopic sentinels standing guard on the huge old head. He embraced me, thumping my shoulder hard with a meaty fist.

"My God, it's good to see you, boy. Missed you. I put my old nose up to the Trade Winds and guessed you'd be blowing in here before long."

"How's Baby Doc?"

"Who? Oh, *Evan*. We call him Evan now, you know. He's a good boy. You'll see him soon. He's fifteen. Lives here with me, you see. Very proud that you're his godfather."

"Way it looks to me, Doc, he could get a wallopin' for that any day now on this island."

Doc grunted and ran his hands back over his forehead. "So you've felt the rumbles already, boy. But surely it must not surprise you? All this rumpus you've begun!"

"*There* yes, in the big world, yes . . . but not here on Hambro."

"Well, what's so different about Hambro! Did you think we would remain transfixed from the moment you left, to wake with a kiss when you returned? Sleeping beauties, eh? Nothing works like that, boy. Never come back *expecting*."

"But you said once that this was the only place in the world you'd found true liberalism. You were always talking about liberalism. What's happened to that?"

"*You* did, boy. You got us into the news too much, and then started bringing all that dirt in here. Nobody knew how to organise it; it got dumped about the place, mounds of it, cluttering up the roads. Brodie wanted to get it worked out but Sidney wouldn't let him. You might say your dirt brought the dirt. Ha! Ha! This Rawlings character came sniffing about, and Sidney fell into his arms like a randy barmaid. Made a deal. Rawlings got cracking like knives and forks on that hotel and golf-course and within the year we'd all changed. We're big time now, boy. Like you. Can't stop a wave breaking, can you?"

"And what about Martin and Quincey Mortimer? Who introduced that black Muslim stuff in here?"

"Aurrgh—that eye-bilge—that came in with a fellow calls himself Mustafa. Comes from Chicago, I think. He's wanted in all fifty-two states, so they say. Anyway, he's made Hambro his headquarters for the time being. When Rawlings arrived with his minions, Martin and Quincey and some other boys like Wilf Buxton and Jemmy Hawks, they all went to work on the building site. Seems like for the first time in their lives they got treated like niggers. They didn't take too kindly to *that*, so when this Mustafa fellow happened along, they were ripe meat. I think they must have done some acts of sabotage because two of them were severely beaten by Rawlings' strong-arm friends, two bouncers he had brought in from Las Vegas. I looked after the boys myself and I can tell you—they were badly beaten. We've got six croupiers and two bouncers from Las Vegas. They say that's where Rawlings get his backing."

"Jesus," I said, "it's worse than I thought."

"You might as well hear the full story. Sidney's been losing at every table in the Casino. They say he's mortgaged himself up to his eyeballs and that means that Rawlings can do virtually what he wishes with all the dirt that comes in on your tankers. Brodie has disappeared down to Snipe's Bay and hardly ever comes up this end of the island. Say's he's going to sell up when Rawlings spreads out, move on to South America. Most able-bodied Hambroans are waiters, caddies, boat-men, laundry-workers and beach-boys at the hotel. They don't mind too much. It's the first time they ever had money handed to them regular. They all got ambitions now, to own cars and radios and such, that is the ones who stay working. The rest of them gone down to Snipe's Bay. Got quite a little settlement down there now. I think they call them 'drop-outs'—isn't that the word?"

I sat with my head in my hands for a few moments. Had to have a little time to let it all sink in. "I've got to do something, Doc," I said. "Throw out a few ideas. I don't know where to start."

"Boy," said Doc. "*Rawlings*, that's the name you want to concern yourself with, Rawlings. Get him off this island and you'll see your way clear to clean up the rest of the mess. As long as that hotel is owned and run by a man like Rawlings you have no influence on this island. And he plans to spread, plans to make this island the biggest tourist resort outside Miami—Bunny Club, Holiday Inn, floor shows, Concert Hall for conventions—the lot. Perhaps you should try to buy him out before the price gets too high. Perhaps you should go to the Jamaican Government for protection, get *them* to put a damper on him. This way, he's king of the cabbage patch and none to deny him doing anything he wants."

We sat in a long silence, sipping our rums. I remembered the silences of my grandfather and the Doc when I was a boy lying listening on the verandah. How unlike those silences this one was! Those silences had been peaceful and fulfilling, this one was ominous and noisy. Doc was waiting for me to make a decision.

I finished my rum and got up to go.

"You're coming up to the house for dinner. Grandma May been cookin' for three days. I have to do some thinkin' and go around the island with Sidney tomorrow. Then I'll tackle Rawlings," I said.

\* \* \*

I sat in a jeep half the next day with Sidney. We began our day at the wharf where the tankers landed their cargoes. Sidney wore tight turquoise silk pants and a see-through shirt straight from some Caribbean Mr. Fish. I felt sorry for him. We were accompanied by Mr. Rawlings' 'representative' who introduced himself to me as Sal Calmette. Sal sat by himself in the rear of the jeep and allowed Sidney to do all the talking. I felt his restricting influence on every word Sidney said, as well as his eyes on the back of my neck. I was not happy.

We watched them load earth into ten-ton trucks and then followed the route to the disposal area where a mountain of the world's most expensive dirt was waiting to be distributed to the Hambro Excelsior Golf Club and Tropical Gardens.

Sidney explained how they were planning to run a small scenic railroad through the Gardens to keep the guests' wives and offspring happy while their husbands and fathers played golf. We walked around the half-finished olympic-sized swimming-pool decorated with green cement dolphins, and I looked back at the hotel. I kept my face perfectly expressionless and only spoke when I had a direct question to ask. A peculiar far-away fear cooled the insides of my mouth.

The workmen and gardeners were all dressed in ugly green-khaki outfits. The only familiar thing about them was the lack of speed at which they worked . . . and though I looked hard into all their faces, there were none that I recognised. None of them greeted me.

Sidney and Sal Calmette showed me around the Golf Course with genuine pride. Even the sallow Sal showed his humanity by addressing himself to an imaginary ball with a borrowed driver and making a vicious assault on the turf. There were groups of players, men and women, all dressed in regulation bermuda shorts of varying colour and size. Each group was followed by four or five small boys humping huge sacks of clubs on their backs. These boys I recognised. They were mostly my cousins or nephews. We shouted to each other across the immaculate greens until Sidney punched me on the arm, "Shut your mouth, Matthew, you make such a noise these white people can't play their shots," he muttered in my ear, one eye fixed warily on Calmette.

"Don't worry, Sidney!" I said, "they on a holiday, no need to play fast. Better they take *our* time when they come to Hambro!" I raised my voice so that big Sal heard too.

On our way to view the two lakes I noticed that the fairways had been planted with hundreds of young trees—jacaranda and poinciana, bird of paradise, flame and eucalyptus, all flowering trees. And they were flourishing. Boys were watering them from thick hoses attached to an underground system fed by the lakes. In a few years it would be a gorgeous place, but I felt only resentment for the whole venture . . . I tried to be pleased that the top-soil was actually *there*, ready to grow things, yield and be fruitful . . . but having Sidney and Sal Calmette point out the future beauties of the place with such a proprietal air, made me retire quickly into myself and stop looking around for fear that I would show my fury.

With mounting dejection, I saw the site for the new Convention Hall. The Holiday Inn ("For a lower income group than the Hambro Excelsior," said Sidney, and Calmette nodded his approval) was only an acre of earth being levelled up by two bulldozers at that moment, but Sidney assured me that in six months there would be accommodation for at least four hundred tourists and a "tie-up with a travel agency for weekly package-deal holidays from every major city in the United States."

"But there are only four hundred people on Hambro!" I cried, startled. "The tourists will outnumber the natives."

"We intend to bring people from Jamaica and the mainland, Mr. Jackson," said Calmette. "Why even now there are sites for luxury homes being prepared around the golf-course." His voice was queerly high and unresonant. A careful eunuch's voice, I thought. It did not go with the rest of him; he was flat-featured but had large rounded limbs that strained his clothing at crotch and armpit and made his head seem tiny.

"Who's going to live in them? And food?" I asked. "How you goin' to feed them all?"

"We fly in regular shipments of everything we need. We will just step up the imports." O you self-satisfied bastard!

"This is not the first time you've created one of these instant holiday resorts, is it?" I asked, but leaving any of the bitterness I felt out of my voice.

"We're professionals, Mr. Jackson," said Mr. Calmette fastening me with small seed-pod eyes. "We have a lot of backing and we don't do anything without planning."

"I can see that, man," I smiled graciously, "but what you plan to do when this whole island filled up and bustin' with tourists? There'll be no place for the people who born here."

"There are fifty-four and three-tenths square miles on this island, Mr. Jackson . . . Mr. Rawlings plans to use every one of them."

"And does Mr. Rawlings allow Hambro islanders to use his exclusive golf-course?"

"The sort of people who come to the Hambro Excelsior are not accustomed to playing in non-segregated conditions, Mr. Jackson. Of course, we would make an exception for you and your father."

So there it was. All out in the open. We had been invaded. If I had ever been unsure that something must be done about the Rawlings syndicate, my meeting with Sal Calmette exploded any doubts.

\* \* \*

I borrowed the jeep in the afternoon as there were no other

new splendours that they could show me. "The other projects are still on the drawing-boards," Sal explained in his eunuch's falsetto. That's where I had to make sure they stayed.

I went down to Snipe's Bay to see Brodie.

Immediately I had passed the busy air-strip, bitumen ended and I raised a column of dust behind me all the way to the settlement.

It was three o'clock in the afternoon when I arrived; the pleasant drone of a sultry tropic day greeted me as I stopped the jeep in the open area where Doc Bates and I had parked his old Riley on my first visit.

There were twice as many houses—ramshackle little affairs—dotted about. Flaked-out dogs lay around in the shade, chickens scratched in the dirt and cackled news of another egg to the world. A woman in a yellow shift sat on the stoop of one of the houses and kept an eye on a group of naked children who played in a pile of old car tyres.

As I walked between the huts towards the beach I heard the sound of school children reciting the three times table. Sweat trickled down my neck.

Brodie's house stood by itself at the far end of the bay. I took off my sandals and ran along the friendly, familiar beach, past fishing nets drying in the sun, past my grandfather's old house which was now just a shell, past a catamaran and two upturned dinghies, till I reached a point directly underneath the house.

"Hall—oo," I shouted through cupped hands, "Brodie! Elliot Brodie! Hall—oo! Anybody home?"

Something shifted on the verandah and a thatch of matted colourless hair appeared. Elliot Brodie unfolded himself from a hammock and stood squinting sightless down at the beach.

After a few moments he saw who it was. "Matt," he said quietly, and then, "Come up."

We did not speak when we faced each other. The frame of him had not altered at all since last I saw him, but everything about the outside of him was changed. His hair was now like old unravelled rope and grey hairs covered his freckly concave chest. He had a perpetual squint-frown and his cheek-bones stuck out like knuckles. The skin was beginning to sag on his elbows and round his knee-caps. He looked like an islander born and bred.

He was examining me just as closely. He had put on a pair of specs.

Finally he grunted and offered me some beer.

"How's Lily?"

"She's gone down to Bobolink Bay to empty her crab pots," he said. "Taken the children with her."

I sat down in an ageing bamboo chair and sucked on my beer.

"Well," he said, "it's no use talking about anything else. What are you goin' to do about it?"

I did not need to ask him what he meant.

"I'll move on in another six months," he said, "nothing else to do, the way things are going. But why did you let this happen here?"

"But I didn't *know*, Brodie! I didn't *know*! I never thought they could step in so quickly and make things so different! I thought Sidney was just spreadin' the earth. He never mentioned going in with a syndicate. All I got was a stack of telegrams: 'Everything O.K., Under control, O.K., Received earth shipments, O.K.' Just that."

"Sidney told me that he was following your instructions all the way along the line," said Brodie watching beer bubbles ooze out of his can. He popped one with his index finger. "We all thought you'd sold us down the river."

"Jesus, Brodie, I swear to you I have never felt so angry or so helpless in my life. I've just been round the whole island with Rawlings' side-kick and Sidney. I've seen what they got planned. They're organised like a fuckin' bank and they've got as much money as one. All the way down here I've been tryin' to figure out some way round them. I can try to buy them out, but they don't need money. I can try to stop any Hambro Islander workin' for them, but it's only a matter of time before they reorganise their labour and import help from Jamaica. I can try to get protection from the Jamaican Government but it will take six months before anyone moves and even then, the Government might decide that the Rawlings syndicate is good for revenue and take *their* side. What else can I try?"

"Look, Matt . . . first *you've* got to decide what you will do with Hambro, provided you get rid of Rawlings and Company. This island is now well on the way to becoming a holiday camp. It can't go back to being a small anonymous dot in the middle of the sea. They've had their taste of 'progress' and it's not going to stop because you tell them that it's no good for them. They can *see* that big hotel stuck there to remind them that *they* can't afford to go into it."

I drank down my beer and asked him for another one. I wanted a cool stream flowing over the back of my throat while an idea grew into a conviction.

*I would have to blow up the Hambro Excelsior Hotel.*

I would try all the negotiations with Rawlings and his team but if they refused me a reasonable say in the future of the island, I would blow their poxy hotel into the sky, and sabotage their Holiday Inn and all their other ventures until they saw that it was useless to go on.

I thought of Sidney. He'd blown tree roots out of the ground when we were making the air-strip. He had been well-known as a dynamiter of fish when well out to sea, in fact he was the only native islander who had an intimate knowledge of the stuff. I would make Sidney dynamite the Hambro Excelsior Hotel. Ironic.

I laughed and swallowed my beer.

Brodie was watching me nervously through his old sun-squint. I did not tell him what I was thinking because I know Brodie of old. He would disapprove so strongly that he would probably go to Rawlings and tell him what I was planning. I love Brodie but I cannot imagine any situation in his life which would allow him to resort to an aggressive act. For him, it would be unthinkable. I was sorry that the only solution I could come up with was a violent one, but that's the way it is sometimes.

Once I had decided what would be the alternative to negotiation, I felt much better.

I knew that Brodie was going to advise me that my best plan would be to leave the island and go back to London, and he did. He gave me a long lecture on the usefulness of my work in integration throughout the world. I listened and nodded, but I knew he could never understand that my destiny was here, that *here* was where I would complete the journey into myself, that getting things right *here* was imperative.

He was still talking when I got up to go. Brodie's always been that way, long-winded and scholarly, urging me on in the same pedantic teacher-pupil way, to read Charles Darwin's *Voyage of the Beagle*, or to study the primates. I even had the same urgent desire to escape once he got started, and found myself shifting my weight from foot to foot, looking out to sea and nodding without hearing one word he said.

He gave up the lecture, and asked abruptly, "Aren't you going to stay and see Lily?"

"I'll see her next time I come down, man. I'll bring my girl. Right now I got some things to do." I hurried down the stairs and ran back to the beach. The sand felt hot and dry under my feet and I looked back at Brodie's house while I put my sandals on. He was leaning on the verandah rail squinting down at me. His face was closed and still but there was a sort of supplication about it that made me feel guilty and sort of crude.

I raised my hand and walked down the beach slowly.

\* \* \*

On the way back in the jeep, I worked out a plan to get everyone out of the hotel while the dynamiting was happening. I did not want anybody's death on my hands.

I would give a free concert with Maggie. A Gala Day. Sunday. Everybody welcome. We could set up a stage somewhere. Sidney could have made his preparations beforehand. He could come and go in the hotel as he pleased. No one would question him. He would see that everybody was out of the place.

It would be organised with the precision of a commando raid.

It was peculiarly *right* that Sidney was to be the guy who did the blowing. He had got us into the shit, now he could get us out.

\* \* \*

I asked Quincey Mortimer to find the musicians and set up mikes. Maggie was very excited and pleased to be performing again. I did not tell her anything about my plans for the blow-up but we moved into the Hambro Excelsior Hotel about a week after our arrival.

Negotiations with Rawlings were a formality. I offered him fifty per cent of all my future earnings in record returns, but would not give him the promise to produce the four long-players and six singles a year, which he wanted. How could I? His syndicate turned me down. I had nothing else to bargain with, so I got on Quincey's wireless and asked every native-born

Hambroan to strike for one day as a protest against segregation at the golf-course. That's when Rawlings shipped in his first consignment of fifty 'skilled workers' from Miami.

I got hold of Sidney and told him what he had to do. It took three days of convincing and explaining before he agreed to move, but once he did, he became more and more excited by the idea. He has had to bring the explosives into the hotel in small amounts, and has planned every phase of the operation with cunning and care. He sees himself as a secret service agent and I suppose he *is*, if you look at it like that.

\*     \*     \*

Today is Saturday, and after weeks of preparation, we are ready. Tomorrow while we belt our lungs out on the stage set up in the Hambro Tropical Gardens and while we have our Gala Day Concert, Sidney will be setting up his fuses.

There are some times in your life when you have to take big steps to change what fate holds in store.

Who said, Give me a point to stand on, and I can move the world.

# 12

## *Maggie Truro*

LOOKING DOWN FROM the Lear Jet, the sea below me changes
continually, from turquoise shallows where I fancy big fish
bask—to sultry green—to creamy ridges of reef—to inky
depths where the shelf of Caribbean coral ends and flat black
deep-sea creatures with huge red eyes and brittle bones live
five miles below. Sometimes, dramatically, we cross an island,
its beaches gleaming in the morning sun, dots of roof-tops—
little scabs on its surface, surf beyond its reefs framing and
disclosing its stability. Big ships are followed by white wakes—
furrows through the blueness of the water; sailing boats tack
into the wind and expose their triangles to me who sits up in
the sky and looks down on their progress.

I am on my way to Hambro Island.

Ever since Jackson first described the island to me I have
been dying to go, to go with *him*, to meet the people who
formed him, to let him take me there.

Ever since I knew we *could* go, I have been breathing deep,
to try and contain my excitement, to hold down the rising shout
of delight, to get enough oxygen into my blood to fill my pumping heart . . . And now here we are, me and Jackson, in Lew
Hamlyn's private jet, slicing through the air on the last lap of
the flight from New York, within minutes of our arrival.

I look across at Jackson. His face is rapt and waiting, and his
eyes are fixed on the sea below as mine have been for the last
hour or so.

"Jamaica will be coming up in about three minutes, time,
sir," the pilot says over his shoulder. "We'll start our descent
immediately after we cross the south coast."

Jackson's face, the face I have been looking at nearly every
day now for three years is in repose. It is a more mature face than

the one I saw at Kew that cold morning; not so raw, not so extravagant, more contained and decided.

In these three years it has grown into its own lines more, like furniture does into a room. It is known and loved by me.

There has always been something about him that I have found mystical and awe-inspiring—the other end of the pendulum from the mad 'energetic' rumbustious Jackson of that day in the snow—the graver side of him has been more in evidence in the last year.

His success was a huge surprise to me—not so much the success, as the nature of it—it was like an explosion that blew all our lives into the air, and we've been waiting to come down ever since.

The most important thing to eventualise from Jackson's fame is that it has created a wedge between the militants—both black and white. They may both deplore him, but he *exists* and that's what matters. (That's Lew talking, not me).

Not one of us—not Lew or me or Cynthia Omerod or Harry Sansom—none of us expected the colossal response to Jackson's magic and message. I have no idea whether Jackson himself was aware of its potency, but once he had the original reaction to 'Hybrid' under his belt, a whole world of ideas and poems, stories, songs and music flowed out of him to consolidate his position and make him into a sort of Oracle-on-legs.

But he has never allowed the humour of the situation to be lost. He has never allowed it to push his original intention of covering his island with earth into the background or be forgotten in the shuffle; he has given me a sense of purpose, a feeling that life is not just filling-in time with as little boredom and distress as possible until we are dead.

I know it's corny to be happy, and people hate your guts for it, but with Jackson, I am a whole woman able to give a whole dedication of herself to someone she loves.

*　　*　　*

"Montego Bay," says the pilot, "down there on the right. We'll pass over Cockpit Country and Mandeville, come out over Old Harbour and Portland Bight."

I crane down to see the inevitable white border of beach, clusters of houses and the broad tarmac lines of the airport.

Golf-courses, speedboats like water-spiders, thin ribbons of road that follow the coastline, or meander off into the deep green and end in a sprinkling of roofs.

Quite soon we are over mountains, ridgy and pitted, densely bushed and connected by a maze of paths.

"This here is Cockpit Country," says Jackson, "where runaway slaves hid out from the soldiers, and set up their own colony. Big trouble for the regular army trying to get hold of anyone in that stuff. Che Guevara land. They're still called Maroons.

"You might not believe it, but we are now flying over the county of Cornwall, and will soon be in Middlesex. That river down there is called the Hector. Troy on the Hector is somewhere down there . . . one day I'll take you right through the islands and you can *really* see it, not just sit up here lookin' down. You got to *smell* it to see it right.

"Oh man," he says, flexing his fingers with delight, "I is lickle-most home!"

*   *   *

More mountains, more black-green jungle, savannah-land, and then a great yawning bay dotted with islands. ("One of them's called Great Goat Island," says Jackson). We are out over the sprawling sea again and beginning our descent; Jackson, squeezing the arm-rests to hold himself down, me, tingling with anticipation, and yet fearful, with that alarm you get when you know you have to meet hundreds of new people and be overwhelmed by a completely new place which is not foreign to your lover.

And there it is—a curling green worm beneath us, a horseshoe in the sea, coming up to meet us . . .

Soon we can distinguish all the features of the island, and when we get to a couple of thousand feet and begin our approach to the air-strip, Jackson asks the pilot if we can't do some low-circlings and see how things are shaping up down there.

So round we go. I can hear the pilot talking to Ground Control. I can see beaches and earth and a golf-course, a hotel that looks like a gravestone, bungalows, a swimming pool, trees, a car-park, more stubbly trees, limpid blue sea, red soil and yellow rivers. We pass a white bird with a long neck hovering beside us on the wind; two yellow trucks move slowly along a winding road. There is a tanker disgorging its belly at the short wharf inside the lagoon, some yachts lie at anchor, their masts pointing up at us; I see a midget man rowing across the flat water raise his hand to shade his eyes as he gazes up at us and ships his oars.

Round we go again, buzzing a beach. I see five boys run whooping along the sand, shouting up at us, palm-trees with graceful ridgy grey trunks leaning out towards the sea, tall spikey plants in a field. ("Sisal", says Jackson.) A woman in a scarlet dress waves her arms at us as chickens scatter around her feet.

Next time round we make our true approach for landing, the flaps go down, and we skim in, touch down with a small bump and a gush of hot air envelopes us. We've arrived.

\*     \*     \*

Oh, the marvellous colours of them as they crowd across the sweltering bitumen that sends its heat into the air to wobble the hangar and shiver the flag-posts; the glorious pinks, yellows; lime dresses and purple parasols, white-teethed smiles in every hue of brown face. There is a steel band playing 'I'll do the same', 'Are you receiving me, Mr. Man?' Jackson songs. There are the cousins and the brothers, the uncles, aunts and sisters, and there is Grandma May, huge and ancient and sturdy as an old tree, her great brown arms sprouting out of a sleeveless floral smock, a hat of violet straw sitting very straight on her head. Lovely!

She stands still, beaming in the sun, while the horde of her descendants hustle and sway around her. Shy little girls with their hair plaited into a hundred tiny braids are pushed into Jackson's arms, small boys punch him in the legs and yowl that the melting tarmac is burning their feet. They skip from shadow to shadow to keep their bare feet from smouldering.

"I'm Matthew's daddy," says a fat man resplendent in white; his small moustache and sweating chops glisten in the sun. "I'm Sidney." And he shakes my hand. He has manicured nails and lots of rings. "Real glad you come here to Hambro," he says.

"This here is Mr. Rawlings, my partner in business," says

Sidney, introducing an out-of-place man with very blue shrewd eyes, who is wearing a smart tropical suit—one of those clever bulky suits that conceal everything about a man's figure except its solidarity. His jowls are very pink and lotioned and well-shaven. I dislike him at once.

"Welcome to Hambro," he says, pumping my hand and smiling with his mouth. "We're just delighted that you-all could fit us in with such a tight schedule and all." What's *he* doing in this family?

Sidney then introduces Mr. Rawlings to Jackson, and I can see Jackson's eyes asking the same question.

"Mr. Rawlings owns half shares with us in the Hambro Excelsior Hotel and the Casino. He got the designer of the golf-course to come out here, and he is our partner in business, man," says Sidney, in a respectful, placating voice which expects rebuke. "He is big hackra here, but I know he is real cool, too. No sweat, sar!" he adds, patting both Mr. Rawlings and Jackson at the same time, one on one arm and one on the other. Mr. Rawlings holds out his hand to Jackson like this is a great moment in his life, cracks his face open again in a smile that exposes two perfect rows of dentists' delights, moved his head from side to side in mock disbelief, and says, "Well, son, you really did it, didn't you. You really made it. You put this place on the map, and this is only the *start*. Wait till you see what we do with this island, son. You really *did* it." He repeats it over again fatuously while I see poor old Jackson squirm like he always does when he doesn't know whether he should just say 'piss off' and leave it at that.

But he doesn't say anything. Just takes my arm and gets hold of his grandmother too; guides us through the mob of family, photographers, band, dancing excited people who fling out greetings and shuffle along behind us, their bodies moving with the beat of the band, fingers snapping, lips mouthing the words of Jackson's songs. It is a great day. Jackson's home!

* * *

It is fantastic the way nobody is in charge of anything, no policemen link arms to hold back the straining crowds, no stitched-up haters call out insults or spit or anything, everybody is jumping and singing and shouting out good things. I suddenly remember the ghastly day we sat sweltering in an armoured car waiting to get through Hyde Park where Jackson was going to give a free concert from behind a bullet-proof screen. Lew had thought up the idea, of course. It was his kind of scene. A brigade of police to protect us. Half a million people turned up on that boiling July day, lugging their kids, wearing their gear, fascist or flower-inspired, wading in the Serpentine to keep cool. They stopped our car near the Park Gates on Kensington High Street, and it took us over an hour to get the three hundred yards from there to where the stage had been set up. I thought they would overturn the car and smash it apart. I was sick with fear and finally just held on to Jackson's hand as tight as I could and pretended they were not there. It's not claustrophobia that causes you the sweat of fear, it's being *looked* to death.

But here, there is the goodwill of relations who are proud and demonstrative.

A buck-toothed man with a microphone presses through the crush. "Quincey Mortimer, H.B.C.! Quincey Mortimer! Hambro Broadcasting Company!" he shouts, holding up the tool of his profession like it was a banner.

"Comin' through! Get your fat batty out the way, man!" he shouts, bullying his way past a large lady with hair standing up stiff as an Airedale's, who is in the act of presenting us with a huge bunch of scarlet poinsettias.

"Quincey!" cries Jackson delighted, "what you doin' wavin' that thing around like you knew what to do with it?"

Quincey thrusts the knobbly old-fashioned mike into Jackson's face to catch these words, and then drags it back under his own chin to shout into it, "This is Quincey Mortimer reporting to you from the Hambro Island Airfield and you are just listenin' to the first words spoken by our conquerin' hero, Matthew Jackson, who has put his foot down on the island after five long years. Standin' here with him, lookin' like a . . . ah . . . a . . . sweet angel vision in bright sunny dress, is his little lady friend, a singer with a nightingale voice, that we all heard so much about, Miss *Maggie Truro*." He pushes the mike at *me* this time.

"An' will you say something to the people of this here island an' all the other places that's listenin' in on us right now, miss?"

235

I speak a few words into the thing. Jackson talks on some more with this Quincey, about how he used to borrow Quincey's old blue-painted bicycle and how Quincey has sure brightened up since the last time he saw him, when he worked on a Mr. Noakes's chicken farm at Snipe's Bay.

Quincey cackles and the words spatter out of him like rain-drops; he edges along with us, still talking up a storm, to where a sleek black convertible is drawn up to take us to the Hambro Excelsior Hotel.

Mr. Rawlings and Sidney climb into the car with me, Grandma May, and behind us Jackson. We are enclosed in an air-conditioned leather-bound saloon, a capsule of cool, with Mr. Rawlings smarming the politesse, and Grandma May talking right through him, telling about how she is preparing a real 'jump-up' evening, a dinner of curried goat, sweet potato pudding, stuffed egg-plant, and all sorts of incredible goodies.

"I been soakin' some beans up overnight. Your favourite . . . them red ones . . . all ready on the stove. Squeeze some coconut milk out . . . Boil it up together with the beans an' rice, and you got yourself his special favourite. Rice and red beans. That your grandaddy's favourite too."

Jackson nods all the while, withdrawn, only his eyes move taking in everything he can see from the windows. The road is wide but the surface is scarred and indented as though tar has been dumped on it by a busy dip-truck merchant who has then gone off to let it settle by itself. The stumpy trees beside the road are stained with a fine grey dust. No crops, no gardens to be seen.

"Sidney," says Jackson, "you and me goin' to take a trip round the whole of this island tomorrow, see what you been doing with the soil and all."

"We'll all go," says Rawlings, bonhomie man, "you'll be amazed at the pro-gress we've made since you left. Our syndi-cate has invested more than two million dollars in the Golf Course alone. We paid Trent-Jones a small fortune to put in a couple of artificial lakes, a waterfall, and design the Club House. Give it two years more, and it will be the lushest course in the whole of the Caribbean." He laughs in a sort of coughing way as though there's some big joke. "It won't be long before *we* can attract the tourists without the publicity *you* give us, son . . . you'll be a bonus thrown in along with golf and gambling . . . Ha! Ha!"

Then he speaks directly to me. "But of course," he says, like an actor switching into his 'this-is-where-we-get-serious' voice; he touches my knee lightly with his index finger, "we could have bought and sold this goddam island five times over and not even noticed it, if it hadn't been for your man here. You really put this place on the map, son," he says to Jackson—the seventh time at least.

Jackson continues to look out of the window, not acknowledging anything Rawlings says but waving occasionally to the straggling lines of people who watch our limousine slide past.

"Gang-gang wanted you to go stay down the old house with her, but we'd already booked you into the *penthouse* suite at the hotel," says Sidney proudly.

Grandma May makes her mouth into an incredible upside-down 'C' and pokes Sidney hard in his bulging solar plexus.

"I not your gang-gang, samfie. I your big black Mammy."

Sidney subsides and we turn in to a drive of neatly shaped bushes.

\* \* \*

A great gaggle of tourists is hovering around the entrance to the Hambro Excelsior Hotel.

You can feel the waves of excitement rippling through the groups of bermuda-shorted tourists. They galvanise into action. Cameras are raised to sun-blinkered eyes, little gasps of "That's him!" and "Oh, he's so cute!", "Who's the girl?", "Is the old black dame his *mother*?" greet Jackson as he gets out of the car.

On the steps leading to the entrance, breathless ladies push forward with their dutiful husbands, who pretend to look as though they are not really there. The women wait expectantly to be introduced by Mr. Rawlings. It doesn't seem to make much sense that *he* should be playing host.

Jackson stops stock-still on the steps.

"What the hell *is* this, Sidney? I'm not doing no goddamn promotional tour for your friend Rawlings or anyone else—I'm coming home to see *you* and Grandma May, Libby and Doc Bates . . . *us* . . . Call them *off* Sidney, or I'm going back to London."

Sidney stands forlorn, making sheep's eyes at Rawlings, awaiting instructions it seems. Nobody moves. It is an ugly moment. A hush has come. The sun is shining brightly.

Jackson turns abruptly comes back down and opens the door of the limousine. He pushes me in. Grandma May still sits sedate in the back. She never got *out*. Perhaps she knew all along that he wouldn't have it. Certainly she's wearing a look of total endorsement on her face. We drive off leaving Rawlings and his guests playing statues on the stairs. Only Sidney runs after us.

"I'll be back to see *you* tomorrow!" shouts Jackson as the bewildered brown Billy Bunter face appears puffing at the window.

*   *   *

Grandma May's house is the best thing I've seen since we arrived. It is made solely of wood, and radiates the feeling that it has grown out of the ground along with the lovely trees that cloister it. There are green oval-shaped fruit hanging from some of the trees.

"Not ripe yet. My granpaw introduced the 'Number Eleven' mango tree from Kingston about fifty years ago, so you could say this tree is the grandaddy of all the mango trees on the island," Jackson says rubbing his hands over the bark and then smelling them. "He brought ackee, woman's tongue, jackfruit, cinnamon, breadfruit . . . this big pretty tree here is breadfruit . . . May, when we goin' to eat some of your saltfish and ackee?"

May is heaving herself up the front steps one by one to a wide verandah where four or five small children are being pushed back and forth in a dilapidated hammock by a pretty girl of about twelve.

Play with puppy, puppy lick your mouth.

Licky-licky duppy, duppy koo south . . . they chant over and over, in time with each push.

Jackson walks me round the garden touching bark and saying names of trees like a litany . . . Spanish elm, broadleaf, wild tamarind, dogwood, mango, bulletwood and breadfruit, Santa Maria, yoke and cedar . . . Lignum vitae, which has a lovely flower, hibiscus and frangipani; tells me how his grandfather has pruned and nurtured all these plants, until they grow old

238

shading and perfuming his family to remind them that he had vision.

We lie flat out on the warm ground looking up through branches. Jackson hums and sings to himself, and I feel tears of joy in my throat. It would be silly to kiss him now, or make any gesture of love that might break the spell. It is enough to lie, suspended in his grandfather's garden, and let the peace of the place enter into me like a love consummation. In the distance we can hear the children and Grandma May's voice giving orders for unseen hands to put flowers in someone called Hector's bedroom, change the sheets . . . "Don't bring me back no jenny crabs!" I hear her shout.

Jackson chuckles softly without opening his eyes.

"Poor old Hector," he says, "Any time anyone come to stay, Hector the first to go."

"Who's Hector?"

"Hector is my uncle. You met him at the airport. Sidney's little brother. Laziest man ever drew breath."

"Aaaaaaah," Jackson sighs, and then breathes in a breath that makes his rib-cage stand right up. "Have to do a lot of things while we here, little girl. Sidney got hisself in real deep with that American syndicate. Casino, golf-course, hotel, night-club . . . that's not what it's all about . . . should a known he'd be playin' some silly game with all that money floatin' about . . . I can see that we all be working for the tourist, the big Buck, before we be supportin' ourselves." He sighs again and opens his eyes.

And now, suddenly, I realise that he is very distressed.

"What's wrong? Is something wrong?" I ask too intensely. I always hear my own voice being much too virulent when I wish it would come out gentle.

"Well, if you were looking down out of that jet when I was, you will have seen that there is a big smart hotel, a golf-course, a yacht dock, some roads, but nothin' much growin' . . . Sidney has used up all that earth on his tourist projects and nobody's planted anything we can eat. Of course, that bastard Rawlings and his syndicate have got hold of Sidney and promised him package tours, percentage of takings at the Casino, a billion dollars, God knows what, I bet . . . and Sidney bitten. He swallowed, man . . . So Hambro bein' turned into a floating crap-game . . . Las Vegas in the Carib . . . a second Free-port

. . . New York businessman's dirty weekend, only three and a half hours door to door . . . Jesus," he says, "you ain't made it easy."

"What will you do?" I ask, daring to touch his temple now. "Will you stop them?"

He lies inert for a while. My fingers feel out the narrow scar on his head where Omerod's bullet cut its crease. I touch its length as a benediction, aching to make him feel my sympathy without using words to tell him about it.

"I wanted to come back here . . . to my *home* . . . find it all growing things," he says quietly, "I wanted to live here . . . fill it up some more with children and trees and plants like my granpaw started . . . drop out of the big world. I've *said* what I wanted to say, let them get on with it. Stay here with you, if you liked it enough."

He rolls over on his stomach and crosses his arms under his chin to pillow his head.

"I want to stop still. Keep still and just grow. Then maybe I'd see a bit clearer. Getting pretty muddied up sittin' in London, ridin' the roller-coaster." There is a silence. In it I hear a sort of trilling whirr and 'tss-tss' sound. Right above my head, about to inject a long slender vermilion bill in a tulip-like flower, the most beautiful bird I have ever seen hovers in the air. It has an iridescent green breast, black head and two long black feathers coming out of its tail.

"Look!" I whisper, mesmerised by this vision of neat flamboyance, "Look! What bird is *that*?"

Jackson glances up.

"Docta bird—he a cunning bird, hard bird fe dead." He says indifferently. "A streamer-tailed humming bird to you, missy."

"Yes," I say, "yes," still watching the bird. "I like it enough to live here. It's like somewhere I've been to before and yet everything is so strange and exotic, the smells and the colours, birds, trees . . . I want to be part of it like you . . ."

"I shoulda had somebody handle the soil distribution at this end," Jackson says, preoccupied, "but I thought old Sidney could handle it well enough . . . Question: Take one island without enough earth. Buy six tankers that bring earth to this one island. Deduction: Put the earth on the island and stick in seeds. Conclusion: you got yourself primary produce—a batch of crops. Right? Right.

"I forgot about Nassau and Freeport and Anguilla. Even Cuba. Same thing has happened in all those places more or less. Big syndicate moves in, buy up land or make a deal with the poor islander who think he makin' the biggest amount of money since J. P. Morgan or maybe even Captain Morgan . . . Syndicate build a casino, big holiday inn, build a golf-course, advertise in all the magazines in the U.S., no tax, no sweat— and before you know what hit you, the people of the island are servants, washing, cleaning up after the rich fat tourists . . . they got no life no more . . . just tips rattlin' about in their pockets. *Got to stop that happenin' here.*"

He leans across, smoothing back the hair from my forehead, cuddling my head to look down into my eyes. "You *really* want to live here on Hambro Island with me?" I nod. "*Really,* really? I mean, not get homesick for that house on Cheyne and all them wigs I had to wear? I think you fancy me more when I in one of them disguises, eh?"

I laugh and nod again, "But you can always put one on for my benefit, right here in Hambro."

"Then you *really* want to *stay* here?"

"Yes," I say. "Yes."

"O.K.," he says kissing my neck and slipping his hand in to feel my breast. "We'll stay, girl."

* * *

"Matthew! Ma—att—hew! Maaaaa—tthew!"
A man's voice is calling through the trees.
"Maaaa—tthew Jack—son!"
"Over here!" Jackson sits up drowsily.
A man in a broad-leaf straw hat, no shirt and a pair of green shorts walks towards us through the grass. I can hear it whisper with his feet. He stops a few yards away and stands looking down on us with a derisive grin on his face. He has marvellously bandy legs and a massive torso.
"Martin? Martin!" Jackson shouts, leaping to his feet. "You old *Martin!*" he says, giving the man a hug, and dragging him over. "This my cousin Martin, Uncle Hector's son. Maggie Truro."
Martin shakes my hand in a very restrained way, resting his weight on one hip.

"Where you bin? I don't see you at the airport. Sit down. Sit down, man, and tell us what going on around here since I left."

Martin squats uneasily and pulls at a piece of grass. I can see a great resemblance to Jackson in his face, though he is darker. His eyes are black under the shade of his hat.

"Got to talk to you, Matthew," he says, pressing a slow aggressive intention into his words. "Got to have a long talk with you by yourself."

"Is it *that* serious?" Jackson sits cross-legged and frowning, hearing the drive in the other's voice. I feel locked out and begin to get up and go.

"Stay!" says Jackson. "If you goin' to live on this island you got to know what goin' on as well as me."

Martin still squats staring down at the grass, his fingers interlaced in front of him. I sit too not looking at him, but I can feel his hostility coming at me like puffs of foul-smelling air.

Finally, he stares into my eyes. "O.K., miss, are you colour-blind? I thought that was a disease only the male of the species suffered from."

When people first started attacking me on this level, making comments, this *sort* of remark, I asked Jackson never to answer for me, to allow me to reply for myself. After all, it's *me* they're speaking to, even if they are hoping to get a rise out of him.

"No," I say, "I am not colour-blind. I would be living with Jackson if he was Chinese, Aztec or English. Does that answer your question?"

"No," he says. "It's not just *you*, it's the whole repeat of things that we will not tolerate."

"What are you talking about, Martin?" says Jackson. "Who's *we*? You can't come here and attack Maggie, and then wander off as though you'd fulfilled some personal duty. You're my cousin and she's my woman, so you'd better tell me what shit-storm is flying about in your skull."

"Did you ever hear of a man called Yacub?" says Martin suddenly, challenging both of us with the intensity of an evangelist.

"Yacub was a mad black scientist who lived about 6300 years ago on an island called *Patmos*. It was when the entire population of the earth was black." He does not wait for any reply from either of us. "This Yacub set up the machinery for graftin' whites out of blacks through the operation of a birth-control system. Whenever a couple on this island wanted to get married they were only allowed to do so if there was a difference in their colour, and by matin' black, with those in the population of a brownish colour—like us—and then brown with brown—never black with black—all traces of the black were eventually eliminated. For many years after Yacub's death the system was continued, until they finally succeeded in creatin' the white devil with the blue eyes of death." He repeats this like a catechism, every word prepared, and it would be impossible to say that he did not believe it, so conclusive is his tone.

"Look at *you*," he says, pointing his finger at Jackson, "you got it staring out your eye. The blue eye of death."

We sit dumbfounded.

"You go to London and start shootin' off your mouth about how white people got to marry black ones, dilute the blood and the genes some more, you bring *her* out here, *and* that white man's syndicate to take over the island. You are a worse traitor to your blood than a hundred black Yacubs."

I feel a terrible fear, as though a razor-edge of hate has just slashed across my face and disfigured me, disfigured the day and the trees, Jackson and all. It seems extraordinary that we should be sitting on the ground in the middle of this calm place, no breath of air to cool us, while Jackson's own cousin pours out invective and calls him 'traitor' to his face.

"Whose blood are you talkin' about, Martin? Yours is same as mine, and that means that your grandfather and mine was white, your grandmother and mine, black. You mean you only acknowledge *hers*? Her blood? Who filled your head with all this Black Muslim shit?"

"I'm as ashamed of my grandfather's blood as I am of you, you ass-licking Uncle Tom," says Martin, venomously. "I wouldn't walk around with the same name as you two if you gave me half-share in all the dirty money you piled up since you started pushing your stinking 'hybrid' crap about.

"When the time come," he says, standing up, his face contorted with impotent rage, "when the time come, see what Whitey does to you—he'll shit on you, and you'll enjoy eating it. You Uncle Tomming mother-fucker!"

He walks stiffly away from us on his bandy legs. At the edge of a clearing that leads back to the house he turns back and shouts, "If you think you goin' to make this island into another *Patmos*, we'll stop you, man. We're ready, I've been sent to warn you! Mustafa says we'll stop you! Just remember that!"

Jackson lies still on the ground for a long minute. Then he gets up and starts walking round in a circle, muttering to himself, holding his shoulders hunched up, hands in his pockets . . .

A fury is building up in me as I watch him. I want to strike out at the hate, end my passivity, smash teeth down the next throat that starts in about Black and White, rage and blister my tongue with abuse against all our sickening attitudes. I stand up and scream out, "Shut up! SHUT UP, EVERYBODY! SHUT UP! WE'RE ALL DRIVING EACH OTHER MAD WITH HATE!" I can't remember what else I shout, except that the shouting becomes weeping and the weeping becomes laughter. It comes from deep inside me, but I am pained, and I am not enjoying my laugh.

Next thing I know, Jackson has grabbed me tight around the waist and is holding me against him, until the awful laughter stops.

"Take off your clothes and let's go for a swim, missus," he whispers into my ear. "Come and lie in the sea with me."

\* \* \*

I sleep in the late afternoon on a brass bed with the pleasant sag of years of heavy men. Not sleep, doze. I don't want to think, in fact I'm incapable of thought at that moment, but my brain won't lie down. It is bristling with inconsequential anxieties . . . like where Hector is sleeping tonight now that we have commandeered his bed, like which of Jackson's half-brothers is called Malcolm and which one is Angus, like whether Grandma May approves of me. Flashes of Martin's eyes under his palm-leaf hat with the leaf bits hanging down; the humming bird, shimmering bill sinking into flower; Rawlings finger on my knee, "You really did it, sonny" . . . buzz about my brain. Martin's eyes . . . those eyes . . . they could look right through a brick wall.

Jackson has gone to see Doc Bates after our swim. He says that Doc Bates knows everything that happens on this island about thirty seconds before it happens, so he's the person to ask. I try to imagine Doc Bates—a sort of West Indian equivalent of 'Dr. Finlay' I suppose. Whirl and turn, crowds, people waving, dancing, Grandma May's arm coming out of her dress, buzz, the cameras thrusting and clicking, praying mantises eating butterflies in the sun, "streamer-tailed humming bird to you, Missy", that's what I'd like to be a 'streamer-tailed humming bird', docta bird, good weather when swallows fly high, love a man's hard small nipple, dripping in the sun, it doesn't matter here whether the swallows are high or not. The weather will be fine. What are jenny crabs?

*     *     *

Seventeen people sit down to Grandma May's dinner, and Doc Bates is not like Dr. Finlay on the telly. He's a mountainous man with a belly that hangs suspended over a thick leather belt. The light shines through the hairs on his head and the pink cranium which I can see underneath looks indestructible. He has a voice that sounds like the growling of a ferocious dog and when he and Grandma May laugh together, it is a true happening, but indescribable. The young girls of the family serve us, their smiles and grace, a sort of lovely reserve, makes me envy them, the hibiscus in their hair, their sweet slow uncomplicated smiles. Doc Bates tells me stories about Jackson when he was little, and we drink rum.

The egg-plant is stuffed with meat and herbs and cashew nuts and the curried goat is hot and filled with coconut, allspice, and rosemary. Huge moths flap against the lamps, girls flit about with more and more and more food, and efficient Libby is directing operations from the kitchen. I wonder if all this will grow familiar to me, if there will be a time when my senses stop being sharpened and delighted by the difference between my own background and this one, a time when the sight of a London bus or the smell of steak-and-kidney pie will have the same intoxication, or even a nostalgia.

We do not discuss anything serious at the table. Nobody mentions Martin, Rawlings or the changes that are taking place in the island's economy. Nobody even says the word 'hybrid' or speaks of Black Muslims, racialism, Quakers, Catholics, Seventh-Day Adventists or Sammy-Davis-style Jews. Jackson laughs a lot and tells them riotous stories of Kew Gardens and how some West Indians went in there and planted gangi root, cannabis, the weed. Nobody noticed that it was growing there until they were caught leaving the premises with a bundle of mature plants under their coats.

After dinner, we sit out on the verandah for a while savouring the sultry night air and slapping at enormous mosquitoes that stick their blood-suckers into your arm with the swiftness of doctors giving injections in a polio scare.

Grandma May, regal in a rocking chair, gently fanning herself with a large orange and green palm-leaf fan on a stick, is the only one they would not dare touch; and maybe Doc Bates, because his blood is sure to be ninety per cent proof.

My eyes begin to close and a delicious weight takes my chest. It is like when I get into bed and try to do a crossword. I only have to look at all those impossible clues and a lovely drowsiness steals over me, taking me out of the necessity to do crossword puzzles, or anything else for that matter, and I sleep in seconds. Crossword puzzles are better than sleeping-pills for me.

"Go on to bed," says Jackson, "I'm goin' to drink some of my granpaw's liqueur rum with the Doc here."

Grandma May hugs me and runs her hand down the length of my hair admiringly, "Prettiest sinting I ever see!"

\* \* \*

I have never slept in a bed with someone before when you both roll into the dip in the middle. That's what wakes me up. I wake to find us melting in an enforced sleeping embrace and seeming to fall ever deeper into the pit every minute. It's so hot. He wakes up too. Perhaps he was never asleep.

"What did lovely Doc Bates tell you about the state of the island," I say, when wakefulness has made me lucid.

"I'll tell you all about it," he says, excited. "We've worked out a sort of a plan. This is it—what's goin' on, I mean. Sidney has let them take over the whole of the soil operation; the Rawlings syndicate plan to turn this island into the most expensive holiday place in the world, with convention halls, Bunny Clubs, Holiday Inns, concert places, another golf-course, Congress Halls, floor shows, gambling joints, tennis, water-skiing, go-carts, the lot, you name it and they'll have it. Rawlings and backers are prepared to spend an enormous number of dollars—that's on paper, of course—but they *will* pump money into Hambro, for sure. Now, because of this financial interest and because of *me*, people are beginning to talk about this island in New York and Chicago, London and Detroit, and it has come to the ears of a man called Mustafa, a black Muslim, that the native population of the island will be overlooked when they're handin' out the bread and the facilities. Because I am an arch-enemy in their eyes, this is the perfect moment to discredit me entirely in the eyes of all the people who believe in hybridisation. They will say that I have used my whole thing to feather my own nest. That I have sold out my fellow islanders to the white capitalist misleaders . . .

"The pity is that they have somehow got Martin and Wilf Buxton, Quincey Mortimer, Jemmy Hawks and his brother, boys from this here island, and these boys have taken oaths to see the white man out, by force if necessary. I don't blame them—I'd probably do the same myself.

"What the Doc says we should do is get governmental backin' before it's too late to stop things taking a real ugly turn. Stop the hammerheads moving in . . . I would say the only way to get things right, is to compensate the Rawlings group for what monies they have sunk in their hotel, golf-course, casino, etc., and *see them out*! So that's what I'm going to try to do, even if it costs me everythin' I ever made, even if I have to make another fifty long-players."

"I love you," I say, glad that the bed has this interesting sag, "I love you, love you, you."

It is all so simple.

\* \* \*

We move out of Hector's distorted bed to the ultra-wide heart-shaped monster in the penthouse suite at the Hambro Excelsior. You guessed it. Pow. Pow. The penthouse suite is also the honeymoon suite, a special for wealthy newly-weds. It is a bit strange sleeping in a heart-shaped bed, but not really uncomfortable because the heart is so big you don't lie in 'V' formation, with your feet touching and heads stretched apart as you'd imagine. Anyway, during my first few weeks on Hambro, I'm very interested in where I'm sleeping. This is because the air here makes me dozy and relaxed and I take a siesta every day. So does J.

Tomorrow is the big day. We have been rehearsing all day today for the concert. I am singing my favourite songs and wearing a floaty backless mauve dress that shows off my tan. I had forgotten how great it is to appear live. We've had some marvellous sessions. Every musician on the island turns up lugging steel drums, tin whistles, bongos, rubbish-tin lids . . . anything that makes a noise when bashed or blown through. There was never a happening like this will be in the whole history of Hambro Island.

Jackson had the idea that we should give a free concert on a Sunday. Then every soul on the island could come. It is going to be stupendous.

I hope old Rawlings appreciates what Jackson is doing for his tourist business; but I don't think we are getting on very well in the negotiation stakes with him. Jackson never says much but he looks so worried after each meeting.

We came to the Excelsior so that he can be near the centre of negotiations, so that we can entertain without putting too much work on Grandma May, and because I need the air-conditioning.

*This* day the air-conditioning has broken down, so Jackson pulls the sliding windows as far back as they will go and opens the door, to pull any air there is through our room.

We are both naked.

I am getting brown all over—living on the top of Hambro Excelsior.

The afternoon is the best time to make love.

It is late.

The sun is sinking to eye-level in the wall-length window. I look across Jackson's sleeping brown body and see the fine white curtains gently lifting in the breeze. And then I close my eyelids in the glow of sunlight that streams through it on us. It leaves gay green and orange spots on the closed screens of my eyes. Watermelons from far away or limes in close-up.

It could be three seconds or three minutes later I hear a noise, the creaking sound of rope being stretched, and open my eyes. The sun is obliterated by the figure of a window-cleaner lowering himself down off the roof. How funny, I think, that a window-cleaner should be cleaning the windows when the glass has been pulled back and there is no window there to clean.

I cannot see the man, only his silhouette against the sun. He is wearing a greeny-khaki outfit and cap of the workmen, I think. He braces himself on the sill and quite slowly I see his arm disengage itself from the solid outline of his body and he raises it shoulder high and forward as though he is pointing. He aims with great deliberation at Jackson's head.

Three shots and Jackson's head whips round to face me. The right side of it is gone and the air is filled with red mist and brain. His lips are already shaking in death. I think I am screaming. I know my mouth is open, I cannot hear anything but a roar. It is like watching something in slow-motion, a dream. I will wake up soon.

I see the direction of the nozzle of the gun change. He is pointing at me now. I put out my hand to stop the bullets.

My hand crashes back against my eye. My eye. My eye. Eye. I. I. I. . .

# 13

## *Lew Hamlyn*

I CAN'T BELIEVE IT.

I can't believe it.

But it's true. I've seen their bodies.

They were staked out in the local ice-making factory. Haven't gotten round to building a proper mortuary on Hambro yet. Mostly when someone dies they bury him quick.

Two poor bodies. Packed with ice, lying on trestle tables in the ice-making factory. Maggie's left eye was covered and they had put a scarf round Jackson's head to cover the wounds.

I flew out from London as soon as the news came through on the A.P. Service.

An old beachcomber doctor had already performed autopsies.

There are only four full-time policemen on the island. No one seemed to know what to do.

The hit happened on Saturday afternoon, but they weren't discovered until after ten o'clock that night.

There was no way we could check the comings and goings of all the boats on the island. Hundreds of people came in on Saturday. Seems Jackson and Maggie were to give a concert on the Sunday. We knew that four planes flew *out* between the hours of four and ten that day—a Cessna, a Piper Cub, one package of day-trippers from Jamaica and the T.W.A. passenger flight to New York.

I immediately hired a firm of detectives from Miami.

I warned Jackson before he left London that he should take a couple of bodyguards along just in case, but he said he was going *home* and that if he couldn't do *that* without goons hanging around his neck, he might as well set himself up in Battersea Fun Fair as target in a shooting gallery.

I talked to the fat beachcomber doctor whose name was Bates; we got falling-down drunk together. He explained the whole situation to me. Told me how a very well-heeled syndicate of dubious backing had virtually bought up the island through the mismanagement of Jackson's father, Sidney. Jackson had offered to buy back control and been refused . . . he then threatened the syndicate with a general strike and removal of all native labour. The syndicate countered by importing staff for the Hambro Excelsior, caddies for the Golf Club, battalions of boat-boys and beach attendants from Jamaica and the mainland of the United States.

Jackson called another meeting and read the Riot Act, said he would seek help at governmental level in Jamaica and have them thrown off the island.

At the same time as all this high-powered brouhaha was going on, a group of militant black-thinking Hambroans led by Jackson's own cousin, Martin, and an American Negro called Mustafa, was seething at the take-over of their island. They blamed Jackson. Jackson, and the white men who were using him as their front.

Poor Jackson had been getting it both ways . . . but which side got to him first?

By Thursday reports began to flow in from the world's press . . .

Tass Agency reported that right-wing extremists had murdered Jackson, *Time* Magazine plugged for the black militants, and the *News of the World* screamed that pop-singer and girl-friend had been found nude, shot in their love-nest, hinted at drugs, orgies, and the usual parade of salacious pastimes.

The funeral was on Thursday. The whole island turned out and we buried them next to Jackson's grandfather.

The only thing to do was to await developments.

So many factions were conducting investigations that leads got crossed and fouled up. Everybody was hearing conflicting stories. Newspapers were paying people for 'exclusive stories' that were pure invention; the situation became an impossible mess. Everybody trotted out his own little theory and there was no one who could say they were false.

I received some very peculiar telephone calls warning me to lay off. Tried to follow them up but got nowhere.

I came back to London last week and since then I have been spending my days looking out the window of my room smoking cigars and thinking.

Baby . . . it's like every time we find ourselves a man who will speak up for civil rights or integration or just plain humanity and the dignity of man, someone gets to him and shuts him up forever . . . The list is getting longer every day— the Kennedys and Malcolm X, Martin Luther King, Yablonski and now my friend Matthew Jackson, the original Hybrid . . .

# 14

## Francis Omerod

I HEARD THE NEWS about the fellow Jackson and his doxie as I was driving back from a shopping exhibition in Estepona. I've retired to the south of Spain . . . bought myself a small finca on the outskirts of a fishing village here . . . labour is cheap, food is cheap, climate good for old bones, and I get good reception from Radio Gibraltar.

Seems someone finished off the job I started a few years ago at the house in Ealing . . . Of course, it was bound to happen . . . probably the fellow had been messing about with another fellow's wife again.

You see, I *know* these half-caste chappies. They're a thoroughly bad lot.

It's as useless as farting against thunder to think that you can mix the bloods successfully. Doesn't work. You've got a perfect example with my bitch Lucy . . . beautiful boxer bitch was Lucy . . . brindle . . . but some cur got in to her . . .